Edward Hoare, John Hume Townsend

Edward Hoare

A Record of His Life Based Upon a Brief Autobiography

Edward Hoare, John Hume Townsend

Edward Hoare
A Record of His Life Based Upon a Brief Autobiography

ISBN/EAN: 9783744661058

Printed in Europe, USA, Canada, Australia, Japan

Cover: Foto ©Raphael Reischuk / pixelio.de

More available books at **www.hansebooks.com**

EDWARD HOARE, M.A.

EDWARD HOARE, M.A.

A RECORD OF HIS LIFE BASED UPON A
BRIEF AUTOBIOGRAPHY

EDITED BY THE

REV. J. H. TOWNSEND, D.D.

Vicar of Broadwater Down, Tunbridge Wells
Author of "Spiral Stairs; or, the Heavenward Course of the
Church Seasons"

WITH A PORTRAIT

London
HODDER AND STOUGHTON
27, PATERNOSTER ROW
—
MDCCCXCVI

Printed by Hazell, Watson, & Viney, Ld., London and Aylesbury.

PREFACE

IT was on the 20th of August, 1864, that the Rev. Edward Hoare, on the deck of the steamer from Boulogne to Folkestone, spoke kindly words of sympathy to a schoolboy returning home after a great bereavement in Switzerland. How little then could either of them have imagined the future relationship of Vicar and Curate, the long years of happy friendship afterwards, the deeply solemn funeral sermon, and, finally, the sacred task of editing the Autobiography and writing the brief sketch contained in the following pages! This work has been undertaken with the greatest diffidence, partly owing to the many duties of a somewhat busy life, and still more from the anxious wish that such a character as that of Canon Hoare should be depicted by one who had known him from earlier years. Another difficulty has been to compress the volume into the small limits desired by the family.

To write a large volume would have been easy,

but to read a considerable correspondence, together with closely written volumes of journal, and give a digest of their contents, has required care and thought. It has also necessitated the putting upon one side of much that was interesting and profitable. Amongst the things unpublished have been many powerful letters upon various burning questions of the day during the past forty years; most of these subjects have now burnt themselves out, and it seemed unwise to rake up the ashes.

It is, moreover, better to say too little than too much, and those who knew him best will acknowledge that the latter error has been avoided.

A man possessing such qualities as those which Canon Hoare exhibited—great kindness and affection, wide views of men and things, strong convictions, ruling powers, commanding intellect, and deep spirituality of mind—was one who could not live without influencing visibly all with whom he came in contact; but it has been the desire of the Editor so to picture this life as it appeared to him, and with the one desire that God may be glorified by the narrative as He was magnified in the life of His servant.

J. H. T.

CONTENTS

CHAPTER IX

CHAPTER I

EARLY LIFE AND BOYHOOD

IT is a common practice amongst remarkable men to leave on record some of the circumstances which have led to the formation of the leading features of their character.

But as the greater part of mankind is not remarkable, I think it just possible that some may be interested, and possibly some profited, by a few details of the life of one whose life has not been marked by incident so much as by abundant mercy, who has been led on step by step in the happy life of a parochial clergyman, and who at the close of it can say with reference to the past, "Surely goodness and mercy have followed me all the days of my life," and can add with reference to the future the blessed hope and determination of David, "I will dwell in the house of the Lord for ever."

Of all the many mercies of my life the one that must ever stand first and foremost is the gift of my beloved father and mother. No words can describe the blessing of such parents, and I never can look back on the unspeakable privilege of

such a parentage without adoring the sovereign
grace which placed me under their parental care.
When I observe the carelessness of some parents,
the inefficiency of others, and the terrible training
for evil to which I see multitudes of poor children
exposed, I can only adore the sovereignty of God
which on June 5th, 1812, committed me as a
sacred trust to the very best of parents.

My father, Samuel Hoare, was a banker in the
City. Both he and my mother, Louisa Hoare,*
had been brought up in the Society of Friends, and
had not formally left it at the time of my birth,
so that I was registered by that body, and at
the time of my ordination I had to apply to the
Westminster Meeting for a certificate of my birth.
But they were both greatly influenced by the
ministry of some devoted Evangelical clergymen,
such as the Rev. E. Edwardes of Lynn, and the
Rev. Josiah Pratt, and I believe it was very soon
after my birth that they were together baptised.
We young people were therefore all brought up as
members of the Church of England, though, as
my father never completely lost his early Quaker
prejudice against infant baptism, we were not
baptised till about the age of fifteen, when we were
considered able to judge for ourselves.

---

* Sister of Mrs. Elizabeth Fry, the famous Christian
philanthropist.—ED.

It was probably the result of his own Quaker education that my father had a strong objection to public schools ; so that his plan was to engage a private tutor, some young man from Cambridge or Oxford, to educate us at home till we attained the age of fifteen, and then send us to a private tutor, preparatory to our going up to Cambridge. This arrangement answered well so long as there were four of us boys at home, and some of our cousins were united with us both in the schoolroom and playground ; but as the elder boys went off, there was a sad want both of healthy amusements and intellectual stimulus for those that were left behind. I was the third, and I remember how difficult it was for my dear brother Joseph and myself to keep ourselves well employed when our elder brothers Samuel and Gurney had been placed under the care of the Rev. H. V. Elliott, the most able and gifted tutor to whom we three eldest brothers were sent, and to whom we were all indebted far more than I can describe. He had a wonderful power of bringing the interest of the University to bear on the education of his pupils, and I never can forget the effect on my own mind, for I never really worked till the day I entered his house ; but I began then, and I have never been habitually idle since. He was a grand illustration of the principle, that the great office of an educator is not merely to cram a boy's head with knowledge, but to kindle a fire in his soul, which will go on burning brightly when the tutor himself has long since passed away.

But though there were great disadvantages in our home education, there were also immense advantages. It was not so effective as my dear parents hoped it would be in preserving us from impure and defiling information, and to this day I rarely pass the back door of what used to be my grandmother's house without a sense of loathing at the wickedness of her corrupt old butler, who on that spot did his utmost to pollute my boyish mind with filthy communication.

But in many other respects I have never ceased to feel the blessed results of those years at home. In the first place, we were all brought under the constant influence of our father and mother. He was a man of great strength of character, and of marvellous perseverance in all that he undertook. He was deeply interested in the improvement of prison discipline, and was one of the " Governors " of the " Refuge for the Destitute." This he used to visit once a week with the utmost regularity, rising early so as to be able to complete his visit before his attendance at the Bank, and I have seldom seen a more affecting sight than when he used to ride off week after week in all weathers, even after the Lord had laid him so low by an attack of paralysis that he could not attempt to ride beyond a walking pace, and it was indeed unsafe for him to ride at all ; but he was a man *tenax propositi*, and nothing would turn him from his purpose. It was his determination of character that made him a most valuable coadjutor with his brother-in-law, Sir T. F. Buxton, in the great anti-slavery struggle, as may be seen in the graphic account given in the Life of Sir Fowell of the great debate which virtually decided the question. Sir Fowell himself was a man of courageous determination ; but it was my father that, during that debate, sat under the gallery of the House of Commons and upheld his hands by his decided and unwavering judgment. It was a great privilege for us boys to grow up under the influence of such a character.

Once a week, on the day of his holiday from the Bank, he used habitually to visit the schoolroom, and hear us repeat what we had learned during the week ; and every Sunday afternoon he used to read with us some good religious book. I fear sometimes one at least of his pupils greatly tried his patience by supineness and inattention, but there were not then the same interesting books for young people that there are now, and such books as Wilberforce's " Practical View " or Doddridge's " Rise and Progress " were not calculated to attract the attention of a set of boys whose hearts were set on cricket.

Then my dearest mother was one of the most lovely women of the day. Beautiful in countenance, gentle in her manners, pure in her thoughts, and most loving in all her intercourse with her family, she exercised over us all a most sacred and refining influence, and one of the most abiding sorrows of my life has been that, when she was teaching me something, I was so negligent that I caused her to shed a tear.

Besides that, she had great intellectual charm. First-rate men such as Chalmers and Wilberforce delighted in her society. She was an excellent English writer. Her letters to her sons at College are perfect models of such compositions, and her admirable little book " Hints on Early Education," containing the principles on which she brought us up, continues to this day, passing through edition after edition, unsurpassed, if I may not say unequalled, by the many more modern efforts to throw light on that most important subject.

It is to her that I am indebted for my first intelligent acquaintance with the Gospel. She used to have us boys to read the Scripture with her every morning at 7.15. Nothing can ever efface the lovely impression made on those occasions. There she used to be by a bright fire in her little room, in her snow-white dressing-gown, looking as pure and lovely as was possible in woman. I fear we boys were often late and sometimes inattentive. But I never forget one morning when she asked me if I knew what faith was, and, finding that I was utterly ignorant, proceeded to teach me those sacred lessons of a Saviour's grace which have been life to my soul from that day till now. Oh, mothers! what an opportunity you have of sowing a seed which will never die!

Another great advantage in our home education was that we became interested in missionary work. Drawing-room meetings were not the fashion then as they are now, and my father and mother, without waiting for the fashion, threw open their large drawing-room to various devoted men. Thus we boys used to enjoy the no small privilege of becoming personally acquainted with many of the most devoted men of the day, as well as of being educated into an interest in missionary work.

But parental influence was not all, for one of the tutors engaged for our instruction was the Rev. R. Davis, of Queen's College, Cambridge, a devoted young man, and deeply interested in the Church Missionary Society. It was he that enlisted the interest of my father and mother, so that I find, in turning to the report for the year 1820, the following entry, which was the sum-total of the then Hampstead Association :—

	£	s.	d.
Contributions by a few children	2	8	0
Rev. R. Davis . . .	1	1	9
	3	9	9

Having been one of those few children, I

remember well the interest that the subject excited
in our minds; and as that interest never died out
in those beloved ones now gone to their rest, and
as I trust it will never do so in myself, I realise
how much I owe to that young man, and I see
how much may be done by a young man who
carries with him wherever he goes the unceasing
desire to be engaged in his Master's service.

This home education was continued until I
reached the age of fifteen, when I was sent as a
pupil to the Rev. H. V. Elliott of Brighton, where
my two elder brothers had been before me. Before I left home arrangements were made for my
baptism. That admirable man the Rev. Josiah
Pratt kindly undertook my instruction, and I used
to ride down to him at his residence in Finsbury
Circus. He was a remarkable man, firm in his
principle, faithful to the Gospel, true to his Saviour,
zealous in Missions, and of remarkable soundness
of judgment. I am not sure that he was altogether
the best instructor for a spirited lad, but I never
shall forget the venerable man, sitting on one side
of the fireplace, finding, I fear, considerable difficulty in eliciting much response from his pupil.
But I learnt one practical lesson from these interviews, which has been a help to many a lad
under similar circumstances :—I was at that time
thoroughly in earnest about my soul, and I looked
forward to my baptism with great seriousness.
It was a matter for much prayer and close ex-

amination. But my dearest mother showed me
Mr. Pratt's letters respecting me, in which he said,
" I hope there is something at the bottom, but
I find it very difficult to bring it to the surface! "
How often have I thought of these words, when
I have been preparing my young people for Con-
firmation ; and when I have seen them nervous,
agitated, and with small development of feeling,
I have thought of myself and of Mr. Pratt's letters,
and remembered how earnest I was at the time,
although he could discover but little trace of it.

The day of my baptism was a very solemn one,
my cousin, the late Sir Edward Buxton, being
baptised at the same time in St. Stephen's, Cole-
man's Street, and I think it was the next day that
we left our homes together and went to Brighton,
to enter upon a new mode of education. I cannot
say how thankful I am that my father sent me
to Mr. Elliott. He was a first-rate man in all
respects, and he had been the means of kindling
an intellectual fire in my eldest brother, who was
passing through Cambridge at the time with high
distinction. He (Mr. Elliott) had a faculty for
inspiriting his pupils for work. I had been an
idle boy until I went to him ; but I had no sooner
crossed his threshold than I felt an ambition for
University distinction, and lost very little time
when I was under his rule. As he took only
six pupils there was the same difficulty that we

found at home in getting good play, first-class cricket.

But there were other great advantages. There were some very choice lads amongst the pupils, one especially whom I can never forget—namely, Henry Goulburn. He was small in stature, but of marvellous ability : for quick perception, clear understanding, for never-failing memory, and a power of seeing through a subject, such as I never saw in any man. I shall never forget his influence when he first joined us as a pupil. There was at that time a good deal of quarrelling amongst us. There was one young fellow who was rich, but very foolish, who became the butt of his companions. I remember well one day, when Goulburn had just come amongst us, and we were all like a pack of hounds upon that young fellow, Goulburn got up from the table, walked round to him, and put his hand upon him, saying, "I will be your friend." That act of his had such a power over the whole party that similar unkindness entirely ceased. I never saw a repetition of it.

But, besides the pupils within the house, we had the immense advantage of the friendship of Mr. Elliott's mother and sisters, who lived close by. That mother was one of the most charming old ladies I ever remember. She was the daughter of Henry Venn, Rector of Yelling, the grandfather of the late Henry Venn, Secretary of the Church Missionary Society. She grew up amongst her father's friends, Berridge, Fletcher, and Simeon in his early days, and nothing could be more charming, more delightful, than her reminiscence of the early struggle of those devoted men. It wanted a good deal to draw me from the cricket field, but she had the power of doing it. I could not have had a greater treat than to listen for half-an-hour to her anecdotes.

Then again it was one of the privileges that we enjoyed at Brighton that we attended St. Mary's Church. Mr. Elliott's preaching was valuable, full of truth, and most beautiful in composition. I used to listen to it with great interest, and from it I first learnt the great and blessed doctrine of justification by faith, which I have had the privilege of preaching throughout my ministry. I never can forget one sermon of his in which he pointed out that there were three great trials of Abraham's faith : (1) His Call (Gen. xii.) ; (2) The Promise given him (Gen. xv.) ; and (3) The Sacrifice of Isaac (Gen. xxii.). He then pointed out that the first and last of these three trials involved immediate action, but that the middle one demanded no action at the time, but required simply a believing reception of the promise of God, and it was of it that the statement was made (Gen. xv. 6) : "Abraham believed God, and it was counted to him for righteousness."

There was a fresh blessing given me in St. Mary's. It was there one sacred day when Robert

Daly, afterwards Bishop of Cashel, was preaching,
that I was led by the Spirit of God to give myself
up to the ministry. I do not remember exactly
what he said; but I am sure that a permanent
impression may be often made without any distinct recollection always of what has been uttered.
So it was in my case, while that noble man was
preaching; and I there and then gave myself up
to the ministry of God, as I told him many years
afterwards. I said nothing about it to anybody
for a year, because I wished my determination to
be thoroughly tested. At the end of the year I
told my father. He informed me that there was
a place open for me in his Bank, but at the same
time he gave his cordial approbation; and so with
his full consent and that of my dearest mother,
I regarded myself from that day as one set apart
to the sacred ministry. That must have been
nearly sixty years ago, and never for one moment
have I had reason to regret the decision.

From Mrs. Hoare to her son at Brighton :—

"*August* 22*nd*, 1829.

"How continually have I thought of you, dearest
Edward, since you left us, with the truest pleasure and
I hope thankfulness for the happy time we have passed
together, with the greatest interest in your present settlement and earnest desire and prayer for your well-doing
in future! You have, my love, gained the confidence
and excited the sanguine hopes of your parents, and if

you do not turn out the *decided, noble, upright,* and *effective Christian* character, we shall be disappointed. I consider the present juncture in your life very important. The more I consider the case, the more I am sure of Mr. Elliott's intrinsic value to you, and the more I am convinced of the wisdom of giving up yourself in the present to his wishes; if you secure his friendship, you secure a treasure for life. In this as in every situation, you will have something to bear.

" 1. Don't stand on your own rights too much or be tenacious in little things.

" 2. Be *very slow* in taking offence or fancying any disrespect or want of favour is shown to you.

" 3. Never *complain* of anything to your companions.

" 4. Encourage a spirit of content, and *be determined* (there is much in this determination of mind) to be comfortable.

" 5. Promote, as far as possible, the pleasure of your companions by yielding in little things. I believe, dearest Edward, you are sensible that, to act with true wisdom, we must seek this precious gift from above, and day by day ask for help and strength and grace for the day.

" 6. Write to me intimately, and the letters may be *entirely private whenever you wish it.*

" The books could not be despatched at once. Sam says the Shakespeare is a bad bargain, but we will talk it over again—oh how I should enjoy a half-hour with thee over this nice library fire!"

EARLY LETTERS.

There are some interesting letters of this period, which have been carefully preserved. The earliest

of these, written when he was eleven years old, is
characteristic. It is addressed to his mother, who
was away from home, and begins with an apology
for not having sent her a letter before : this is
based upon an accident at cricket, which he describes graphically, the ball " ascending to a great
height " having fallen upon his thumb and so
disabled him, etc., etc. ; but the pathetic narrative
is followed by a burst of honesty—" however, as
that happened only yesterday it is not much of
an excuse "! Another, a year later, written from
Ryde, after describing a boating and fishing ex-
pedition, relates further a conversation with the
boatman, whom they saw doing something to the
dogfish that they had caught. " He replied " (and
here the young scribe phonetically renders the
local pronunciation), " ' O Lar, I'm only termenting
'em.' We asked, ' Why ? ' ' Because 'em has a
pisonous prick on 'em's back.' We asked him how
they could help that. ' Oh, I knows 'em needn't
have it if 'em didna like ! ' "

The letters that follow were written from
Brighton, and describe his arrival at Mr. Elliott's
house, and sundry events that took place from
time to time ; they are full of affection to his
mother, and abound likewise in touches of humour,
but they show also a diligence and steadiness of
purpose, and a liking for good things, remarkable
in a boy of that age. Subjoined are a few extracts
as specimens :—

" I suppose Jack told you of the famous hunt we had the other day when we were going out riding and met the hounds, half by accident? We had a run of above an hour, and the hounds were in full cry all the time; but, alas! the other day a bill came in from the horse-keeper, which informed us that we were to pay a pound for each of the horses because we had been with the hounds. . . . I like Abercorn * very much, but he is excessively idle, as my shoulders will bear witness, as it is his great delight to get up and thump Ted Buxton and me on the shoulders; but fortunately he is tired of hitting me, as I repay the blows tenfold with a single-stick, and the consequence is that poor Ted gets double his former allowance."

" We have capital walks on the Downs almost every day, which are very pleasant, and capital exercise, as we go a considerable distance; the other day we went nearly to the Dyke. Before seven [a.m.] we three have delightful readings together —we have nearly done Matthew; at seven we come down and read till breakfast, and after that till two; we then go out for our walk till dinner. . . . On Thursday we are to have our debate about the battle of Navarino, in which I am going to be exceedingly eloquent—only there is one great barrier to my eloquence, which is that I can think of nothing to speak about. Robert and Jack are going to attack the battle; and Ted, Abercorn, and I are going to defend it. I think they have got much the best side."

This extract, written in a boyish hand, is dated February 19th, 1828. The next, on October 4th in the same year, is remarkable for its transition

---

* The late Duke of Abercorn, one of his fellow-pupils.

into the formed hand of the young man, and its
resemblance to the writing of all his later years.
He was then sixteen. The letter is full of manly
thoughts, kind sympathy for some relatives in
trouble, great thankfulness to God for restoring
him to health after an illness, and then the schoolboy reappears towards the close as he longs for
a share in the partridge-shooting which his father
and elder brothers were enjoying at that time,
and "the plumcake after church, and then the
walk on the lighthouse hills" at Cromer, concerning which he winds up by saying : "I do not know
two things that live so pleasantly in my mind.
How far superior to all the strutting finery of
Brighton!"

The letters written during his residence in
Brighton show that Mr. Elliott, besides being a
very kind tutor, had the gift of inspiring his
pupils with great diligence and love for their
work. The year 1830 was the last spent under
his roof, and they testify to a great deal of hard
reading, with the University constantly in view.

At the end of a letter dated "Brighton, September 20th, 1830," young Hoare writes : –

"I may tell you that this is the last letter you are ever
likely to receive from me from Brighton. My two years
and a half (that but yesterday I thought would never
end) are now nearly come to a close ; I am sure if I had
time I ought and could write a long letter of gratitude
to you and my father for having given me such oppor-

tunities of improvement. Oh that I had made full use of them ! what a capital fellow I should be ! At all events, of this I am quite certain, that if your sons turn out either rascals or blockheads (the latter of which I fear is the case with the third *), it can never be laid to your charge. And so, with regard to the course we are now likely to enter upon, I feel that every reason which ought to influence a person in the strongest degree binds me to read with thorough diligence and perseverance, and I only trust that I may be enabled to show my gratitude for your kindness by taking thorough advantage of it."

"O si sic omnes !" is the thought that rises to the mind after perusing these schoolboy letters ; they contain the germs of all the characteristics that made Edward Hoare the power that he after-wards became—manliness, gentleness, remarkable diligence, reverence for religion and the Bible, a loving and thankful spirit, and, last but not least, a keen sense of the humorous side of things.

---

* Himself.

CHAPTER II

CAMBRIDGE

IN the year 1830 I went to Trinity College, Cambridge, one of the finest places for education. My dear brother Gurney was there at the time. Goulburn followed a year afterwards. Canon Carus was in his years a Fellow of Trinity, and my beloved friend Bishop Perry was there as a tutor. I had many friends, and we were a happy party. I have outlived almost all of them. I owe more than I can express to my College life. I read hard, and I have often observed that hard-reading men look back upon their College days with the greatest pleasure. I was surrounded by a set of steady men, and, above all, I had the advantage of Mr. Simeon's ministry. There was something very wonderful about his preaching ; it was not eloquence, and he had none of the brilliance of Mr. Elliott. But it was as clear as a noonday ; his statements of truth were unmistakable. He was raised up to preach at Cambridge the great Evangelical doctrines of Scripture. And he taught them with a clearness, a distinctness, and a courage such as could not well be surpassed.

Many and many a time did I return to my rooms after church, "sport" my door, and kneel down in earnest prayer under the solemn conviction produced by his most spiritual and awakening ministry. Thus the three years of my University life passed rapidly by. I was very eager in boat-racing, and very keen at the game of cricket, although I could not play much of it, as it took too long a time. But I am thankful to say I had the ministry always in view; and I remember well that on the morning I went into the Senate House for my degree, I knelt down to pray for success, and I thought at the time how much higher gifted I would be if the Lord would make me wise to win souls.

University Letters.

Although the autobiography contains but a brief reference to his career at Cambridge, it seems a pity to pass too hastily over this most important time of a young man's life. A great many of his letters to his mother were written at this period, and, like his boyish letters, they are all carefully stitched up into a series of sets, as if his parent foresaw that one day they would be valued by others. They form delightful reading, and it is unfortunate that want of space forbids more than a summarising of their contents and a few extracts.

The first of these, written to his mother, October 22nd, 1830, two days after he had taken

up his residence at Trinity College, describes the
purchase of cap and gown, the first dinner in Hall,
the rooms in which he was settled, the prospects
of College life, which he greatly relished, and the
determination to keep clear of " harum-scarum fellows." A characteristic sentence is worth quoting :
" There is only one point I really dislike, which
is the profane manner in which the Lessons are
gabbled over at chapel, so that you can only hear
a hurried mumble, and not one word of the sense."

Various incidents enliven the letters at this time :
descriptions of his friends, a very nice set ; allusions
to some " glorious sermons " of Mr. Simeon, who
was then the great power at Cambridge ; his reso-
lution to join a boat ; and the excitement caused
" by an attack on the Anatomy Schools, when
the Vice-Chancellor sent round to the Colleges
to call the men out to fight, which summons we
obeyed with great alacrity, though little necessity."
Surely the last item must make Cambridge men
of this generation envy their predecessors of sixty
years ago ! On his nineteenth birthday young
Hoare thus writes to his mother :—

" I don't know whether you recollect that I shall
never again see nineteen years. So I am now entering
a new year—oh how earnestly I do hope that, through
His grace who alone can keep me, it may be a year of
profit and advancement in holiness ! I have thought
a good deal about it, though not so much as I could
wish. How many blessings I have to be thankful for

that I have received during the past year, when sorrow and affliction have been scattered all around me! How wonderfully all of us have been preserved in perfect health and enjoyment!"

A few months after this, in a letter from Hampstead, he mentions walking across the fields one Sunday morning to St. John's and hearing a sermon from Mr. Noel that greatly impressed him; the subject was "The necessity and efficacy of diligence in religion."

"He really seemed as if he had meant it for me, for I had been thinking a great deal how far more diligently I pursued my mathematics than my religion."

Yet at this time he was teaching in a Sunday School every Sunday—rather a rare thing for an undergraduate in those days.

Here occurs an allusion to one who was destined to occupy a warm share in his affection during years to come :—

"I met the other day Perry, who was Senior Wrangler and fifth on the Classical Tripos, and finding that he was going to take pupils I have engaged him for next term, provided my father intends to be so liberal as to let me have a tutor."

For over sixty years the friendship was strong and deep, and after Bishop Perry's resignation of the See of Melbourne their intercourse was frequent and loving up to the end. In the Lent Term of 1832 he writes :—

"I have been getting on this week tolerably in my reading, and intolerably in my rowing, having been bumped by the Johnians on Thursday for the first time in my life, and that too when we might have got away with the greatest ease if all our crew had exerted themselves."

Half a century afterwards his curates were often exhorted to work together with a will, and the exhortation was enforced by allusions to the disasters experienced by a crew whose members were not absolutely one in "go" and sympathy.

The following letter from his father has reference to College events at this time :—

"London, *March* 19*th*, 1832.

"DEAR EDWARD,—A hasty opinion is not always worth having, but you may safely take my advice and try the new boat, bump the first Trinity, and wait for further orders. Let your mother's letter compel you to watch yourself, and if you find the effects of rowing at all prejudicial give it up, but if you find your health and strength on the wax go on, tempering your zeal with moderation, and I will do my best to make peace at home—a work which I shall accomplish with more ease and in less time than you will be at the head of the river. It came across me that, after having vanquished all Cambridge, you might wish to carry your victorious oars to Oxford !"

A fortnight after the last quoted letter from the young collegian, there was another which recounted that, although his boat, of which he was stroke, had gone down as low as fifth, yet on the last race-day it had recovered its old place of second. Then follows a groan concerning the difficulties that attended his post as captain over a discordant body of twenty men : " The crew, when successful, get all the credit, and in the time of misfortune make me their scapegoat."

Fortunately he did not adhere to his original intention of resigning the captaincy, and ultimately his boat attained the proud position of head of the river. Edward Hoare's success in rowing did not make him idle, however : nothing could do that ; into whatever he undertook he threw his whole heart and soul, and the very next letter, a few weeks later, May 4th, 1832, begins thus :—

"Here I am a scholar of Trinity safe and sound, as the master calls it ' discipulus juratus et admissus,' and not a little pleased am I at the thought. But what pleases me most of all is that, so far from being last of all, as our list declares, I have come in very high on the list. I do not know exactly where I am, but, as you wish for all the reports, I tell you one which I don't quite believe, which is that I was the second in both years. I beat all the third year, and all my own except the great lion Stevenson, and I got within a respectable distance of him, and Peacock says I have gained upon him since the last examination, whereas I never expected to get within miles of him. In fact I am altogether happier than I can express, and really think that I never spent so joyful a night and day in all my life "

Referring to this success his father writes again :—

"MY DEAR EDWARD,—Of advice and congratulations you will partake abundantly without an addition from me, but your mother wishes me to write, what I have no doubt Sam has already written. What may be the best course for you to pursue I have not made up my mind, but as you are at Cambridge it is as well to remind you that a man may be happy without mathematics, and that the glory of being Senior Wrangler (supposing the possibility of such an event) may be purchased at too high a price. I attribute the greatest proportion of your late honours to solid understanding and reading, some part to good luck or accident. Had you not then better see the result of the class examination before you take the plunge? With the blessing of God you will be rooted more deeply than ever now in all our hearts, and, what is far beyond extending growth here, you attain that eminence which is quite out of the sound of wrangling.

"I am most affectionately yours,

"S. HOARE."

A few days later he receives the news of the sudden death of a relative, Mr. Powell,* and various letters describe the effect that this event had upon him. His sympathy was warmly expressed for all the mourners; and then, as was natural to a thoughtful mind, the remembrance of the shortness of life made itself felt. Strong

---

* Killed by lightning.

and athletic as he was, he too might be cut off suddenly : was he ready for the call?

But his recent success at the scholarship examination, and his future hopes, seem to have had a strange light thrown upon them by this bereavement, and he began to ask himself the question which some of us have had to face in hours of success or failure—"What *are* College honours? Are they an end, or only a means?" He writes thus :—

" I never felt so strongly as I do now the utter worthlessness of the objects at which I have been aiming with so much zeal. What does it signify whether I am fourth, fifth, sixth, or anything else in this examination, when at one stroke all one's honour and all one's learning may be dashed from you? It has impressed me very strongly with the feeling that to read because it is my duty and because it is an admirable preparation for after-life is a glorious object, but to read (as I must confess I have done) for a place and a place only, and slur over higher things for it, is indeed vanity of vanities."

The summer of 1832 was spent with a reading party in Wales. The start was made from Highgate, where the coach "Wonder" took in its passengers and conveyed them to Shrewsbury "with *wonder*ful rapidity," the journey commencing at 6.40 a.m. and the destination being reached at 10.30 p.m., or one hundred and fifty-six miles in nearly sixteen hours!

Thence sometimes on coach, sometimes on foot,

they made their way to Llangollen, Llanrwst,
Conway, and Bangor. The beautiful suspension
bridge was an object of immense interest. The
travellers went over to the Anglesea side, and
down into the chambers and passages of the
rock where the chains are fixed that uphold the
structure; the letter recounting this visit contains
diagrams descriptive of it all, showing the fascination that it exerted on the mind of the writer.
Various accounts of the magnificent scenery fill
pages in these interesting letters, and also allusions
to the kindly way in which Welsh tracts were
taken by the people, and the excited gratitude
which the gift sometimes caused. At last Bar-
mouth, the "ultima Thule" of their wanderings,
was reached, lodgings were taken, and the party
set steadily to work.

They were fortunate in the parish clergyman,
whose name was Pugh, and young Hoare's letters
often speak with gratitude of the guidance from
above which led them into the parish of this
excellent man. Michaelmas Term found them
back at Cambridge, and now his younger brother
Joseph * joined the party, and Edward's feelings
with regard to his duties towards him are expressed in a letter to his mother, of which nearly
the whole is taken up with a loving interest in his
brother's plans and prospects. He writes :—

* In later years so well known as a Vice-President of the
British and Foreign Bible Society.

" I most earnestly hope that I may be able to assist him, and, what is far more, that he may have that far better assistance which can alone be all-sufficient. . . . I have had a most happy vacation, and cannot say how I have valued it. I only trust that I may be able to repay a hundredth part of your and my father's kindness to me by fraternal affection towards Joe. My motto with regard to him is—

> "'Men must be taught as if you taught them not,
> And things unknown proposed as things forgot.'"

During the month of September, in the year before this, his elder brother Samuel was married to Miss Catherine Hankinson.* There was a warm attachment between the brothers. Edward often writes in terms of great admiration of "Sam," and now the new sister was received with equal affection into his heart. It was a feeling which grew and strengthened to the last day of his life, and was returned by her, being specially manifested in the tender care which she bestowed upon his motherless children more than thirty years afterwards. This, however, is anticipating, and it is suggested only by a letter from Cambridge dated November 9th, 1832, full of delight—

"at the joyful news of the week. I am highly proud of my new avuncular honours. I begin to feel quite a strong affection to my new niece, which I never expected to do, at all events till I had seen her !"

---

* Afterwards Lady Parry.

The same letter writes thankfully about the interest which he had been able to arouse in the University in connection with the British and Foreign Bible Society.

There had been one collector in Cambridge previously, but young Hoare set to work and had the gratification of sending in more than a hundred guineas, fifty of which came from Trinity. He says, " I only hope that this success will encourage us to work hard during the next year." His interest in the Society never waned, and it did well many years afterwards in making him one of its Vice-Presidents.

We have an insight into a College Sunday in one of his letters at this time :—

"We have had a delightful Sunday, and a most edifying sermon on the Conversion of St. Paul. After Hall I had a large party in my rooms, and we read one of Blunt's Lectures on St. Paul. Our party after Hall has become rather a burden to me, it has grown so very large, as I have invited any persons who I thought would come and employ their time better than elsewhere ; and now I feel that it is an opportunity which ought to be employed to good purpose, and I don't know exactly how to go to work to do so."

In a letter written early in 1833 he refers to all the dignities of the third year upon his head, and his desire to use them aright ; it will probably be the opinion of any who read the extracts above quoted that the young collegian rose nobly to the ideal which he had set before him. There are those now living who can testify to the rich harvest of good which sprang up in his generation from the seed of manly Christian influence so freely scattered round him in those undergraduate days. Yet a crisis in his life was approaching, which we must leave to the next chapter to describe.

CHAPTER III

RELIGIOUS STATE, AND EXAMINATION FOR DEGREE

A FEW months after Edward Hoare took up his residence at Cambridge he commenced to keep a journal, which practice he continued for more than thirty years. Into its pages he poured his thoughts and communings with God, and, as he says in different parts of the journal, he did so that, looking back from time to time, his faith and love might be increased by noticing the way in which God had led him.

At the same time he was determined that there should be no repetition in his case of the grievous mistake which has been made by some well-meaning biographers; over and over again therefore he has inscribed upon the top of a page the word "Private"; and at the end of the first volume, written at a time when he thought that he was very near his end, he distinctly directs that his journal is not to be published. His wish has been carefully observed; no one has read the journal except the editor of his Autobiography, and he only to get a clearer view of the character

which he wishes to place before the reader, with
the one object laid down in the closing words of
the volume referred to—"Let nothing be done
with it or said about it except to extol the
goodness of God by the weakness of the creature."

It is evident from a perusal of the journal at
this time that he was dissatisfied with his spiritual
state, and a letter to his mother, dated July
21st, 1833, gives such a particular account of the
remarkable crisis through which he passed that
it is here given in full :—

"You have often expressed a wish that I would write
you a full and intimate letter about my own religious
feelings, but I have not done so hitherto, because I
lament to say they were too feeble to authorise any
expression, but I have had a time of very deep interest
since my return, and I do not like to withhold it from
you.

"When I arrived at home, I ought to have been
smarting with a guilty conscience, but I had succeeded
in stifling things, and though I cannot say I felt irre-
ligious, I was far from a Christian walk with God. On
Sunday morning Dr. Chalmers preached his sermon
upon the enjoyment and preparation for heaven, and
told us that the fruition of heaven was already begun
in the Christian's mind by the work of sanctification and
regeneration in his heart. I began to think how this
work was going on with me, but I found it so difficult
to bring my thoughts to bear upon the subject that I
carried the process of examination very little way, but
that little brought a whole array of irreligion before me.
I felt that my heart was not right with God, that I had

not that love towards the Saviour, nor that detestation
of sin, which it appeared to me that any one must feel
who had in truth participated in the Christian covenant,
and I was surprised and horror-struck at finding that
I had been guilty, not only of neglect, but of some
actual violations of God's law. Still, with all this I
could not bring my mind to dwell upon its own state,
and my serious thoughts were constantly supplanted by
others of a trivial nature. I tried to go and pray as an
offending sinner, but I could not collect my thoughts,
and though I daily said my prayers they were heartless
and cold, and did not at all reach the deep sensation
of need which I every now and then experienced, and
I felt that I was making no progress, though I was
growing very anxious. Every now and then my faith
almost gave way, and I thought that I had resisted the
Spirit so long that God had taken it from me. Then
again I thought of some passages such as these : 'It
is the Father's good pleasure to give you the kingdom
of life,' and those beautiful verses in the third of
St. John, ver. 14 ; and I heard Dr. Chalmers' morning
reading upon the generality of the Gospel offers, when
he dwelt upon the words 'whosoever' and 'every one,'
and I thought too upon the great Sacrifice that had
been made for sinners, and I had times of alternating
hope and despondency, but I was never happy because
I found I could not pray with my whole heart in faith,
and I did not think I was under the influence of the
Holy Ghost. This went on till Sunday evening. I
then heard an excellent sermon from Mr. Fisk about
the enthusiasm which a Christian must feel towards
God and the Saviour, and I felt that the state of my
own heart differed widely from this description. I
came home very unhappy, but even then I could not
get rid of wandering thoughts, by which I was so dis-

couraged that I began to think that God had cast me
off. Then I thought of the promises, especially 'Come
unto Me, all ye that labour and are heavy laden, and
I will give you rest'; but then I felt that I could not
number myself with them, for if really burdened with
sin I could think of nothing else. I walked about my
room for a long time and I knew not what to do, for
my faith was so weak that I felt a fear of approaching
God. At last, however, I felt that I could offer a
silent prayer to Him to teach me to pray, and *He heard
me.* I knelt down and felt as if a thick cloud had been
removed from me, and I was enabled to approach God
and entreat Him to pardon and to sanctify me. Oh,
dear mother! I cannot describe to you the joy I experienced when I felt that God had vouchsafed once
more to hear me.

"I afterwards went and told Goulburn all that I had
been going through, and was cruel enough to wake him
up in the midst of his night's rest. He satisfied me
very much upon the generality of the promises, and I
went to bed full of joy and thankfulness. The next
evening we met together and read the '1st Ephesians,'
and he offered up a most satisfactory prayer that the
Holy Spirit might manifest Himself in our hearts, and
I am most thankful to say I do believe his prayer has
been heard. We have continued to read and pray
together every evening, and I have found it perfectly
invaluable, and I trust, dearest mother, I have been
able to cast the whole burden of sin upon the Cross.
I feel still, however, that my heart is corrupt before
God, and I feel a want of devotion towards Him, but I
can pray that I may be strengthened with might in the
inner man, and I *know* I shall be heard. Oh how
unspeakable is the love of God! Oh may Christ dwell
in my heart by faith, that I, being rooted and grounded

in Him, may be able to comprehend with all saints
what is the length and depth and breadth and height,
and to know the love of Christ that passeth knowledge !
I need not say that this letter is perfectly private. I
should, however, have no objection to my father or
Elizabeth seeing it if they wish. I will include too
Sam and Catherine, but I don't wish anybody to be
told about it.

> "Believe me to be
>
> "Your most affectionate and grateful Son,
>
> "EDWARD HOARE."

Just at the same time in his journal he chooses
as his "text for life" St. Peter's words—"Casting
all your care upon Him, for He careth for you."
But a great sorrow was at hand. Shortly after
those lines were written his eldest brother Samuel
was struck down by a hæmorrhage, and in less
than three months he had passed away peacefully.
This was a sore trial to Edward, and his letters
abound with messages of deepest sympathy with
his brother and the young wife soon to be left a
widow. The words which he writes to his mother
read like the experience of an advanced Christian,
and the firm trust inspired by the "text for life"
breathes through them all. The examination for
his degree was rapidly approaching, so that study
could not be neglected. This year the reading
party went to Derbyshire, and the letters thence
give delightful accounts of visits to the Peak, etc.,
but the coming cloud casts its shadow across all

his thoughts; yet even so faith triumphs, and passages like the following, in a letter to his father, occur from time to time :—

"Oh what a thing it is to think that the Peace which can never be taken away is not only bestowed upon you and upon him here, but that if it should please God to realise our fears, it will soon be bestowed upon him in perfection above! Sometimes when I think of his prospects, as far as he is concerned, I can scarcely wish him well again, and, if it were not for all of you, could almost desire to go with him."

On Sunday, October 23rd, 1833, the beloved brother passed away, and the journal records that Gurney and Edward sat beside him all through the night and to the end. Early in November Edward Hoare was back at Cambridge. His first letter is full of sympathetic thoughts concerning the bereaved ones at home, and it is not until the last paragraph that there is any mention of his work; this, however, is particularly interesting from one point of view. The great anti-slavery struggle was nearing its climax; and, considering the prominent part which Sir Fowell Buxton took in the movement, it was not remarkable that his nephew should have thrown himself warmly into it. Accordingly we read :—

"I believe you were interested in my declamation. I have not got the prize, but they put me up on the paper as having made a very good one. The other three men, however, made better. I believe if I had not been so hot about slavery I might have got the prize, for at the time they expressed their great dissatisfaction at what I said about it."

Even as a young man he was not afraid to champion a cause which was unpopular with some who were in authority.

As the year draws near its close he describes his position as one of "overwrought excitement" when his mind dwells upon the approaching examination, which gives way to "a state of despondency" as a single thought of his sad home passes before him. Either this depression or the natural humility of his character makes him now "expect to take a fair second-rate degree"; when within a fortnight of the examination his mind becomes calmer, and he is enabled to make a good forecast of the result.

"I have good reason to hope," he writes, "for a place upon which I shall look back with pleasure and gratification all my life. . . . My own desire is to get into the first six wranglers, and if I accomplish that I shall be delighted. . . . I am not sanguine, but neither am I anxious. I desire to leave it altogether in the full assurance that I shall get the place which is best for me, whatever that place may be."

Surely the influence of the "text for life" is visible here! And those who knew him in later years will remember that this was his leading characteristic to the close of his life, making every preparation, using every endeavour, and then leaving the issue tranquilly in the hands of Him who "careth for you."

Christmas Day was spent with his Uncle and Aunt Gurney, and two or three days at the beginning of the New Year given to his home, to turn away his mind entirely from mathematics for the last day or two before his examination. Then two letters appear in the carefully preserved bundle, one to his mother at Hampstead :—

"I have not time to write much, but I have the unspeakable pleasure of telling you that I am 5th Wrangler and Robert Pryor 4th. I cannot say how thankful and happy I feel about it."

Written hastily, and in suppressed excitement, the date at the head of the letter—"December 17th, 1833"—is wrong both in the month and year (as the postmark testifies). The same day he writes more fully to his father in London ; to this letter there is no date at all. Never surely in all his life did he make either of these mistakes again! (The postmark on this is the same as on the former letter, viz. January 17th, 1834.)

"I have had a hard fight to-day in the bracket, the result of which is that I am 5th Wrangler, and Pryor 4th. I cannot say what unqualified pleasure and gratitude I feel at this result of my College labours, and the pleasure is not a little increased at Robert being the person to beat me ; there was no person in the examination to whom I would so willingly yield a place. I have had a hard fight to-day in the brackets. I was well aware, from the failure I made in two of the problem papers and the first class, that I was hard-run by some of the men in the bracket, so that I felt rather dismayed at finding myself with a good prospect of being 8th, whereas 6th had been my ambition. However, I set to work steadily and well, and, as I have since heard, gained three places, for I began at the bottom of the bracket. Peacock is very anxious that I should go in for the Smith's prize, as most men of my standing generally go through that ceremony. The list of our bracket is :—

Pryor
Hoare
Main
Bullock
Bates."

Robert Pryor, his "twin cousin," as he used to be called, was Edward Hoare's playmate from his earliest years. Educated together, together they entered the University, and came out, as we have seen, side by side in the list of wranglers. Pryor went in for the scholarship, but failed, and in a letter at the time his successful cousin writes of him as "behaving nobly," thinking nothing of his failure, and only setting to work twice as resolutely as before, with the happy result above noted.

Here follow letters of congratulation from the relatives with whom he spent the Christmas before his examination. The event to which they refer may well terminate a chapter of this book, as it certainly was the close of an important chapter in his life.

Congratulatory letter on his success at Cambridge from J. J. Gurney :—

"NORWICH, *June* 18*th*, 1834.

"DEAREST EDWARD,—I think it would be very flat of me not to acknowledge the receipt of thy letter. I understand from Geo. Peacock's letter to Hudson that the examination took an unfortunate turn for thee, or thou wouldst have been still higher ; however, I am sure thou art quite high enough—and we have nothing to do but warmly to congratulate thee on thy prowess and well-earned honours. Certainly I for one should withhold all congratulation, did I not feel assured that thou hast aboard thy vessel plenty of good ballast in the shape of humility, simplicity, and Christian principle. Therein I do and will rejoice, more than in the flag of victory. I should now advise a polite treatment of thyself—a journey—a frolic—a good long holiday, yet not absolute idleness, which is good for nobody.

"I am thy truly affectionate Uncle,

"J. J. GURNEY.

"My congratulations and kind regards to Rob. Pryor. I told thy mother that I was ready to be £50 towards thy expenses, shouldst thou take a journey—to be had at Overend's any day, on my account."

Congratulatory letter from his aunt :—

"UPTON, 1834.

"I must, my dear Edward, add one line of expression about my pleasure in hearing of thy success ; my only fear for thee seems to be lest thou mayst not feel humble enough, and continue to remember from whom thou gained thy excellent talents and powers of perseverance. To Him thou art, I know, desirous of dedicating them. I am writing by my dear John, who unites with us in our feeling for thee, and begs to unite in love to thee; thou wilt, I am sure, have felt for him in this trying relapse, but we desire to be enabled to believe it is permitted in mercy, and the favourable recovery from the operation is very cheering to us. Thy uncle with Sarah and Pris⁰ dined at Hampstead yesterday; the dear circle there as well as one could expect.

"Thy very affectionate Aunt,

"E. GURNEY."

Letter of congratulation from his cousin :—

"UPTON, 1834.

"MY DEAR EDWARD,—We are all so much interested and delighted at hearing of thy capital success, that a few lines must go to tell thee how warmly we congratulate thee, and how heartily we rejoice in it; it was most kind of thee to write and let us know of the result of the battle; we were longing to hear, the uncertainty of yesterday's report being so disappointing. It is pleasant to hear of Robert Pryor's doing so nobly, though I must confess my cousinly feelings would have been quite as well satisfied if you had changed places. Kitty desired me to give her love most particularly, and to tell thee she had set off directly to tell the Frys and the Listers about thee. Thou wilt have heard of the great anxiety we have gone through lately on dear John's account; we have now the great comfort and mercy of seeing him recovering as well as possible from this attack. The horses are at the door for a ride, and all the party waiting for me, so I must say no more.

"Thy very affectionate Cousin,

"S. GURNEY."

CHAPTER IV

VISIT TO IRELAND, AND PREPARATION FOR HOLY ORDERS

WHEN a young man distinguishes himself by taking a brilliant degree, the question is asked, "What profession is he going to adopt?" No doubt many were curious to know how Edward Hoare intended to make use of the talents that he possessed and the position which he had attained, and the following letter to his father, dated "May 17th, 1834," supplies the answer:—

". . . Now as to plans. With respect to the opening in business, I feel quite satisfied in declining it entirely. I am well aware that it might lead to an extensive field of usefulness and to many and great advantages in every point of view, but still I have long looked to the Church as my profession, and feel every day more and more decided in my desire to devote myself to it ; and I earnestly hope that I may be strengthened in the feeling, and that when, if ever, my hopes should be realised, I may be taught to be a useful minister both to myself and others."

In reply his father writes as follows :—

"Your letter conveyed the intelligence which I fully

expected to receive. I have only to pray God to bless you and make you a bright and shining light in His sanctuary.

"You have chosen the better part, and I confidently hope and expect that a blessing will rest upon it, and although you may not be blessed with the fat of the land, that you will be with the springs of living water springing up into everlasting life."

This was a distinct turning his back upon wealth, and perhaps social or even future Parliamentary distinction; but he had made up his mind. "The joy of the ministry" was the object of his young life, and surely thousands have had good reason to thank God for his choice, for thousands by his means have become sharers in that joy.

He did not, however, seek ordination at once. Being still too young for Holy Orders, and having been strongly urged to read for a Fellowship, he determined to set to work for another year of diligent study, and arranged at once to take a reading party of undergraduates to Killarney for the summer.

Many entertaining letters describe this period. We are rather alarmed in these days by the Race to the North between the trains of rival railway companies; the same spirit was not unknown sixty years ago, and showed itself in racing coaches!

The first letter describes such an event: two opposition coaches raced down a Welsh valley;

one passed the other at full gallop, but soon began
to sway fearfully, and at last went over with a
terrible crash. Providentially and most marvellously no one was injured ; had it happened a few
yards farther on several lives would have been
lost. Our travellers were deeply thankful for their
escape, and proceeded on their journey *via* Holy-
head to Dublin, and thence, after a short stay
in the Irish capital, which they much admired,
travelled southwards to the famous lakes. The
exquisite scenery made a great impression upon
the young Englishmen. "Fairy-land" was the
first brief summary of opinion, and they agreed
that it had surpassed all their expectations.

Great thankfulness is expressed frequently for
the excellent parish clergyman, Mr. Bland, and his
sermons are often described with interest. All
were reading steadily, but frequent excursions were
made, and rowing, fishing, and climbing of mountains kept them well occupied. One difficulty
not met with on former occasions was the great
hospitality of the surrounding gentry, who would
have entertained them at dinners and balls every
evening of the week if they had been disposed to
go. Some of the young men could not resist the
social charms of the place, and their chief writes a
little despondently of the responsibility upon him
of managing so large a party. He does not shrink
from it, however, and the first letter mentions
the regular "family reading" every day, to which

they invited their landlord and his family. The condition of the poor Celtic population around served to excite at different times feelings of amazement, humour, and almost of disgust. It must be remembered that some considerable changes have taken place in the manners and customs of the poor of Ireland since then; still much that is said in the following letter is true, not only of that neighbourhood, but also of large portions of the South and West; and yet, as he used often to remark in later years, this ignorant, pauperised, and superstitious population have proportionately more representatives in Parliament than the intelligent artisans of England!

" I had no idea of such want of comforts. You may travel for miles and yet meet with scarcely any one whom a Brewhouse Lane pauper would condescend to speak to. I do not complain of their having no shoes and stockings, because that is not their misfortune but their choice, but what few clothes they have are a mere bundle of rags : you see women about in worn-out men's coats, and the men do not cast them off till no strings can hold them together any longer. And then their cabins ! you never saw such places ; they generally consist of one room, though sometimes there are two. In the better sort there is a hole in the side by way of a window, but nowhere any glass in it ; then there is a large aperture above the fire, which I believe is intended for a chimney, but the smoke decidedly prefers to pro- ceed (after it has spent some time with its masters) by the more fashionable entrance of the door. This is a great convenience, as they smoke all their dried meat on the ceiling instead of in the narrow passage of the chimney. Their furniture consists of perhaps a table, two or three low chairs, a long box which serves for a bed for two or three by night and a seat by day, and a long bench for the younkers. Besides this there is some straw in one corner for those of the family who have no room in the box, and in another for the pigs ; a large coop to fat the young chickens in, and some bars across the top which serve to dry the hams on and as roosting poles for the hens. In the third corner they may stow a young lamb, and in the fourth throw a heap of potatoes. I went to a place arranged as I have attempted to describe. At first I could not see for the smoke, but was soon told that if I were to stoop low enough I could breathe if not see ; I accordingly sat me down on the low form, and when I was accustomed to the darkness I perceived the form of my hostess, bustling about with no shoes or stockings, and scolding hard at all the little urchins. Then there ensued a conflict with the pig, who could not understand on what grounds he was to be excluded, more especially when he saw the woman pour out a whole pot of hot potatoes on the table, and give a basin of goat's milk to each of us, which I can assure you that we and the chickens feasted on with no inconsiderable relish. Now for mathematics !

> " Your most affectionate Son,
>
> " Edward Hoare."

Men who have not forgotten the sensations of College life will recollect the rapid way in which age accumulates at the University ! This comes out amusingly in some of the Killarney letters, *e.g.* :—

" There could not be a place better suited to our purpose, nor a party better suited to each other ; the worst of it is I feel such an old man in comparison to the other two. Still we get on uncommonly well."

And again :—

" I am not reading hard, for we have all agreed that, as we have come so far, we will see the country well, and that I am too old and the others too young to fatigue ourselves with reading."

A vast gap of about two years separated the leader of this reading party from his juvenile companions, and though the outer world may not recognise much difference between young fellows of twenty and twenty-two, University men will recognise at once the historical accuracy of the feeling and its expression! It is very hard to put aside all the amusing letters written at this time, with their picturesque descriptions of the exquisite scenery, their accounts of duck-shooting and stag-hunts and expeditions of various sorts, and their droll description of novel experiences in his present surroundings. The following extract from a letter to one of his sisters must suffice as a specimen :—

" I must tell you of our evening yesterday. I was reading away as hard as could be when I heard the bagpipe in the next room. I found it was Gandsey, the celebrated piper, and all the village crowded into the house to hear. However, the ladies who had him would shut the door, because, as our landlord said, ' one of them was a dumpey,' *i.e.* deformed, and did not wish to be seen, so that we were disappointed. When he had done with them we thought that we must give ourselves and all the listeners a treat, so we said he must play for us too; and as our room was not large enough for the party, we adjourned to the kitchen, which, though a large room, was soon as full as it could comfortably hold. We had several famous tunes, to the great delight of all parties. As I felt my own feet quite a-going with the music, I proposed that those who wished should have a dance. We soon had some volunteers, and a famous Irish jig was the consequence. The partners were to me so un-tempting, as by far the best was the cook-maid, that, though I longed to dance too, my pride would not come down, and I looked on. Upcher and Merivale, however, danced hard with two of the maids, but they could not learn the jig, so the latter gave up. Upcher, however, went on with more perseverance than skill. But I can assure you it was a grand scene—a fine old blind man, the best piper in Kerry, playing with all his might, and the more active dancing in the middle of the room to correspond, and, if any by chance had a pair of shoes, taking them off to be the more active; while all along the walls were the ragged Irish watching the dance and sucking in the music with the greatest animation. Now just think what a difference there is between our two situations: you sitting quietly in the comfortable library with my father and mother, and I giving a ball in the kitchen, with nothing but a clay floor and naked walls; with scarcely another sound coat in the room except our own!"

The summer at Killarney passed pleasantly, and October found the travellers back at Cambridge, Edward Hoare reading steadily for fellowship, but with a growing desire for the work of the ministry evidently uppermost in his thoughts. There are hardly any letters at this period, but his journal is full of the holy aspirations of the young man's heart.

The following June (1835) found him at Keswick intent upon his studies, and at the same time full of increased longing to help others in spiritual things. Writing thence to his mother, he alludes to a brief visit to his rooms at Trinity, where he spent a busy week preparing and collecting papers to take with him. Almost all his old friends were gone, but his influence had reached men of junior standing, and the consequence was—

"I was quite delighted and touched by the warmth of affection which I received there. Goulburn and Merivale were both out, but I could compare my reception to nothing but the prophet's in Israel. I thought there were no friends left, but there were nearer seven thousand, and most affectionate they were. Mr. Simeon especially was full of love and kindness; he spoke of you with the deepest interest, and said he longed to see you, and that he thought he could be a help to you as the messenger of the Gospel; and he spoke to me most beautifully about the Three Persons of the Trinity all assuming to themselves at different times the character of our Comforter, as also upon the fellowship existing between Christians through the Saviour."

In the same letter, speaking of Keswick, he writes :—

"I regard this opportunity as likely to be one of great usefulness, and I look forward with great pleasure to the prospect of quiet repose, withdrawn from all active service, as a preparation of my own mind and a thorough sifting of the foundations, before I enter upon the more active duties to which I trust it may please God before long to call me."

He was not content with mere meditation, however. Being desirous to give some help to the parish clergyman, he was asked to take some cottage lectures in a neighbouring farmhouse. As an old man he often referred with great joy to this time as the beginning of his ministry. The farmhouse was an old building with low rooms, having great deep beams running across the unceiled kitchen. The tall young figure could not stand erect in the low-pitched room, except by *fitting his head between the beams!*

But the difficulty and humour of the scene were both forgotten in the sight of the crowded, attentive listeners, and the evident signs of the presence of the power of the Holy Spirit in the midst. Long, long afterwards Canon Hoare revisited the place, found the farmhouse, entered the very room, and was overjoyed to meet some who had never forgotten the addresses of the earnest young collegian more than fifty years before.

CHAPTER V

ORDINATION AND FIRST CURACY

HAVING failed in his fellowship examination, Edward Hoare was in perplexity as to the right course for him to pursue. His heart longed for the ministry. On the other hand, his former College tutor and many old friends urged him to stand again, saying that it was impossible for him to fail in obtaining fellowship. For three months he was in sore perplexity, looking for guidance, sometimes inclining to one plan, sometimes to the other. At last the leading came. The Rev. E. G. Marsh, Incumbent of Well Walk Chapel, Hampstead, called upon him, and his conversation settled the matter at once ; the fellowship was given up, and Edward Hoare began to think of a curacy and speedy ordination.

Just at this time, and as if to try and hinder the young earnest heart from entering upon active work, the great enemy of souls assailed him with vehemence.

There was a long struggle, dark and intense. Probably the most faithful have had to go through terrible times of testing, and have known what it was to endure dark hours, aye, and days and weeks, "when neither sun nor stars appeared, and all hope that we should be saved was taken away." It may be a comfort to many who in his ministry have been upheld by the firm faith of their teacher to know that Edward Hoare once passed through a time like this. It is no breach of confidence to give here the following lines written in his journal at this time :—

" Forsake me not, my God! my heart is sinking,
   Bowed down with faithless fears and bodings vain,
  Busied with dark imaginings, and drinking
    Th' anticipated cup of grief and pain :
    But, Lord, I lean on Thee ; Thy staff and rod
        Shall guide my lot ;
    I will not fear if Thou, my God, my God,
        Forsake me not.

" Forsake me not, my God!
   Though earth grow dim and vanish from my sight,
  Through death's dark vale no human hand may take me,
   No friend's fond smile may bless me with its light ;
   Alone the silent pathway must be trod
        Through that drear spot—
   For I must die alone—oh there, my God,
        Forsake me not !

" Forsake me not, my God! when darkly o'er me
   Roll thoughts of guilt and overwhelm my heart ;
  When the accuser threatening stands before me,
   And trembling conscience writhes beneath the dart,
   Thou who canst cleanse by Thy atoning blood
        Each sinful spot,
   Plead Thou my cause, my Saviour and my God!
        Forsake me not !

" Forsake me not, O Thou Thyself forsaken
   In that mysterious hour of agony,
When from Thy soul Thy Father's smile was taken
   Which had from everlasting dwelt on Thee :
   Oh by that depth of anguish which to know
             Passes man's thought,
By that last bitter cry, Incarnate God,
            Forsake me not ! "

But the storm passed, and was followed by
" clear shining after rain." The adversary meant
it for harm, but God overruled it for good ; and
surely one of the secrets of Edward Hoare's great
power of helping troubled souls, for which he was
so remarkable in after-life, lay in the fact that
he had passed through the time of spiritual darkness, and had come out into the light.

AUTOBIOGRAPHY (continued).

After taking my degree at Cambridge I continued to reside there for a time, taking mathematical pupils and reading for a Trinity Fellowship ;
but not having succeeded in my first examination,
and being anxious to be at work in the great
calling of my life, I could not devote another year
to the study of mathematics. So I threw my whole
heart into immediate preparation for the ministry.

In those days there was no Ridley or Wycliffe,
and I was thrown upon my own resources for my
study ; but I worked hard and brought all my Cambridge habits to bear on the great subject of theology. If I had learnt nothing else at Cambridge,

I had learnt never to be satisfied till I got a clear
view of what I was about, and that habit of mine,
acquired through mathematical study, has been of
the greatest possible benefit throughout my life.

During those important months, to use Cambridge language, I "got up" some of our best
books, such as Butler, Pearson, and Hooker. What
I learnt from the latter especially has been invaluable to me through life. Butler's "Analogy" has
again and again been helpful to me, when there
has been a tendency to a shaking of the faith.
But that which helped me most during that time
of preparation was the study of great doctrinal
truths from Scripture itself. I took up such subjects as *The Divinity of our Lord, Justification by
Faith, Baptism, The Lord's Supper, Election,* and
Final Perseverance, one at a time; and I read the
whole New Testament through with especial reference to the one subject which I was studying, carefully noting every passage referring to it. I then
analysed and grouped those passages, keeping careful records of results. Having thus dealt with one
subject, I went on to the second, then to the third,
and so on. I have no words wherewith to convey
the immense value these studies have been to me
throughout life. They have told upon the whole
of my ministry. After more than fifty-two years
I am habitually using the results first obtained in
that preparation period.

I cannot speak too strongly, therefore, of the

vast importance of our young men, when preparing
for the ministry, devoting themselves to the careful
study of theology. I see dear young men, full of
zeal and holy earnestness, who seem, indeed, so
zealous that they cannot wait to study ; and they
are to my mind like men who are in such haste
to fire their guns that they cannot wait to put any
shot in them ! The result is that, when they are
sent forth as ministers of the Gospel and as teachers
of the truth, they are themselves ignorant of the
clear definitions of the truth they are going to
teach, and, while they can make fervent appeals,
are utterly unable to build up others in great
fundamental truths of the Gospel. It is not fervour only that makes a minister valuable, but a
fervent exhibition of truth ; and if we are to be
able ministers, we *must* be able ministers of New
Testament truths.

I consider, therefore, that an immense benefit
has been conferred upon the Church of England
by the foundation of Ridley Hall at Cambridge,
and Wycliffe Hall at Oxford. How thankful
should I have been myself to have been under
the teaching of either of the two able Principals
of those Halls ; and how earnest should we all be
to secure to our young men the benefit of these
institutions, and not to let them go forth as
evangelists or scripture-readers, to be giving *out*
before they have taken *in*, and to be teaching
others before they have learnt themselves.

At length the day came for my ordination, and I had the inestimable privilege of being ordained as curate to my revered and beloved uncle, Mr. Francis Cunningham, Vicar of Lowestoft and Rector of Pakefield.   An ordination in those days was a very different thing to what it is now.   At that time Bishop Bathurst was Bishop of Norwich, and too infirm to undertake his own ordinations. He therefore gave his candidates dimissory letters to the Bishop of Lincoln.

I cannot say that much was done to deepen the impression on the minds of the candidates.   As we all had to go to Norwich first for examination, and to Buckden for ordination, it was necessary to show some consideration for us, as there were no railways then.   I often think that the Chaplain showed a great deal of good sense in his examination.   It began on Wednesday morning, and he told us that he should give us hard questions at the beginning, that they would grow easier and easier during the three days of the examination, and that he should let us go as soon as he was satisfied.   So we had a good stiff paper on various subjects at the first sitting, while he walked about the room and looked over the papers as we were writing, but having nothing to look over from a great many of the candidates.   It was a great satisfaction to me, when that first sitting was over, to be told that I might go, and that I should find the necessary papers at Buckden.

Most of us Norwich men had to put up at Huntingdon, as the little inn at Buckden was full of the men from the Lincoln Diocese ; and as I imagine that the Bishop did not like to have the Norwich men in addition to his own, he gave us no share of any of the privileges that his own candidates may have enjoyed. We signed our papers, etc., on the Saturday morning, and were told that we Norwich men were not wanted any more till the next morning. Accordingly the next morning we were in the church at the appointed hour, and that evening, to my great joy, I read prayers at the parish church of Huntingdon. How wonderfully different is the careful pains taken by all our present Bishops ere young men are admitted to the ministry, and what a wonderful improvement has taken place in this respect!

Letter from Rev. E. G. Marsh, on his entering the ministry :—

"HAMPSTEAD, *February*, 1836.

" MY DEAR FRIEND,—Knowing with whom you are connected in the great work which you have now undertaken, I feel that I might fairly excuse myself from saying anything to you upon an occasion so interesting to all your friends ; and my natural indolence would readily yield to the suggestion, and withhold me from interfering where others are more competent to advise. Yet on the whole I could not be quite easy if I suffered you to enter upon an office, far too high

and holy to be approached by a sinner, but for that
infinite condescension and love of our Saviour which
has called us to it, without saying to you, in the words
of St. Paul to Archippus, ''Take heed to the ministry
which thou hast received in the Lord, that thou fulfil
it!' This is indeed a solemn charge, even more so
than that which you have just received from the Bishop.
I can add nothing to its weight, and can only pray
my God to forgive all our deficiencies, and to supply
all our need, according to His riches in glory by Christ
Jesus. Nevertheless there are one or two hints which
I will venture to suggest, in case they should help you
in taking a practical view of the obligations thus laid
upon you. In the first place, although this is a work
which can only be successfully prosecuted in the spirit
of prayer and in the strength of the Saviour, it is very
desirable that the greatness of it should not dishearten
us, or render us insensible to the duty of doing what
we can. My simple advice to you in the beginning
of your ministry is this—never to let a day pass, if it
be possible, without doing some act in fulfilment of
it. I mean some act having respect, not to your own
personal salvation, but to the salvation of those to whom
you are an ambassador for Christ: to your parishioners,
while you are among them; to others, when you are
absent. And this act, whatever it be, should be made
the subject of special prayer. My second advice is to
give sufficient time to each act, that it may be done
properly, and rather to let many be neglected than to
do any one perfunctorily, for on that which is performed
indifferently and without due attention we cannot con-
sistently expect a blessing. To do one thing at a time
is the only way, either in spiritual duties or in temporal,
to do many things well. Do not, therefore, attempt too
much at once. Many break down and are discouraged

by this error. Again, I would say, 'Attend more to the living than to the dying.' However important may be the clinical department of ministerial duty, we must always be greatly on our guard against encouraging the notion that the work of religion may be done, as doctors' degrees are sometimes taken, *per cumulum*, or that anything can be done by a clergyman at the last hour which can reasonably be expected to produce a change in the spiritual condition of a person who has neglected to seek it before. Thus the ministry which you have received may be continually carried forward, independently of those occasional calls, caused by the alarm of sickness or the apprehension of death, which are most valuable seasons indeed, but on which too much stress may be easily laid, to the neglect of more hopeful opportunities. I hardly intended to say so much, and indeed, on what I have now said you may naturally ask me whether these have been my maxims in the course of my own ministry. But, alas! my dear friend, I do not propose myself as an example to you. I rather wish to see you avoid my errors and supply my defects; and happy shall I be if, in the arduous duties on which you are now embarking, you can derive the least aid from a single word of mine. Commending you to God and to the word of His grace who alone can make you an able minister of the New Testament,

     " I remain ever, my dear friend,

       " Your faithful and affectionate fellow-labourer,

            "E. G. MARSH."

From Mrs. Hoare to Mrs. Catherine Gurney on Edward Hoare's first sermon :—

" I must send thee one line, dearest Catherine, to tell thee what a remarkable day of interest we passed on Sunday. Our dearest Edward read the service in Well Walk in the morning and in the evening preached. It was deeply interesting, and I longed to have my heart melted in love and gratitude. Such heartfelt satisfaction to have this dear child so devoted, and adorned with so childlike, lovely, and devoted a spirit, and thus enabled in our own chapel, amongst our friends and neighbours, to proclaim with grace and fervour the great salvation of the Gospel of Christ! This appeared to me to be remarkably the case with him, and, independent of a mother's feelings, his countenance and manner, his manly grace and childlike humility and simplicity, were striking. The congregation had, I believe, much fellow-feeling with us, and the expression of it from different friends has been touching to us. Never was I less disposed to boast, and deeply can unite in that expression ' Where is boasting ?—It is excluded '; and yet I *long* to say with the Psalmist, ' My soul shall make her boast in the Lord,' and in the blessing He has been pleased to vouchsafe. Of course we feel the prospect of parting with Edward ; one of the many cheering points in the prospect is his vicinity to Earlham, and to thee and our dearest brother. How kind has Joseph been to him, and what an opportune visit was his last to Earlham !

" I went to see Anna Tooten yesterday at Tottenham, as I had left Upton before the arrival of thy letter. Catherine has been very much cast down lately, and I am but a poor helper. The dear babes are with me to-day, while their mother is in Devonshire Street.

" My dearest brother and sister, nephew and niece,

and dear Rachel included, I know they will all unite with us in the interest of Edward.

"Your truly affectionate
"L. H."

AUTOBIOGRAPHY (*continued*).

It was not long afterwards that I went to my curacy. Pakefield was a bleak village on the top of a cliff, and I never shall forget what the guard on the coach said to me as I was approaching it for the first time. I had complained of cold, and he said to me, "Don't talk about the cold yet; wait till you get to Pakefield—there you catches it genuine!" And so we did. Aye, and I witnessed many a gale of wind, and during the year that I was curate, there were no less than fifty shipwrecks off the coast of my own parish.

But no words can express my thankfulness to God that He placed me at the outset of my ministry in that village. My dear uncle had laboured there for more than forty years. In his day there were none of the new plans for evangelisation; the high-pressure system had not yet dawned. He had worked hard with parochial work, and he had faithfully preached the old-fashioned Gospel. There was no particular brilliancy about him; his sermons were not equal to his character, but they were like himself, full of Christ, and he and his most remarkable wife lived such a life of Christian holiness in the midst of those rough fishermen, that the late Rev. Henry Blunt once told me that he considered Mr. Francis Cunningham and Mr. Haldane Stewart to be the two holiest men he had ever met with in his life. And what did I find in that village? I found large congregations of fishermen and their families ; but more than that, I went diligently about from house to house, and was soon acquainted with every house in the parish, and there I saw unmistakable evidences of the blessing that had rested upon my uncle's ministry.

There were noble men among the fishermen, nobly working for God and for the cause of truth, and there were refined and well-instructed women in the different homes, many of whom had been brought up in those schools. There was a most marked and unmistakable difference between the converted and the unconverted, so that it was impossible for a young man to go from house to house without seeing with his own eyes the manifest results of a faithful Evangelical ministry. I have no words to express what the benefit was to myself. I learnt in that village what I was to expect, as well as what I was to do.

I saw in Mrs. Cunningham the most beautiful example of a clergyman's wife, and I saw in numbers of young women of the parish the conspicuous evidence of God's blessing on her work amongst them.

There were amongst those men fine, noble,

rough, powerful fellows—men who, till Mr. Cunningham went there, had been living without God in the world, but now devout consistent believers, and splendid men for dashing through the surf to save life from shipwreck, knowing not what fear was, yet who would kneel together in devout Communion at the Table of the Lord. I never can forget one fearful snow-storm accompanied by a heavy gale. Two of these true men, Nath Colby and Robert Peck, brought in their boats through the gale, wet, cold, and half-frozen, but there I saw them at the service on the Thursday evening, drinking in the Word of Life, and evidently regarding it as their greatest pleasure to be able to be present on that occasion.

That was the last time I ever spoke to dear Robert Peck. He went out again in command of his large fishing boat, and early in the following week I heard that his boat had been found bottom upward. It was my solemn duty to walk through the village, where, everybody being so awed by what had happened, no one spoke a word, to go up to that cottage to tell the poor woman her husband and her son were gone. As I went up the alley where she lived, I heard voices in one of the cottages; turning in, I found some Christian friends assembled there, praying for the poor bereaved woman. I then went into her cottage, and I suppose she read in my face what had happened, and she said to me, ere I could open

my lips, "Then they are both lost?" Then she
added : "'A bruised reed shall He not break, and
the smoking flax shall He not quench.' These
were the last words that Robert spoke to me—
and I am sure the Lord will never fail me!" Oh
that every young curate had the opportunity of
learning as much from his Rector, and his Rector's
family, as I did from Mr. and Mrs. Cunningham!
I do not hesitate to say that their example, and
the blessing which God gave to their ministry,
have given character to the whole of my own
ministry for the last fifty-two years.

These were not the only advantages I enjoyed
in Pakefield, for I was within easy reach of
Earlham, the seat of my dear Uncle Joseph John
Gurney. He was a very remarkable man, and
his home was one of the most charming homes in
England. He used to collect there many of the
most distinguished men of the day. Nothing
could be more delightful than the great gatherings
under his hospitable roof on the occasion of
the Norwich Meetings which were held every
autumn.

I had a horse at that time which taught me a
great lesson in practical life. It was a splendid
trotter, but pulled like a steam-engine if I pulled
against it ; but if I treated it gently and with
confidence it was as gentle as a lamb. How often
have I seen the same effect produced amongst
mankind ! Try to force them, and they resist ; deal

gently with them, and they will be your most active and kindest helpers. So I used as often as possible to ride over to Earlham.

There I had three friends. There was my uncle, who was far in advance of the Quakers of his day in theological knowledge, being a good Biblical critic and well made up in the great doctrines of the Gospel. The great point in his conversations with me was the Divinity of our Lord and Saviour. It was he that taught me of the goings forth of the pre-existent Saviour with the Name and Attributes of Jehovah. Then there was Mr. William Forster, the father of the late statesman, who was most earnest with me on the importance of definite theology. He recommended certain books for my study, and at his advice I purchased Brown's "Natural and Revealed Religion," Guise's "Expositor," and Dwight's "Theology," which three books have been of the utmost value to me throughout my ministry. The latter book indeed has been made the text-book for my son's theological students in China. Thus is Mr. Forster's advice being still acted upon in that far distant region.

Besides these two men was my very dear friend the Rev. Robert Hankinson, at that time Curate of Earlham. He was a man of remarkably sound judgment, as well as fervent piety ; and never can I forget the profitable hours which I spent with him in the Earlham Parsonage, learning from him maxims of practical wisdom to carry home for my ministerial work.

But that was not all that happened to me at Pakefield; for while I was there it pleased God to take home to Himself my dearest mother. My dear brother Sam had died of consumption in the year 1833, and she deeply mourned his loss—nor could we wonder, for he was a noble young man, full of high principles, dutiful to his father and mother, and devoted to the Lord. His influence over us his younger brothers was of infinite value to us all, as we had ever before us a spotless example. He had married most happily, was settled in his home near to our father's house, when he was suddenly seized with hæmorrhage, and very rapidly sank, full of faith in God. I remember well, when I sat up with him on the last night of his life, how he spoke to me of the bright hope of the coming Resurrection, how he exhorted those around him to be ready for their Saviour.

I believe it was the shock as well as the sorrow of parting with him that so deeply wrung my mother's heart. She was in his room with him on the morning of his death, and thinking that his dear, wife required attention, she went out for a few minutes to see after her, and when she returned to her surprise, he was gone. That was in the autumn of 1833, and for nearly three years we saw her gradually fail, till at length in the summer of 1836 the end came.

There was something most interesting in the character of my mother. She was not one of those who spoke much of present salvation and present peace; such subjects were not spoken of so much throughout the Church in those days as they are now. Good men in those times seemed to think more of the future than the present salvation. I am not sure that we have not drifted rather too much into the dwelling on the present, to the forgetfulness of the future life, and surely it is important for us to keep the balance. But while there was very little of the modern language of assurance, there was in its most perfect form the great reality of the hallowed Christ. I can never forget the language of that dearest mother to me as I stood by her bedside during her dying illness: "I can reverently say, with the deepest humility, 'Lord, Thou knowest all things, Thou knowest that I love Thee.'" And she did love Him with her whole heart and soul. How well do I remember her words in the garden at Hampstead in the afternoon of her son's death! While she wept over his loss, she exclaimed, "How little it is in comparison with sin!"*

---

* An old friend relates that, when he was going to be ordained Deacon at Ely, Edward Hoare, with whom he was not then acquainted, was to receive Priest's Orders at the same time, and as they passed into the Cathedral he heard young Hoare say with great solemnity, "Now may the Holy Ghost fill this place!" The words and tone made a profound impression upon the younger man.—ED.

Pakefield Letters.

"Pakefield, *June 20th*, 1836.

"My dearest Mother,—Having paid my bills and seen after the schools, I commence my usual Monday's letter. . . . As for myself, it is needless to give you my history, for you know it already, the life of a country curate not being subject to much external variation. The internal changes, however, are indeed numerous— more frequent and uncertain than those of our most changeable climate. I never had an idea how many ups and downs there are attendant on the ministerial work. At times it is delightful ; all seems easy and pleasant, and the only difficulty is to keep within bounds. At others there is a deadness and barrenness which words cannot describe. I speak under a very vivid recollection of this low estate, for I was down at the very bottom yesterday. I fought my way pretty fairly through the morning sermon (on Isa. xxviii. 16), but in the evening I had a real trial of my faith. I had good notes, and had well considered my subject. But as soon as I began it all appeared to leave me. I was much in the position that Robert Hall was when he broke down, and I thought I must have stopped. There were my notes, but they seemed to tell me nothing, and I had the pain of going through my lecture hardly knowing while I was delivering one sentence whether I should ever find another to follow it. You may easily imagine, from such a description of the performer, what was the character of the performance. However, I can look back to it, painful as it was, with great thankfulness : for (1) I know that in weakness He is strong, and the good done may perhaps be greater than that which would have followed a clear and well-

delivered lecture ; and (2) if it did no one else any
good, it was a fine lesson for myself, and one that I
wanted.   I knew I wanted to be kept down, and had
prayed for it.   This was the appointed means."

Writing to his mother at various times upon his
work at Pakefield there occur passages such as
these :—

"Preaching is becoming more and more a pleasure
to me. The great difficulty of addressing people appears
to pass away.   The knowledge of all the congregation
is partly the cause, and also the encouragement derived
from visiting."

"You see there is a good deal doing here, but what
is it all if the Spirit of God be absent ?—a sounding
brass and tinkling cymbal.   It is there that the difficulty
lies.   Nothing is easier than to get through the duties
of a parish, and to get through them, as man thinks,
well ; but to go to your work in the Spirit of Christ,
carrying with you the unction from the Holy One,
there is the difficulty.   May God forgive my great short-
comings !   Sometimes I dread Jeremiah xlviii. 10."

Upon the spiritual life he writes to his sister :—

"The characteristic of the new life is that we have
fellowship with the Father and with His Son Jesus
Christ ; it must therefore follow that all interruptions
will increase a deadness of faith, and total separation
cause death.   It is one of the privileges of my office
that all my work is for God (though He only knows
how little I keep this end in view), and therefore the
busier I am the more I am compelled to pray. This,
however, is not sufficient, though delightful. We cannot

live without that 'freedom of speech,' translated 'boldly' in Hebrews iv., in which we pour out our heart before Him. When we know that we know in truth that God is a refuge for us, this is the balm of Gilead that can heal every wound, the power that can say to the troubled waters, 'Peace, be still!' In order to the attainment of it let us allow nothing to impede our private communion with our God."

Writing one Sunday evening to his mother he says :—

"I have had somewhat to contend with in myself from very cloudy views of the doctrines I was preaching. At the same time I have found comfort in the recollection that the work is not mine nor dependent upon my own feelings. I began work at a quarter before nine by opening the boys' school ; at ten I was really refreshed and humbled by just dropping into the prayer-meeting ; there was a most beautiful spirit amongst them, and they were praying most delightfully for me. I left them deeply impressed with the sense of their far greater fitness to teach me than mine to be their minister."

In the postscript of a letter dated August 1st, 1836, he writes : "Congratulate Uncle Buxton upon the glorious events of this day." An entry in his journal dwells joyfully upon it also—and well might his and every Englishman's heart be stirred by the thought that from that day every slave standing on British soil was free !

CHAPTER VI

RICHMOND

BUT my Pakefield curacy was soon to terminate. Whether it was the cold, or whether
it was the pressure of ministerial interest, which I
have often known to break down young men in the
outset of their ministry, or whether it was the
death of my dearest mother, or the three together, I cannot say; but I had a bad cough, and
I went away for a time to my father's home to
nurse it. I had no idea at the time of leaving
Pakefield, but my kind and valued friend the
Rev. J. W. Cunningham, brother to my Rector,
recommended me, without my knowledge, to the
curacy of Richmond, Surrey.

He was a true friend to me and to my family.
He was a very different man to his brother; he
had taken a high degree at Cambridge, and he was
a polished scholar, one of the best writers of the
English language that I ever met with, an admirable friend as a scholarly critic to a young man
entering the ministry. I am much indebted to his
advice, and only wish I had followed it more carefully. It was his doing that introduced me to the

Rev. W. Gandy, Vicar of Kingston and Richmond ;
and through him the curacy was proposed to me.

I must say that it was a desperate experiment
on his part, for there were peculiar circumstances
connected with the position, and I had never run
alone in the ministry, but always had the friendship and counsel of my beloved Rector.

The position of the parish was this. There
were four parishes lying together along the banks
of the Thames—Kingston, Petersham, Richmond,
Kew—all in the gift of King's College, Cambridge.
It had been thought desirable that there should be
only two Vicars instead of four, and therefore it
had been arranged to group them, two and two.
Of course the most natural arrangement would have
been to have put together the small parish of Petersham and the large parish of Kingston to which it
was adjacent, and the small parish of Kew and
the large parish of Richmond which also ad-
joined. But in those days there used to be a
good deal of jobbery, and, for some reason or other
which I never could explain, it had been decided
to unite together the two large parishes, Kingston
and Richmond, skipping over Petersham ; and the
two small parishes, Petersham and Kew, skipping
over Richmond ; so that the Rev. Mr. Gandy was
Vicar of Kingston and Richmond, while another
gentleman was Vicar of the other two smaller
ones.

Mr. Gandy was a man altogether incompetent

to have the charge. He was a most interesting man, and a deep student of Scripture—a man of heavenly mind, one in fact who seemed so occupied with heavenly views that he was unfitted for the practical business of this lower world. Mr. Simeon once said of him, " All of us are going stumping along on the surface of earth, but Mr. Gandy rises right into Heaven ! "

It may easily be imagined that he found his great double charge far too much for him, so Mr. Cunningham advised him practically to give up Richmond into the hands of some trustworthy curate, who should find his own assistant, and undertake the entire responsibility of the work. This was the charge to which I was called by the providence of God in those early days of my ministry. I have just said it was a desperate experiment, and looking back to that time I can see plenty of mistakes, and I learn from my own experience that it is a possible thing to mistake the irritation produced by our own blunders for opposition to the Gospel which we preach ; a man may be true to the Gospel, but he may not infre- quently make very great mistakes in his mode of putting it forth.

In looking back to those days I am thankful to believe that I went to Richmond true to my Master, and I am profoundly thankful for the help given me ; but I should make a great mistake if I were to lead anybody to suppose that, in my earnest desire to exalt my Saviour, I never did anything to irritate. At one time I had great difficulty with one of the churchwardens, which led to a considerable correspondence. I kept that correspondence carefully, and after ten years I looked it over. That revision taught me a great lesson, for I found that in the heat of the controversy I had written very differently to what I should have done in the calmer review of ten years afterwards. That was one of the lessons I learnt at Richmond.

That which I look back upon with the greatest thankfulness is a confirmation by my Richmond experience of the great lesson I learnt at Pakefield respecting the results to be expected from the ministry. Mr. Gandy had been Vicar for some twenty-five years, during which time he had appointed a series of curates, the first of whom was the Rev. Stephen Langston, who resigned the curacy about twenty years before I was appointed. But when I set to work in the parish, the first thing that met my observation was a body of Christian men and women who owed their conversion, through God, to Mr. Langston's ministry. There they were living consistent lives and most truly glorifying God, in some cases under sharp opposition, and the twenty years that had elapsed since Mr. Langston left only tended to confirm their faith and establish their character.

Both in Pakefield and Richmond, therefore, it

was my unspeakable privilege to see the effects
produced by the faithful ministry of the Word of
God. And yet the two cases were entirely different. Mr. Cunningham was an admirable pastor,
but not a particularly interesting preacher; Mr.
Langston was a poor pastor, but the grandest
preacher I ever heard. I have heard many able
men preach many excellent sermons, but there was
a richness, a fulness, a power about Mr. Langston's
such as I never met with in any other to whom
I have listened. The two instruments, therefore,
were entirely different, but God made use of them
both. They were both blessed by Him; and it
taught me the lesson that I must be prepared to
meet with great differences of administration, but
in the midst of those differences it is our privilege
to look for a blessing. God did not withhold from
Mr. Cunningham His blessing, because he had not
the preaching power of Mr. Langston; nor did He
withhold His blessing from Mr. Langston, because
he had not the pastoral zeal of Mr. Cunningham.

The lesson taught me was not the only blessing
bestowed upon me through the friendship of those
excellent people. I had in it the enormous advantage of the ripened experience and tried wisdom
of some of the most excellent Christian people
living. Never can I forget the friendship of Sir
Henry and Lady Baker, of Dr. Julius and of Mrs.
Delafosse, to whose loving sympathy and Christian
counsel I used continually to resort; and amongst

the humbler classes there was Mrs. Abbott, a grand old Christian who had loved the Lord before she heard the preaching of the Gospel, and the moulding of whose faith was drawn from the Prayer-Book. She often used to express to me her astonishment that when people were brought to Christ it did not make them love their Prayer-Book more.

And down a row of cottages at the bottom of Water Lane there lived a blind woman named Mrs. Woodrow, whom I shall ever regard as one of the best of my many friends. I had been preaching one day on the importance of praying for the ministry, and when visiting her a few days afterwards I said, "I'm sure you pray for me." "Indeed I do," she replied with great emphasis, "morning, noon, and night." She spoke with such earnestness that I could not refrain from asking her what she prayed for, when she said, "They tell me you're a very young man, so I pray that you may be kept from the sins of young men." How much do I owe to the prayers of that blind widow!

In addition to these advantages I enjoyed the intimate friendship of my beloved and honoured friend the Rev. James Hough, founder of the Tinnevelly Mission. After his return from India he had settled in the incumbency of Ham, and I never can forget his first visit to me. I had taken a lodging just beyond the bridge, and I had scarcely finished my breakfast on the first day after my arrival when the venerable man entered the room. He spoke very kindly to me, and before he would say a word upon any other subject, he told me that many Christian friends had been praying that the right appointment might be made, and afterwards for me when they heard that I was appointed, and that he had come on the first possible occasion to commend me solemnly to the Lord. He then fell on his knees and pleaded for me before God that I might have grace and wisdom for the difficult post to which I had been called. His subsequent intercourse with me was in harmony with that beginning. His house was always open to me, and whenever I wanted counsel I always used to go to him, as I never failed to find in him one who seemed to bring his wisdom fresh from the throne of grace.

With these advantages I set to work. I wonder at the grace of God that kept me from making more blunders than I did; for having had no experience I had not the slightest fear of difficulty. Things in those days were very different to what they are now. Ritualism had not then been invented, nor had that loose vague system now so popular under the name of Undenominationalism.

Among those who professed to be Churchmen there were only two classes—those whose Churchmanship consisted in maintaining things as they were, who were living for the world; who, if they cared for their own souls, were utterly unconcerned about the souls of others ; who showed not the slightest sympathy in any Christian object, and who seemed to consider that anything that disturbed them must of necessity be unorthodox. To avoid such disturbance one of those gentlemen stumped out of church every Sunday morning as I went up to the pulpit, and others used to take refuge in the chapel of Archdeacon Cambridge on the other side of the river.

On the other hand, there was a body of people, drawn from all classes of society, who " had passed from death unto life," who had been quickened by the Spirit of God, and who were taking their stand nobly on the side of their Saviour. Thus there was a much wider line of demarcation between the converted and the unconverted than we meet with in modern times, and a clergyman's work was simpler than it is now, inasmuch as there was much less to entangle and confuse the application of the message to individual souls.

But there was in some cases sharp opposition. It may seem extraordinary to some that at the visitation of the late Bishop of Winchester,* then Archdeacon of Surrey, I was publicly presented before the Archdeacon by one of the churchwardens for having been guilty of giving a Wednesday evening lecture in the infant schoolroom ! What was more extraordinary still was that, when I was

---

* Wilberforce.

called up before the Archdeacon and all the clergy
to answer for my fault, the Archdeacon said with
great solemnity that it was an important matter,
and he must refer it to the Bishop. And what
is more wonderful still, in consequence of that
reference I had to give up the lecture.

The Bishop was in a great difficulty. He
thoroughly approved of such lectures, and had
advocated them in a charge recently delivered,
but he believed that they were not strictly in
accordance with the Act of Uniformity, so that he
felt it impossible to support me, while at the same
time he did not at all wish to have the responsibility of stopping me. This led to a somewhat
painful correspondence with that excellent man,
and after full consultation with my dear friend
Mr. Hough, I thought it best to give up the
lecture, stating that I did so in obedience to the
Bishop's wish. One blessed result of that whole
transaction was that a bill was carried through
Parliament distinctly legalising all such services.

But of all those whom God raised up as counsellors and friends, there was no one to be compared to the beloved one whom God gave me to
be my loving wife,* on July 10th, 1839. She
combined the ability of her father with the
devotedness of her mother, and it is perfectly

---

* Maria Eliza, only daughter of Sir Benjamin Collins Brodie,
Bart., the eminent surgeon. Her mother, Lady Brodie, was
Ann, youngest daughter of Serjeant Sellon.—ED.

impossible for me to say what she was to me in the parish, in her home, and our own private intercourse. One thing only I would especially mention respecting her, viz. that it was to her that I owe what I believe to be the most useful characteristic of my ministry—I am thankful to say that from the very beginning I always quoted a great deal of Scripture in my sermons, but I used to do so interweaving those texts with my own composition. But she taught me the use of proof texts—she said that my preaching was not so profitable as that of the Rev. H. H. Beamish, to which she had been accustomed, and instead of merely quoting a passage, he used to give a chapter and verse, and allow the people time to look it out in their Bibles.

As he was constantly engaged in the exposition of the Word of God, and laid a solid foundation of the truth taught, I was thoroughly convinced of the wisdom of her words; and for the last fifty years I have systematically acted on her advice, so that, although I never heard Mr. Beamish in my life, I have always regarded his ministry as the model on which my own has been formed; and when I have seen the blessing which the exposition of Scripture has been made to very many souls, I have never ceased to thank God for that dear young wife who did not shrink from pointing out to her husband his defects.

It was during the period of my Richmond

curacy that I had the high honour of being invited by my dear friend the Rev. Henry Venn to become a member of the Committee of Correspondence of the Church Missionary Society. I think it was in the year 1844. I am not quite sure respecting the date, but I have no hesitation in expressing my thankfulness to our Heavenly Father for the wisdom, the fidelity, for the true missionary spirit with which the affairs of that great society have been conducted during the many years of my intimate acquaintance with its business and its leaders.

My love for it when I was at Richmond once brought me into a serious difficulty with the late Bishop Wilberforce, and taught me his marvellous power in controlling the minds of men. He was at that time Archdeacon of Surrey, and as such he proposed a scheme for doing away with all especial interest in particular societies, and to raise one general fund to be laid "at the feet of the Apostles," and divided by them according to their discretion.

We did not exactly know who the Apostles were. We thought that probably they were to be the Archdeacon and the Bishop, as they were to be the distributors.

Against this scheme the friends of the Church Missionary Society rose as one man. We held a meeting to consider what should be done. We decided that we would all attend the Archdeacon's meeting in order to oppose the plan, and engaged conveyances accordingly. When the morning came I had such a headache as I never remember to have suffered from, either before or since, and I was utterly unable to leave my bed, so off drove the others, full of zeal and holy courage. But what was my astonishment when they returned in the afternoon, and one of the most faithful, earnest, and trustworthy of the whole party came to tell me the result. He said they had found the plan was not so objectionable as they had thought, and at length reluctantly acknowledged that the Archdeacon had not allowed them to separate till he had made every one of them, dear old Mr. Hough included, sign a paper agreeing to the introduction into their own parishes of the Arch-deacon's scheme.

So then I stood alone, and thanked God for the headache which had saved me from the fascination.

But Richmond was the parish that was doing more than any other in the rural deanery for Missions, and it was most important for the success of the plan that Richmond should be included. So nothing was left undone that could induce me to join the others. But I was still free, as all my other brethren began to wish they were, and I stuck to my point. I was invited in the most cordial manner for a visit, with my dearest wife, first to Alvenstoke and then to Farnham Castle. I was addressed in the language of warm affection,

6

not only towards myself, but to my beloved mother. But I considered that by the Providence of God I had been preserved from the fascinating power, and that my only wisdom was to keep clear of it when I was free; so we went on independently till the next visitation of the Bishop. My heart was filled with thankfulness when I heard him announce in his charge that he had advised his beloved friend, the Archdeacon, to give up his scheme.

This curacy I held for more than nine years, for seven of which I had the unspeakable help of my dearly beloved, most faithful, and most able wife. During the time I had different livings offered to me, and I believe that, if I had regarded my worldly interest, I should have accepted some of them. But I had a great conviction of the importance of my position, and strong belief that the Lord had called me to it. So we both agreed that we were most likely to do His will if we persevered in the curacy.

To Mr. and Mrs. Cunningham at Lowestoft Rectory :—

"RICHMOND, *February* 19*th*, 1837.

" MY DEAREST UNCLE AND AUNT,—You will be glad to hear that I am myself very comfortable. Of course there is a large field of enjoyment from which I am wholly excluded; I am no longer a social being. In all the difficulties and responsibilities of this place I am absolutely alone. I have no dear Rector within two miles, whom I may consult over all my affairs and discouragements. I compare myself to a ship finding its way alone across the ocean, and sometimes well-buffeted in the journey. I certainly miss friendship wonderfully, and I cannot say how greatly I long after you all. My heart this day has been full of tenderness to Pakefield. I think of that attentive congregation at Kirkley, of the prayer-meeting, of the schoolroom lecture, and of that close and, I trust, heavenly bond of union which God permitted us to enjoy, and I know not how to bear the thought that we are separated. However, the more I look at my present position, the more am I satisfied that the change is of the Lord. The need of this place is grievous. The little flock is scattered and disheartened; the poor have been totally neglected, the sick unvisited, and the societies are all fallen to decay. The short time that I have been here has not been without its encouragements. Our tender Father has been pleased to favour me with some cases in which my private ministry has been greatly valued, and I hope blessed. I think also He is with me in the pulpit; the evening congregation is rapidly increasing, and we have had some very solemn occasions. All this is encouraging, but I desire not to build upon it, for I well know that such encouragement has not strength enough to bear weight. In health I think I am better than I have been since August. I find my power for work increases, and the cough is gone. Join with me in praising a merciful Father. ' Praise God, from whom,' etc."

To Mr. Cunningham :—

"RICHMOND, SURREY, *September 24th*, 1838.

"My DEAR UNCLE,—You ask how we are getting on here, and you must know how difficult it is to answer such a question. I think that, whenever God permits encouragement, He sends at the same time some draw-back, as if to prevent encouragement lapsing into self-confidence, and self-gratulation taking the place of a spirit of thankfulness. And this is just the case with our parish : there is much to call forth the most unfeigned thanksgiving—great kindness amongst the people, large congregations, a capital collection yesterday for the Pastoral Aid Society—but on the other hand a continual worry about our schools, and, what is most of all to be considered, very little evidence of the regenerating power of the Holy Ghost in individuals. I see that the messenger has a far wider influence than he once had, but I do not see the message itself attended with the same saving power. This is a cause of great sorrow to me, and the more so because I fear it may be in a great measure explained by a want of spirituality in myself. There is a wonderfully close communion between the power of preaching and the power of feeling, and when a man's own heart is very dead, he is not likely to produce much life in others. I think, moreover, there is great danger of spending our energy on our machinery. I am doing all I can to work the parish efficiently, and set all the machine in active operation, and I feel the effect of it in a forgetfulness of the spiritual end of the whole. It is something bordering upon leaving the Word of God to serve tables. However, in the midst of all, I trust there is a real progress. I find unspeakable comfort in Hebrews xii. 2, and whether a want of spiritu-ality in myself or a want of spiritual power in my ministry be the cause of sorrow, I find the universal remedy in 'looking unto Jesus,' and I believe that to be the whole of the Christian's secret. The more we can keep our eye on Him the stronger shall we be in every point of view, and one moment's forgetfulness of Him must produce weakness, if not a fall."

To his uncle :—

"*December 7th*, 1838.

"I should be inclined to question how far it was well to leave a curate altogether to himself, so as not to know what he is doing. There seems to me a great difference between keeping him under orders, and so checking his independent action, and by constant intercourse maintaining a vigilant superintendence. The plan that I adopted with ——, ——, and Frank himself was to point out clearly at first their line of duty, and then to leave them entirely to themselves in the discharge of it, at the same time making the pastoral ministry a subject of constant conversation, so that I always knew exactly what each was doing. By this means you get (1) the advantage of division of labour ; you (2) know exactly what is going on, which parts are comparatively neglected, and which have an extra supply, and, like a general, you can by a recommendation apply your forces just where they are wanted. There is another thing which I should be inclined to suggest, especially with a beginner, viz. that you follow out the territorial system and assign him a district. My own plan is this. I divide my visiting into the aggressive and the extraordinary. By the aggressive I mean the regular stated visiting from house to house. By the extraordinary I mean those visits which I pay in consequence of some providential call, such as sickness, affliction, religious impression, etc. I then divide the parish into two parts, and give —— the whole aggressive work for one district, and take it myself for the other. For the extraordinary I make no local divisions. I find then in practice that the calls are sufficiently frequent to keep a measure of connection with the whole parish, while the limitation of the aggressive brings each district tolerably within the compass of its minister, so that he is able by perseverance to gain an influence."

To Mr. Cunningham :—

"RICHMOND, SURREY, *March* 14*th*, 1839.

"MY DEAR UNCLE,—I am always greatly rejoiced to hear of your well-doings at Lowestoft, but I am more pleased than ever now, for I have something of a parental as well as filial interest—filial because I was trained amongst you myself, and parental because Frank stayed six months with me. I have no doubt that the change of ministry is likely to prove a real refreshment to your people, and I should not be surprised if it were to be the means of calling out some, and leading to true conversions. You must not let all the ladies turn Frank's head by flattery, of which there always appears to me great danger for young clergymen, for good people seem to suppose that religious interest gives a licence which is allowed in nothing else, and make the Gospel an occasion, rather than a check, for unwholesome conversation. I have felt the danger of it very much here, and though I have been very much preserved by a culpable want of sentimentality, I fear that I have suffered from the evil. I find that I often return from my intercourse with them thinking better of myself instead of worse. I was much interested by your remarks about the country. How completely does it prove that 'Christ is the head over all things to the Church'! Men appear with wicked designs and ungodly purposes, but Christ is Lord, and when they are just ready to strike He paralyses their aim. I regard these failures of wicked men not so much as the effect of a state of society as evidences of the controlling power of the Lord. He allows them to form their wicked schemes, and just when all is ready for an explosion, He defeats them, that so He may prove His power and their nothingness. Thus it is that these very men who are most opposed to the Church of Christ become the occasions for adding to its strength, for they call forth the protecting power of God, and so increase faith by experience. I have been inexpressibly cheered lately, amidst the sins of this ungodly world, by the thought of the final triumph of the Church. 'The God of Peace shall bind Satan under your feet shortly.' It is therefore certain that the day will come when Satan and all his agents will be overthrown, when we shall no more suffer from sin and its effects, and then all the elect people of God shall be visibly gathered under one Head, enjoying a perfect union with each other and with Christ. All this must take place. Popery, atheism, infidelity, and the spirit of schism may unite their unholy ranks and lend all their strength for the overthrow of our Lord's kingdom, but 'the gates of hell shall not prevail against it.' How is it that our hearts are not filled with holy joy at the prospect, and that we do not ride triumphant over all the fears, the sorrows, the sins, with which on every side we are beset?

"Your most affectionate Nephew and Curate,

"EDWARD HOARE."

To Mr. Cunningham :—

"HAMPSTEAD, *April 6th*, 1839.

"MY DEAR UNCLE,—How are the mighty fallen! I am going to be married!! I have been spending a delightful week with the Brodies, and am come home engaged hard and fast to Maria. I am exceedingly happy, though I scarcely can believe it. I have the greatest hope that the thing has been undertaken in a prayerful spirit, and that we may look for God's abundant blessing on us. We both particularly beg that you will marry us.

"Your most affectionate Nephew,

"EDWARD HOARE.

"Give my dearest love to my aunt, Frank, etc."

To Mrs. Cunningham :—

"RICHMOND, SURREY, *May* 30*th*, 1839.

"MY DEAREST AUNT,—As for myself, I am exceedingly happy, though so unusually busy that I hardly know how to think much about my happy prospects. Never was a person less loverlike, for I am expecting a confirmation here next week, and having more than one hundred and thirty young persons under my care, I am so busy from morning till night that I find my whole mind occupied. I think it is a good thing for me, for it fixes my thoughts upon my work, which otherwise they would be very much disposed to wander from. I am every day more and more happy in the thought of my marriage, and more and more thankful for the prospect of a wife who, I fully believe, has given herself to God. There is not a single feature in the whole thing that I could wish otherwise, and, besides all living circumstances, the recollection of my dearest mother's wish makes the connection to my own mind quite a hallowed one. I only hope that we may be enabled to devote ourselves unitedly, as we have desired to do separately, to the service of that Heavenly Father who has laden us with so many blessings. We expect to be married on the 2nd of July, about ten days after their return; we then hope to go to the Isle of Wight for a fortnight or three weeks. I do not wish to take a long holiday, because of the expense, and because I am very anxious to take the lady into Norfolk and to Lowestoft in the autumn. I doubt, however, whether I shall be able to accomplish it."

A letter from one of his sisters describing the wedding :—

"Broom Park, *July 9th*, 1839.

" Here we are in peace and safety, Edward shut up with Maria, Kate and I looking tolerably neat in white poplin, having just dressed in our little room, our only misfortune being that we have no gloves. We found dearest Edward most bright and sweet; the drive down with him has been not a little pleasant; nothing could have answered better than our journey with him, and we did quite enjoy it. Here is Maria come for us! She looks so quiet, and is so nice, only she has got a bad cold. When we went downstairs the Buxtons were just arriving; they had joined our phaeton party, and all arrived together. The only mishap has been that by going to London for her gown Miss Foreman entirely missed them, and we are fearful that there is but little hope of her arrival now; it is most provoking and quite a tribulation. Caroline arrived from Bury Hill, looking most sweet with a beautiful bouquet of orange flowers. Lady Brodie very kind and like herself, Sir B. B. detained in town by patients. When we had had a satisfactory tea, some went back to the drawing-room, others for a walk; the party consisted of all our own clan, and, as in most parties, there was a flock of girls in white, the belle on the Brodie side being Miss Beamish, on ours of course Chenda. Mr. T. Hankinson arrived in the middle of the evening, having stopped to climb up Box Hill and ford a rivulet. The house

is beautiful, and the whole place pretty and cheerful.
Maria behaves herself capitally—so much spirit, yet so
quiet, and thinking little of herself ; she looks two years
younger than when we saw her last. *We* are in Mr.
Brodie's room, and, as Laydon says, there is so much
shooting tackle ' she don't know where to put away our
things.' Edward is most happy ; it truly is a pleasure
to look at his beaming face. How I wish you could see
them both together, dearest sister ; it is most interesting. . . . The party now assembling for church all in
good heart ; Mr. Hankinson making the eight bridesmaids and about six other ladies laugh in the dining-
room, the rest dispersed. . . . Half-past five o'clock (in
the room which we had at Gurney's wedding). After the
above followed a lengthy waiting—people arriving, but
no Bishop. Maria and Lady Brodie appeared, quite
ready, but had to abide for a long time till the Bishop
had arrived and arrayed himself. About eleven o'clock
we went to the church, six bridesmaids in one carriage,
and two with Caroline in another, all the gentlemen
having walked previously and were ready at the church-
yard gate to receive us ; four bridesmaids with their
gentlemen stood on each side of the path till the bride
had passed and then closed in behind her. In the
church the positions were capital—the relations round
the altar, and her bridesmaids standing on a step behind
her. The Bishop read the service beautifully, and they
both spoke very clearly—she was perfectly composed.
Signing and kissing as usual afterwards, with the bells
ringing, and home as we came. After some congratulat-
ing in the drawing-room we all sallied forth for a walk,
stimulated, as in everything, by Mr. Tom Hankinson.
Maria then went in to rest awhile. We gathered in a
group round Mr. Hankinson (in the garden) and heard
all the poem about Sir Rupert and Lorline ; then down

to the water, where all the eight bridesmaids were put into the boat and our dear bridegroom (taking off his coat) rowed us about. This filled up the time capitally till the breakfast, for which we were very ready, though we had to wait some period for the Bishop, who was lost on the strawberry beds. The breakfast was very nice and *very amusing*. The first health was proposed by the Bishop in a most nice little speech; it was of course 'Mr. and Mrs. E. Hoare.' Our sisterly vanity was amply satisfied, and how I wish you could have heard Edward's reply. It was so gratifying and nice to have him make such a truly nice speech, which he ended by proposing 'Sir B. and Lady Brodie.' A most feeling reply from Sir Benjamin, speaking so highly of both bride and bridegroom, but he could scarcely get on once or twice from feeling it so much. He proposed the Bishop of Winchester, and that was greeted by another three times three; which he thanked for, observing that 'he had not expected to make so much noise in the world.' Then Gurney proposed 'The Bridesmaids,' and Mr. Goulburn thanked for us, though, alas! he nearly stuck. Then 'Papa'—and he made such a nice speech in return, observing that his three daughters-in-law being an increasing and untellable blessing to him, he had no small reason to rejoice in his new acquisition. Breakfast done, we went away, Maria to dress. The parting scene with her father and brother (in tears) upstairs was trying; but she passed by all of us who were waiting in the hall and went off very brightly. But I must leave off, though I fear this is an unsatisfactory history, though in all the muddles we have done our little best. Ever, dearest Sister,

"Most affectionately,

"C. E. H."

CHAPTER VII

HOLLOWAY AND RAMSGATE

IN the year 1846 the time came for a change. My friend the Rev. Daniel Wilson wrote to invite me to the Incumbency of St. John's, Holloway, about to be vacated by my dear and honoured friend the Rev. Henry Venn, one of the wisest, the ablest, and the most trustworthy men I have ever known in this life; and there were many circumstances, amongst others the illness of my beloved father residing at Hampstead, that led both of us to the conclusion that we ought to accept the offer. It was one of deep interest in many respects, more especially in consequence of its connection with the Rev. Henry Venn. In early days he was curate or lecturer at Clapham, when he used to attend the Committee of the C.M.S., and was urged by some of the fathers of those days to undertake the Secretaryship; but his heart was devoted to parochial work, so he accepted the living of Drypool, near Hull, and so broke away altogether from the work of the C.M.S. And then it pleased God that he should meet with, and ultimately marry, a lady of some property, in consequence of which he was no longer absolutely dependent upon his profession for his maintenance. He was led, however, to return southward, where the Vicar of Islington offered him the Incumbency of St. John's, Holloway, a new church just built out in the fields. To the interests of that parish he devoted his whole great energy, and he returned, as might have been expected, to the old committee room in the C.M.S. There his power was felt more and more, while his own heart became more and more drawn into the deep interests of missionary work, till at length he decided to give up his parochial work, as he could now live without the income derived from it, and devote the remainder of his life, without one farthing of salary, to the sacred work of the Secretaryship of the Society.

I felt it a great honour to succeed such a man under such circumstances, as it was a great privilege to be brought into closer contact with him, as he continued to reside within the parish. The time at Holloway was not one of encouragement. I met with a great deal of kindness, and I had most interesting Bible classes—not merely one for the young people, but one for the gentlemen after their return from business in London—but still I longed for more of that marked decision which I had left behind me at Richmond. Evangelical truth was "the proper thing" at Islington, so that it was very generally preferred; but I often wondered how far it was a reality in the souls of the people, and sometimes I used to think that the spirit of antagonism at Richmond was really more healthful than the spirit of assent at Holloway. It certainly brought out more decision of character.

But I have learnt many lessons respecting that period. I have often said that I regarded that year as the most fruitless period of my ministry, but as I have gone on in life I have met with so many who have ascribed their conversion to the ministry of that short period, that I have been taught the lesson that a clergyman is utterly unable to form any estimate of what God the Holy Ghost is doing through his ministry.

However, we were not to remain there long, for the Lord Himself made it perfectly plain that it was His will for us to remove. My dearest wife was very unwell, and I was lame in the right knee. My father also was quickly gathered to his rest in Christ Jesus, so that one of the great motives in going to Holloway was removed. Though I had great difficulty in walking, I was able to ride, and one day I rode in to call on my father-in-law, Sir Benjamin Brodie, whom I consulted respecting my knee, and he said to me,—

" I tell you what, Edward ; you must go to the seaside."

" Well," said I, " I did think of going for a short trip after Easter."

"Oh, I don't mean that," said he. "You must go to the seaside for a year at least."

"But what," said I, "is to become of my parish, my work, my family?"

"I don't know," he replied, "but this I know, that if you don't go to the seaside for at least a year you will die, and so what will become of it all then?"

This was indeed a very heavy blow to me, and I rode home that day solemnised in spirit, and thinking how I should tell my dearest wife what her father had just said to me.

It was a very solemn and sacred ride that I had that morning, but on my arrival, before I went upstairs to her, I opened my letters that had arrived during my absence, and almost the first one was from my friend John Plumptre, in which he said that he was one of the trustees of a new church nearly complete at Ramsgate, and it would be a great satisfaction to him and his colleagues if I would undertake the first Incumbency. To describe the mixed emotion with which I went upstairs to tell my wife, both of her father's opinion and Mr. Plumptre's letter, is impossible.

But the remarkable coincidence did not at first thoroughly satisfy the sound judgment of my friend Mr. Venn. When I spoke to him on the subject, he said that the text which had guided him in his important decisions was Prov. xvi. 3 :

"Commit thy works unto the Lord, and thy thoughts shall be established." He said that at first he would frequently be divided and perplexed in judgment, but that as he went on waiting on the Lord for guidance and trusting Him, the whole matter would gradually appear to him so clear that it left no possibility of doubt. How often, acting upon his advice, have I found it true, so that I have seen my way perfectly clear in cases in which there seemed at first nothing but perplexity! Was not this the secret of that singular wisdom which he showed in the affairs of the C.M.S.? and is there any one who sat with him habitually in the committee room who does not remember the frequency with which he put his hand over his eyes, without doubt "committing his works unto the Lord"? But his thoughts, which were as mine, were established with reference to our removal to Ramsgate, and we never had reason to regret the change.

Letter to his Uncle Cunningham :—

"HAMPSTEAD, *November 28th*, 1844.

"MY DEAR UNCLE,—I quite agree with you that it is a bad thing never to write to those we love. Real good, strong affection can stand the long lack of communication, as strong plants can stand a long drought, but it is an unwise thing to put it to the test. . . .

"I fully sympathise in what you say of the Church. I can imagine nothing more deplorable than the foolish

men, both curates and bishops, scattering the very best
of the laity from her fold, and all for their empty, worth-
less baubles. Oh, what a blessing it would have been
for our Church and country if people had spent half the
strength in lifting the Cross and spreading the Bible
that they have wasted over surplices and rubrics! But
it is not mere waste. As far as I can see, it is down-
right suicide, a wilful destruction of the Church's influence over her people. But do you not think God is
teaching us a lesson? Are not His waiting children
taught by all this to rally round their risen and reigning
Lord, and to cease from man whose breath is in his
nostrils? Is not the Church always exposed either to
pressure from without or delusion within? And are not
those the two great instruments by which He keeps His
elect people pure? Oh, may God grant that we may
be amongst the Lamb's faithful followers! . . .

"In our parish we have had but little visible encouragement since our return from Norfolk. Before we went
out we were blessed with several interesting cases, but
since our return we have not known of one. It is a
great sorrow to me. I hope, however, the Lord is really
owning His word. We are desiring to honour Him and
to set forth Christ crucified, and though our labours
are most miserable, I delight to think that from the in-
most soul it is our desire to honour Christ in them. I
have just finished a course of four practical sermons on
the Bible, in which I found great interest, and am now
preparing another course for Advent on the following
subjects: *How our Lord will come; when; what to do;*
and *what we should be doing till He comes.* Our prophetical meeting this November was one of the most
delightful hours I ever knew. It was so sober, so
serious, so practical, and so full of Christ that I think all
felt it a time of true blessing to be there. I never heard

anything more completely to my mind than the addresses of Mr. Auriol and Mr. Goodhart on the 'practical bearing of the expectation of future reward.' . . .

"Your most affectionate Nephew,

"EDWARD HOARE."

AUTOBIOGRAPHY *(continued)*.

The position was one of the greatest possible interest. The circumstances of the town were quite peculiar. The Vicar of St. George was a High Churchman who did not hesitate to employ curates who went far beyond himself in their opinions, and the result was that two of them went over to Rome. There was an amiable man in Trinity Church who had no sympathy with St. George's, but yet had but little power in satisfying the hearts of those who loved the Gospel, and the result was that many of the most devoted people in the place were driven either into the dissenting chapels or into general unsettlement of mind. Meanwhile Mr. Pugin* was erecting a large establishment on the West Cliff, and the chapel was already opened, and an active priest at work amongst the distracted and unsettled flock.

Then it was that God raised up a very remarkable man with wonderful energy to erect the new church. He formed a small committee, but he himself was the moving spirit and the one centre

---

* The eminent Roman Catholic architect.—ED.

of power. He was a lieutenant in the Royal
Navy, with no general acquaintance and nothing
of what the world calls influence, but he was God's
powerful instrument. I refer to Lieutenant (afterwards Commander) Hutchinson, R.N. As he knew
nothing of Church matters, he wisely took counsel
with Mr. Plumptre, who put him in communication
with some London lawyer, I forget who, who might
direct him in the use of what was then called the
Church Building Act; so he served the proper
notices on the Vicar and patrons, and having
secured to trustees the patronage of the new
church which he proposed to build, he set to
work single-handed to raise the funds and to complete the undertaking. He wrote countless manu-
script letters all over England. He was a man
of wonderful energy, as he afterwards proved by
reducing Balaclava to good order, and all that
energy he devoted with unsparing zeal to the great
work to which God had called him. How many
letters he wrote I do not know; I know that I
received several. His first letter would be a
general application; if that brought him a contribution, it would be quickly followed by another
rejoicing that the work was so much appreciated,
and asking for a second gift; but if it brought no
reply, then came a second convinced that the only
reason for delay was the great importance of the
work, and earnestly appealing for the help which
he was sure was contemplated. Thus letter

followed letter in quick succession; the contract was signed on his own responsibility, and Christ Church was quickly reared as a monument to show what might be done by one man whose heart was in earnest, and who, like Mr. Venn, "committed his works unto the Lord."

It is not to be supposed that these letters written were in a very complimentary strain with reference to the existing order of things in the Parish Church, nor were they likely to make Christ Church acceptable in the eyes of the Vicar or his staff. I myself went to the Parish Church in the afternoon previous to the opening of Christ Church, and I heard a sermon descriptive of the persons who would attend the new church, upon the text "He went away in a rage," and I there heard my future congregation all classed with Naaman. But apparently there were a great many such Naamans in Ramsgate, for the church was well filled on the 7th of August, the day when it was consecrated by Archbishop Howley, and I may say has been so ever since.

I found Ramsgate to be a most interesting sphere of ministry. There were three great sources of interest. First, the shipping. My original Pakefield interest in the English boatmen was more than revived by my acquaintance with the "hovellers," two hundred of whom were dependent for their bread on helping ships in difficulty off the Goodwin Sands. I fear that some of them

thought more of their own earnings than they did
of the lives they were so brave in saving. I can
never forget the reply that I received from one
of the best of them when I asked him one bitterly
cold winter's morning how he was getting on ;
upon which he replied that now they had got all
their lights, and buoys, and chain cables, there
was nothing left for an honest man to do. He
said : " There we were at the south end of the
sands about three o'clock this morning, when up
came one of these foreign chaps, and was running
as pretty upon the Goodwin Sands as ever you'd
wish to see, when, all of a sudden, he saw one of
these here nasty staring buoys -- port helm and off !"

But though it was a pretty sight to them to see
a foreign chap go straight upon the Goodwin
Sands, it was a magnificent sight for any one to
witness the skill and daring courage with which
they handled their luggers and dashed through the
breakers in order to save the lives of the shipwrecked men. They were noble fellows, and when
their hearts were touched by the grace of God,
they were fine, manly witnesses for Christ.

Then there were the sailors on board the various
ships that put in for shelter. As the harbour was
at that time free, it was sometimes crowded with
vessels, and I used to have a grand opportunity
for out-of-door preaching. At first I used to go
down in my cap and gown on Sunday afternoons,
but I found that a sermon out of doors, combined

with a walk on the pier, was more agreeable to
many people than either Church or Sunday School,
so I had to give it up, and seize such opportunities
as wind and weather permitted. But I never was
at a loss for a large congregation, and when I took
my place on the poop of one of the ships, I had the
deep interest of seeing crowds of people, some on
the pier and some on the tiers of ships and some
on the rigging, amongst whom I had the sacred
opportunity of scattering the seed, without the least
idea to what point the wind would carry it.

On one occasion I was greatly solemnised. I
selected the ship best suited for my purpose, and
the Captain and his men gave me the kindest
possible reception ; the only inconvenience to which
they put me was that they would insist upon my
preaching against the wind, as they did not consider it sufficiently dignified for me to stand in
the hold of the vessel. There they listened most
attentively. In the evening the wind changed,
and all the ships hurried out of harbour, and how
deeply affected was I to hear next morning that
the one on which I had received so kind a welcome
had been lost with all hands during the night.

The advantage of the harbour was that throughout the winter months there was always something
going on in it, so that we could not settle down into
stagnation. One morning, for example, my friend
the harbour-master, Captain Martin, sent up to
me to say that he expected a crew of shipwrecked

emigrants to be very shortly landed ; so I hurried
down to the harbour, and there I saw one of the
most piteous sights I have ever seen in my life.
There was a small schooner just entering the harbour, with one hundred and sixty German emigrants crowded together on the decks. Their
ship had been wrecked over-night, and one boat
containing seven women was sent off soon after
the wreck, but was supposed to have been lost in
the breakers. The remainder were subsequently
taken off by the schooner that brought them into
Ramsgate. There they stood, huddled together,
in the clothes in which they had sprung from their
berths on the striking of the ship—that is, almost
in a state of nakedness. The sea had been breaking over them from the time the ship had struck,
and they had no food. What was to be done with
them was indeed a question, but all parties set to
work with vigour.

An infant schoolroom was set apart for their
accommodation, and another large room was obtained in connection with one of the public-houses ;
so they were very quickly housed, and such vigour
was shown by the ship agents, consular agents, and
all connected with the harbour, that something
warm was provided for every one of them, even
upon their landing.

But they were still unclothed, and to meet this
difficulty bills were put out, so soon as possible,
to request gifts of clothing, cloth, or flannel, and

also the help of any persons who could assist us in making up clothing. It was wonderful to see the zeal and liberality with which piles of goods were poured in upon us. These were not always very suitable, and I remember seeing amongst the goods sent *some muslin-ball-dresses!* There was a great quantity of good useful clothing, added to which numbers of ladies came together and worked hard all through the day, while the various agents laboured at the distribution, so that I believe that not one of those hundred and sixty emigrants lay down that night without having some warm, comfortable piece of clothing provided for him, and without being well fed with a comfortable meal and well housed for the night's rest.

For this they were most grateful, and I had a grand opportunity of preaching the Gospel, as they stayed with us about ten days. But here, alas! was the grievous difficulty, that I did not know German ; but this was met by the ready help of two young ladies in my congregation, to whom German was as familiar as English, and, as far as preaching and other addresses were concerned, a great difficulty was removed.

At length, however, there arose one for which I was not prepared. The poor emigrants, in the fulness of their hearts, were not satisfied with the service provided for them in the schoolroom, but were anxious to come together to the Holy Communion. But here a fresh difficulty arose. They could not be satisfied to come to the Lord's Table without first coming to confession. This appeared to me to be a matter of mere formalism, as they insisted upon it that it would not make the slightest difference whether or not I understood their confession, nor did they even see any objection to their confession passing through the medium of the young lady who was kind enough to act as my interpreter ; and I fear they were but partially satisfied when I told them that confession to a priest was not required in the Church of England, but that in it we were taught to confess direct to God.

I have seldom known a more solemn and sacred service than when we all knelt together in one spirit, if not in one tongue, to commemorate the dying love of that blessed Saviour who shed His precious blood that whosoever believeth in Him should receive remission of sins. The next day they were sent off to London, and I have never heard of any of them since. But I believe the record of those days to be written in heaven, and I must say I took great delight in the testimony borne by the German Government to the zeal and hospitality of the good people of Ramsgate, more especially as particular mention is made of that dearly beloved one to whose zeal and loving-kindness the whole movement was chiefly due.

But the chief interest was in the sailors themselves. I was deeply impressed at the hardness of the life of those engaged in our coasting trade, and I met with many who, living in the midst of every possible temptation, seemed wholly abandoned to utter recklessness, both for time and for eternity. But they all appeared to have a heart, and some of them were eminently Christian men.

I never can forget one fearful Sunday morning, when it was bitterly cold and blowing such a north-easterly gale as it can blow at Ramsgate, before church I went on to the cliff to see what was going on, and there opposite the mouth of the harbour I saw one ship sunk, not very far from the entrance of the harbour, with its crew clinging to the masts. Our brave hovellers were doing all they could for their rescue, and I saw another smaller vessel, "with sails ripped, seams opened wide, compass lost," struggling if possible to make the harbour. Oh, how I longed to run down and take my part in the efforts that were being made for their rescue! and I cannot answer for my thoughts during the time that I was obliged to be at church. No sooner was the service over than I was again on the cliff, and not a trace could I see of the sunken ship or crowded mast. It had fallen before any help could reach the poor fellows who were clinging to it, and all hands had been lost; but the little sloop was just entering the harbour, and I cannot describe the scene I witnessed when I went on

board. There were five poor fellows completely
worn out, wearied, hungry, cold, and frost-bitten,
and I never shall forget the master of that vessel.
As long as he was in the harbour I had a great
deal of most happy intercourse with him, and in
the course of it he gave me the following narrative
of his voyage.

He said he had one very dear friend, the mate
of a collier brig, and they were together at Sunder-
land. His friend came to him in the evening of
Christmas, and they had a delightful evening
together, till at length his friend returned to his
ship, and both vessels sailed for the South. All
went well with him till he reached the mouth of
the Thames, where he was caught by the gale
and took shelter behind the long sand; but after
a time the wind shifted, and his position became
one of the utmost danger. He found his only
hope of escape was to pass by the end of the sand,
and he doubted whether this would be possible,
and he knew that if once stranded on it he must
be lost without a hope. The first thing was to
hoist a sail, but in order to do this they had to
clear the ropes of ice with their axe. They then
hauled in the anchor, and the little vessel was
soon in the midst of the boiling surf. The master
himself took the helm, and said to the crew that
their only help was in God, and bade them come
and kneel around him while he steered and prayed.
Very soon a huge wave appeared to lift the little

ship right upon the bank, and let her down with
a fearful scrape upon the sands. A second followed, which did the same, and then came the
third, which seemed to carry them with still greater
fury than either of the others; but when it let
them down, what was their joy when they found
that the spur of the bank was passed, and that
their vessel was safely afloat. Their Heavenly
Father had heard their prayers and saved them.
But though immediate danger was past, everything
was so shattered that the ship was almost un-
manageable, and they were driven about in the
Channel for some three or four days before they
could reach Ramsgate Harbour.

And what was the sorrow that awaited my
excellent friend when he found himself safe. As
he entered the harbour he passed through the
wreckage of the vessel I had seen before church,
but when he learnt the particulars he found that it
was the ship of that dear friend with whom he had
spent that happy Christmas evening, and that he
was one of those who had perished in the wreck.
But in the midst of it all he was kept in a calm,
hallowed, peaceful communion with God, which
proved indeed how the Lord sitteth above the
waterflood, when the Lord can give peace unto
His people.

It was one of the sorrows connected with
Ramsgate that we seldom saw those brave men
a second time. So my friend stayed awhile till his

ship was refitted and his men cured of their frost-
bites, but the wind shifted and she was gone, so
that we parted never more to meet till we stand
together before the throne of the Lord.

Another great object of interest at Ramsgate
was the conflict with Rome. I had had some little
experience in the controversy when at Richmond,
as a zealous man had given some controversial
lectures there in favour of Romanism, and so compelled me to get up the subject. This had led me
to preach a course of Sunday Evening Lectures,
which I afterwards published under the title of
" Our Protestant Church." I have had reason
to believe, with great thanksgiving, that God has
made them useful to others, as, I thank God, He
made the study of the subject exceedingly useful
to myself. I remember a remark of Dr. McNeile,
that nothing tended more to set forth the glories of
the Gospel than the dark background of Popery.

At Ramsgate the conflict was in full activity.
A chapel had been recently erected through the
liberality of Mr. Pugin, and the Roman Catholic
party had all the enthusiasm of a new and hopeful
enterprise ; so we were soon brought into collision,
sometimes in private conversation, and sometimes
in public lectures, in which I freely invited any one
who could to answer me.

And there are four lessons which I learnt and
which possibly may be useful to my brethren.
Firstly, the Romish controversy does not require

a great amount of learning. The Romanists themselves are exceedingly ill-instructed in the principles of their Church, and there are very few points on which their convictions rest. Secondly, it is of essential importance to be perfectly accurate in every statement made and every quotation given, so as to be able, if need be, to give proof of that accuracy. Thirdly, it is essential that all quotations should be made direct from the original documents, and not taken second-hand from any Review, Catechism, or Handbook. Those books may be extremely useful for our own instruction, but they are worse than useless if we are in conflict with a Romish controversialist ; if we wish to be strong on such an occasion we must appeal to the "ipsissima verba" of some authoritative document, such as the decrees of the Council of Trent, or the Creed of Pope Pius IV. Fourthly, we must bear in mind that numbers of those who are led away by Rome are truly and conscientiously seeking peace. I believe that there is no state of mind so open to the persuasions of Rome as when a person is awakened but not at peace in Christ Jesus. It is then that Rome steps in with a promise of peace, and the more earnest the awakening, the more dangerous the seductive power.

I had one fearful instance of this at Ramsgate, in the family of one of our tradesmen, who had taken sittings in my church. I heard one day that his daughter was in habitual attendance at the Roman Catholic chapel. So I went at once to pay a pastoral visit to the mother, and she confirmed all that I had heard, and more than that, she told me that on the Sunday following her daughter was to be publicly received into the Church, and that her dress was already prepared. " Oh," I said, " how I wish I could see her before she joins ! " and I invited her to come to me that evening at eight o'clock. The mother said she would give my message, but did not think it very likely that her daughter would come.

However, at eight o'clock precisely the bell rang, and the daughter was there. She was a woman between thirty and forty years of age, fine features, and strong in intellectual expression of countenance. She confirmed all that her mother had told me, and when I asked her what had led to it, she informed me that she was engaged to a young man of very superior position to her own, that when walking together one evening the year before they had turned into Christ Church, and there heard a sermon that had made them both so uneasy that neither of them had ever been happy since. They were afraid to go again, for fear that their trouble should be increased ; so they had wandered hither and thither, seeking rest and finding none, till at length somebody told them that if they only joined the Church of Rome they would be at peace. She added that the young man had joined already, and that she hoped to be received on the Sunday following, when she trusted that both their hearts would be at rest.

It was clear that the poor thing was really anxious about her soul, so instead of saying one word to her about the Romish controversy, I asked her the question, " *Must you be holy first, or forgiven first ?* " She was very much surprised and almost affronted by my asking her anything of so simple a character. " Of course I know that," said she. " I daresay you do, but it will do you no harm to tell me what you know." " Of course I must be holy first," was the reply. " Then there is the secret of all your difficulty : you have been for the whole year striving to be holy, and you have utterly failed, so that you have had no peace, and could have no peace in the forgiveness of sin." " Do you mean to say then," said she, " that I can be forgiven first ? " I said, " That is exactly what the Scripture teaches," and I set before her a series of passages, showing first how the forgiveness is bestowed through the perfect propitiation of the Son of God, and then how it is granted at once, before the fruits of faith can possibly be developed. The poor thing was amazed, and I believe that that very evening, before she left the house, she was enabled to trust her blessed Saviour for the present perfect forgiveness of all her sins.

She left the house declaring that nothing should

induce her to join the Church of Rome, and now followed the most fearful struggle that I ever met with in the whole course of my ministry.

The young man had been already received, and the more she saw of her Saviour, the more she felt the impossibility of their union. What was to be done? She could not go forward to unite with him, and he would not go back to be one with her. Rome brought all its armoury to bear upon her. Bishop, priests, and Romish friends united all their strength in persuading her to give way. But God helped her to stand firm, and though she passed through a most fearful conflict, she lived and died in great peace of soul, resting in Christ Jesus. The young man became a Jesuit priest, and died suddenly when officiating at the mass. The case taught me the lesson, which in fact I had learned before, that in a great number of Romish perversions there is a real desire for the peace of God, and that our wisest course is in all such cases to go direct to that one point, instead of perplexing the mind with the erroneous points of Romish teaching.

But the chief interest of all consisted in the blessed privilege of carrying the Gospel of salvation to a number of persons who were really hungering for the Word of Life. There is no class of persons in the world that has a greater claim on those who know the Lord than that consisting of real inquirers after the way of life.

Now I met at Ramsgate with many who had had sufficient knowledge of the truth to make them utterly dissatisfied with the Tractarianism in the Parish Church and the Chapel of Ease, but who were longing for something more than they had already found. It was most interesting to see them flocking back to the Church of England after having been driven hither and thither, and I can never forget a conversation I had with one of the curates of St. George's some two or three years after Christ Church had been opened. I was remonstrating with him on the bitterness which was still shown toward us, but he justified it by saying that we were working against the Church of England.

This was too much for me to take in silence, so I asked him whether he would bear with me if I told him plainly what each of us had been doing since our residence at Ramsgate. And I then told him that I had been occupied in winning back to the Church those whom he had driven away from it. This surprised him very much, and he replied, " Yes, they will come to hear you preach, but not become communicants," to which I replied that I could not speak with accuracy, as I had never counted, but that it was my firm belief that on the previous Sunday I had administered the Lord's Supper to no less than fifty persons who had been driven from the Church of England by the teaching of St. George's. My friend was deeply impressed by that fact, and our future relationship was of the most friendly character. Would that all clergymen would consider what they have to answer for, when by their own erroneous teaching they scatter the flock committed to their charge.

But if it was a joy to see the dispersed of the flock brought back to the Church of their fathers, how much greater was the joy of seeing precious souls brought into living union with the Lord Jesus Christ Himself; and this, through the great mercy of God, we were permitted very quickly to do. They were of two classes. There were many who had looked forward in earnest hope, and often prayed for a blessing on the new church, and we cannot be surprised that, when the church was opened, they received that for which they had been praying; but there were others who had no such expectation, but were rather prejudiced against the Gospel, and altogether astonished when for the first time they heard its blessed language.

Let me give two cases in illustration of what I mean. About two miles off there was a mill, at which was working a young man named John Brampton. On the day of the consecration of the church, he left his work to attend the service, and in that service it pleased God to open his heart, so that he received the blessed message of life in Christ Jesus. He became at once one of the most active of our helpers, and was amongst the first, if not the very first, of the teachers in our new Sunday School. During the whole of our residence at Ramsgate he was a zealous, faithful fellow-labourer, and when we moved to Tunbridge Wells, and I wanted a Scripture-reader, I considered that there was no one who would help me more effectually than my zealous young friend from Ramsgate, so invited him to join me, which he did with his whole heart, labouring most diligently till after twenty-four years the Lord took him to his rest. He had had no experience as a Scripture-reader before he came, but the Lord taught him, and he was most effective as a helper. He identified himself so completely with all that we were doing that he would sometimes entertain those who did not know him by speaking of "our house," "our field," "our grounds," etc., etc. It was a pleasure to me to hear him, and it was an evidence of that oneness of heart which he felt with us in everything. He was indeed a helper to his Vicar, and for many a long year have I had to thank God for the gift bestowed on that young man, on occasion of the first service ever held in Christ Church.

The other case was altogether of a different character. I have already mentioned the bitter hostility that some persons showed toward the new church. This was manifested not very long after the consecration by some bad fellows, of whom we know nothing except that they wore the coats of gentlemen, climbing over the iron fence by which the church was surrounded, breaking down the young trees which had been recently planted in the enclosure, and throwing several stones through the windows into the church. The outrage excited, as might be expected, a great deal of conversation in the town, and a few days afterwards I was told that Colonel Williams and Mrs. Williams had called to see me. I had no idea who they were, and on my entering the room he told me, with that remarkable honesty and directness which characterised all his conversation, that he had come as the representative of several of the Parish Church congregation to express their extreme disapproval of the recent outrage. He told me also that he was a great friend of the Vicar, and had extremely disapproved of the erection of Christ Church. He also added that, in order to show the sincerity of his protest, he intended to take two seats in the church, and that possibly, as he then lived in the neighbourhood, he might sometimes attend, but that he had no intention of doing so habitually, and merely took them to assure me of his sincerity.

I assured him that I did not require any such evidence, but the seats were taken, and it was not very long before I saw him seated in one of them, and I was deeply interested that his attendances became more and more frequent, until at length one day he was again announced as calling at the

house. But this time he wished to see me in
my own study, so he came, evidently full of deep
emotion. He opened the conversation by saying
that he was not come to ask for help, as he did not
want it, but to tell me what the Lord had done for
his soul. He said that he had been deeply impressed by something he heard in church, and for
the last six weeks had passed through agonies
of soul. He had been walking all over the Isle
of Thanet, earnestly seeking peace, till at length
God had brought him to see the fulness that is in
Christ Jesus. Now he had come to me to ask me
to unite with him in giving thanks for the blessed
peace which God had bestowed upon him in
Christ Jesus. He then fell on his knees, and
we both poured out our hearts in thanksgiving
to God for the wonderful mercy which He had
shown, and the blessing of His salvation in Christ
Jesus the Lord. From that day forward he took
his part boldly as an earnest advocate for the
truth. He was a man of strong convictions, and,
when convinced, he carried out those convictions
with prompt and firm determination. So he did
on this occasion. To myself he became one of my
most warm, faithful friends, and in the support of
every good and holy work carried on at Ramsgate,
for the rest of his life, he was the faithful and
unwavering standard-bearer.

Thus the wicked outrage of those men who
violated the sacredness of our church was over-

ruled by God to the giving to me one of my most faithful friends and efficient helpers, and to the town of Ramsgate one of its most active, energetic, and faithful maintainers of the great Protestant principles of the Church of England.

The schools at Christ Church were built by Mr. Hoare when at Ramsgate. The Seamen's Infirmary and General Hospital in that town also owes its existence to his exertions.—ED.

CHAPTER VIII

TUNBRIDGE WELLS

BUT these bright and stirring days at Ramsgate were at length brought to a close by Sir Charles Hardinge inviting me to undertake the living of Holy Trinity, Tunbridge Wells, in the year 1853.

At first I thought very little of the offer, as I expected Sir Benjamin Brodie to put his veto upon my removal from the sea. But when I went to consult him upon the subject, I was not a little surprised by his saying that, as in 1847 he had judged it necessary for me to go to the seaside, so now he considered it very desirable that I should leave it. So that impediment was removed, and I had to face the question whether I was called to remain where I was or to remove.

It was a very difficult question, and I was greatly perplexed as to the decision. But, according to Mr. Venn's principle already referred to, my thoughts were ultimately established, and I have never seen reason for a single moment to

regret the change. I can scarcely imagine a better
sphere for the ministry than that which I have
been permitted to occupy for nearly thirty-six
years. I have had a large parish, which, after
four parochial districts have been taken from it,
still contains more than six thousand persons,
the population consisting of a well-proportioned
mixture of gentry, tradesmen, and poor. I have
had in my church a stream of visitors from all
parts of England, and not from England only, but
from India, Australia, and America. I have had
very many most kind, faithful, and affectionate
friends ready to help me in everything, so that,
on the whole, I believe we have been able to keep
pace with the rapid growth of population ; and I
have had an excellent church, which, though I do
not suppose it would satisfy the ecclesiologist, I
have found to be most commodious for the worship
of God. There are three things in it quite at
variance with modern fashion : instead of an open
roof to generate cold in winter, heat in summer,
and echo at all times, we have had a flat ceiling
to protect us from all changes of the climate ; and
instead of having the people spread far and wide
on the ground floor, there are deep galleries along
three sides of the church, containing nearly six
hundred persons, all within ear-shot ; and instead
of a low pulpit scarcely raising the preacher
above the heads of his hearers, there is an old-
fashioned "three-decker" of sufficient height to

enable the preacher to see the whole of his congregation.

At Tunbridge Wells was much less to excite
than at Ramsgate. There were no shipwrecks,
and no such activity on the part of the Church
of Rome, but there was a great increase of solid
pastoral work, and I firmly believe that our removal was of the Lord. In no period of my life
have I experienced greater mercies.

After ten years of happy work together, it
pleased the Lord to take from me my dearest
wife, at which time He showed His abundant
mercy in so strengthening her faith, that she gave
a glorious testimony to the power of that Gospel
which she had earnestly desired to teach, and
which had been the subject of our whole ministry.
She was kept at perfect peace through a long
and suffering illness, and fell asleep in full and
unbroken trust in the blessed Saviour whom she
loved. Shortly before she died, she quoted to
me the words of Mr. Standfast : " I have loved to
hear my Lord spoken of ; and wheresoever I have
seen the print of His shoe in the earth, there I
have coveted to set my foot too," and He was
faithful to her to the end.

But, speaking of mercies at that period, I must
not omit to mention the help He raised up for
me in my valued friend Dr. Richardson, and my
beloved sister-in-law Lady Parry. Dr. Richardson
was the greatest help to me in the management

of my large family, and would come in again and again as a friend to give me any advice he thought necessary, and tell me whether he thought it important I should call in medical help, and again and again has he told me that they wanted no more than their faithful nurse could give them. As for my dear sister, she was everything that a widower could desire, tender, wise, considerate, the best of counsellors and the truest of friends. What she was to me at that time of my bereavement no words can ever describe.

Then amongst my many mercies at Tunbridge Wells I must reckon the severe illness which I had ten years afterwards, which I am thoroughly persuaded my Heavenly Father sent me as a blessing. It called forth the same unbounded loving-kindness from my parishioners and fellow-towns-men which I am now experiencing while dictating this sketch of my history, and I felt at the time that it brought us into a closer relationship with each other than we had ever known previously. But, above all, it burnt into my heart those words of the Apostle Paul in 2 Timothy i. 12 : " I know whom I have believed." Those six words contained the whole of my religion as I lay for weeks unable to think and pray, for they do not say, " I know *how* I have believed Him," nor do they refer to any qualification in my own faith, but simply to this qualification as taught in the following words, " And am persuaded that He is

able to keep that which I have committed unto
Him against that day." It was the entire persuasion of His perfect sufficiency that kept my
soul at peace, and has made me ever since thankful
to God for having brought me into the happy
experience of that sufficiency for one who, like me,
was altogether insufficient in himself. I enjoyed
also many proofs of the Lord's providential care,
one of which was so remarkable that I think it
ought to be recorded.

After my degree in 1834, I continued to reside
at Cambridge and took mathematical pupils. One
summer I took a long-vacation party to Killarney,
and in the course of our residence there a young
man came over from Cork to see me. He had a
great wish to go to Cambridge, and having heard
that there were Cambridge men at Killarney, he
came over in order to obtain information. The
result was that he came up the next October, and
I was glad to help him in his work, in which he
made good progress. But after some time he told
me that the expenses had exceeded his estimate
and that he feared he should not be able to
complete his University career. If richness be
measured by the proportion of income to expendi-
ture, I was a richer man then than I have ever
been since, as, in addition to my father's allowance,
I received a considerable income from my pupils.
I therefore told him that he must go on to his
degree, and with the help of my dearly beloved

friend Henry Goulburn gave him a cheque which he considered would be sufficient. The result was that he took his degree and left Cambridge. After that I altogether lost sight of him, and wondered what had become of him.

Thus twenty-six years passed by, and I was very much interested at Tunbridge Wells in the erection of St. James's Church, and had issued a circular requesting that all subscriptions might be paid in by January 1st, 1862. But though the world gave us credit for being extremely rich, my account at the bankers was so low that I found I could ill afford the £100 which I had promised. That 1st of January was therefore to me a day of real anxiety, and in the early morning I committed the matter solemnly to God, and my Heavenly Father was "thinking upon me" when, after our family worship, my letters were brought to me, and there was one from my young Irish friend in which he said that, though I regarded the money given at Cambridge as a gift, he had always considered it a loan and now wished to repay it, so enclosed a cheque of £100. It was that cheque that I paid into the bank with a thankful heart that morning, as my contribution to St. James's Church. So my young friend was employed by my Heavenly Father to take care of the money until the time when I should require it.

In addition to the deep interest of my own parish, the proximity to London brought me into contact with various movements of a more public character. This involved a conflict between my duty to the parish and my duty to the Church of which I was a member. But I firmly believe that the parish was the gainer, not the loser, by my interest in those general objects, and nothing tends more to wither up a man's ministry than such an isolation as brings him into contact with his own limited surroundings, and leads him to stand aloof from the general work of the Church of God.

Then it has been my desire to attend as far as possible to diocesan interests, those connected with the rural deanery, the archdeaconry, and the diocese, such as ruri-decanal meetings, visitations, and diocesan conferences. It has appeared to me that when, by our position, we have a right to attend on such occasions, we ought to do so, and that if we hold back from taking our legitimate part, we have no right to complain if things are said and done of which we disapprove.

On the same principle I have attended Church Congresses, and have been thankful for the opportunity of publicly maintaining those great principles which are inexpressibly dear to my own heart. I have never hesitated to state what I have believed as clearly as I knew how to put it, and my experience is that, if a person will attend them in the Name of the Lord and as a witness for Christ, and will speak without either reserve or compromise, he will not only receive courteous treatment from those in authority, but will find a grand opportunity of spreading the truth through the length and breadth of the land.

I have myself received letters, from all parts of England, thanking me for words which I was enabled to speak at one of the Church Congresses, and I have known more than one instance in which words so spoken have been blessed to the permanent peace of conscientious inquirers.

I have been deeply interested in the large lay and clerical meetings of the Evangelical body. When I was quite a beginner I listened to an address at the Islington Clerical Meeting, by the Honourable Baptist Noel, which has affected the character of my whole ministry. He was speaking on the subject of spiritual power, and said that, whenever any attempt at ornamentation became apparent, power ceased. On those words of his I have acted ever since I heard them, and I am persuaded that those meetings are frequently the means of making permanent impression on many of those who are brought together by them. Thus I have always availed myself of every opportunity of attending such meetings. In the course of fifty-four years I have missed the Islington Clerical Meeting only three times, and then from no choice of my own, and they have led to a very sacred relationship with many of my beloved and honoured brethren in all parts of the country.

But I have known none that I have regarded as

a greater privilege than our own Aggregate Clerical
Meeting at Tunbridge Wells. From that I have
never been absent, except when detained by severe
illness, and nothing can exceed the sacred privilege
which I have enjoyed in those happy gatherings.
We have met as brethren in the Lord Jesus, as one
in the great privileges in which we live, as fellow-
labourers in our happy ministry, and as fellow-
partakers of the grace of God. We have often
taken counsel together, and though in the course
of thirty-four years almost all the original founders
have passed away, there is still the same spirit
of brotherly harmony, and the same loving interest
in each other's welfare. I often wonder how it is
that some dear brethren appear to me to under-
value such gatherings of those who fear the Lord.

But of all the objects away from home there was
none that called forth my deepest interest like the
Committee of the Church Missionary Society. I
do not know exactly how long I have been a
member of it, but I was invited by Mr. Venn when
I was Curate of Richmond to join the Committee of
Correspondence, and as I left Richmond forty-three
years ago, I consider that I must have been at
least forty-five years a member of that body, and
I regard that membership as one of the great
blessings of my life.

It has been the practice of its management to be
always on the look-out for men who had distinguished themselves and could bring to the

Committee their own experience of the work of the Gospel in those countries where their lot had been cast, and the result has been that there have been in that committee room a body of men, many of whom have filled highest positions under the Crown, but who gladly gave their time and talents to the patient consideration of the many difficult questions that have arisen in the progress of the work.

I can quite believe that the business of the Committee might be conducted with more despatch, and I have myself desired to see some changes in that direction, but for calm, patient, and prayerful consideration of the business before them, I have never known anything to exceed the conduct of the C.M.S. Committee. I cannot express the confidence that I feel in the fidelity of that Committee, and when I have heard men finding fault with their decisions, I have often wished that, before finding fault, they would attend our deliberations and see for themselves the prayerful process by which they have been led to their decisions. Again and again have I known them kneel down in the midst of their business, and plead with God for His guiding hand. And although it would be absurd to expect, upon every difficult question, forty or fifty independent minds should think exactly alike, yet I do not remember ever to have known an interruption of the unity of spirit, and there are few things that I have felt more, since it

has pleased God to lay me very much aside, than
the necessity of quitting my place in that committee
room, and losing the privilege of uniting with such
a body of men in such a work as that of the
Church Missionary Society. I trust God will
bless them with His own rich and abundant
blessing. They have a noble work before them,
not merely in spreading the Gospel amongst the
heathen, but in uplifting the banner of truth at
home, and I trust it may never happen again that
dear brethren, in their earnestness for the maintenance of a pure Gospel, will ever think of weakening
the Church Missionary Society by forsaking it, and
so rejoicing the heart of the great adversary of
souls.

With these words the brief Autobiography is
closed, and it is characteristic of the writer that his
faithful heart, like the compass-needle ever pointing
to the North, should, after a brief deviation to his
personal affairs, turn finally to the contemplation
of the glorious work of that Society whose cause
he loved to plead.

It is, however, impossible to close the volume at
this point. The forty-one years of ministry at
Tunbridge Wells were the most fruitful and important of his life, yet their events are barely
noticed in the last pages that he dictated. We
must therefore devote some space to the work and
character of Edward Hoare in that sphere where

he became best known, in which he bore the greatest trials of life, and whence from pulpit and press that teaching flowed forth by which the Holy Spirit blessed thousands of anxious souls.

Extract from the Journal, May 1858.

Thoughts about Personal Holiness.—Nearness to Christ. Likeness to Christ. Singleheartedness to Christ.

The Whole Work of the Holy Spirit.—In Christ. With Christ. For Christ.

Peculiar Importance to Ministers.—Because we are acting under a strong religious stimulus which may be mistaken for true holiness.

Must not expect to draw souls nearer to God than we are ourselves. " Be ye followers of me."

Because by-ends mar and impede God's blessing. " My glory will I not give to another." "Ye ask and ye receive not," etc. God has too much regard for the minister to trust him with success.

By-ends strike at the root of faith. " How can ye believe ? " etc.

Nearness to God carries a man humbly through success, and peacefully through discouragement.

If we live in Christ we shall be carried through the dying hour.

The Visible and Invisible Life.—Men see Christ's Gospel in us. We are the visible representatives of an Invisible Presence. Thousands read us who never read their Bibles.

Questions.

Is there the same desire for salvation of souls when others preach ?

Is there never pleasure in finding others less than ourselves?

Is there real gratification in the progress and success of others?

" Search me, O Lord " (Psalm cxxxix.). " Cleanse the thoughts of our hearts." Lev. xxii. 2 : " Profane not," etc.

" Pardon iniquity of our holy things." " Be ye clean, ye that bear the vessels of the Lord."

Pardoned sinners the only witnesses to converting grace.

CHAPTER IX

WORK IN VARIOUS PLACES

THOSE who knew the subject of this memoir only in his later years were often struck by his physical strength and vigour. Yet from his earliest years and up to middle life there were signs of constitutional delicacy which caused anxiety. On various occasions he was laid by through attacks of illness, and it is plain from passages in his journal that, although physically an athlete, he quite expected that his life would be a short one. But God had other plans for His young servant: true, he was to be disciplined by frequent illnesses —Pakefield had to be resigned in a year owing to delicacy of the chest; his work at Richmond (where he caught smallpox in his parish-visiting), and Holloway, and Ramsgate, was interrupted by periods of ill-health; but these were perhaps the training by which faith was strengthened and spirituality deepened for the great work of middle life, and a hale and saintly old age.

The close and topical study of the Scriptures to which allusion is made in the Autobiography, and in which, no doubt, the mathematical training

of the University was a great assistance, gave him
a clear view of the doctrines of the Church of
England ; combined with this was an intimate
acquaintance with the formularies of the Prayer-
Book and the writings of the Reformers, also the
result of years of careful reading,—consequently
Mr. Hoare was in great request all over England
to speak at gatherings of the clergy and devotional
meetings of various kinds.   Soon after his appointment to Tunbridge Wells, we find in his letters,
of which a few extracts are given in the following
pages, references to these journeys ; in fact he
literally seemed to go up and down the country
speaking and preaching.   It was no unusual event
for him to address great audiences in remote towns
on the same day.

The following letter, written to one of his
daughters just after her Confirmation, for which he
had prepared her, alludes to this kind of work,
but it is inserted here more particularly as a
specimen of his tender interest in the spiritual
welfare of his children :—

"YORK, *May 28th,* 1856.

"I do not yet know whether or not I shall be wanted
at Pontefract to-morrow, and if I am not I may reach
London as soon as this letter ; but you have been so
much in my thoughts lately that I cannot forbear sending
one line of affectionate remembrance.

"I have felt the last three months to have been a
profitable time for us both, and I trust it has brought

us into a closer union with each other than we have
had before. I consider that as dear girls grow up they
become not merely the children, but the companions
and fellow-helpers with their parents, and therefore I
rejoice at all that brings us together, as I believe the
Confirmation has done, and as I believe that our uniting
together in the Lord's Supper will yet further tend to
do. I cannot tell you with what a deep feeling of
interest I look forward to the joy of receiving you as
a Communicant on Sunday next. I trust that it may
be a help to you in drawing nearer to God than you
have ever yet done, and in feeding on Christ by faith
to the very end of your course. I am sure of this, my
dear girl, that there is no joy like that of knowing
Christ, no place like that to be found in His love, no
happiness like that which springs from His grace, and
it is no small comfort to me to rest assured that you
feel this yourself, that you have not merely felt the
importance of it, but have also known something of
the joy. It is a great thing to have the knowledge
of our real and great necessity, but that cannot give
us peace ; it is the sweet assurance of His sufficiency
that can really give rest to the soul. That sufficiency,
dear girl, is for you, freely offered to you in Him,
without money and without price, and I trust sweetly
enjoyed by you through the teaching of the Holy
Spirit. May He lead you forward day by day, and
graciously prepare you for His kingdom !

"Since beginning my letter the post is come, and
your letter with it. I knew the good news before I
came away ; but I am not quite sure whether I shall
come, for I do not know whether I am wanted here.
Tell your mother I am very well, and am taking the greatest
care of myself. I got on very comfortably yesterday,
and was not overdone. This afternoon I go (D.V.) to

Leeds. I am quite concerned about baby. Dear love
to your mother.

"Your most affectionate Father,

"E. H."

His love for the Church Missionary Society
made him ready to go anywhere in its service,
and in 1862 Mr. Hoare visited Cork for this
purpose; some mistakes appear to have been
made about dates by local friends, and accordingly
there were one or two days in which there was
no work for him to do. This, which would have
been a natural source of vexation at all times,
was at this juncture particularly hard to bear.
Mrs. Hoare's serious condition had just been
discovered. It was therefore with considerable
unwillingness that he had consented to leave her
at all; but when, through the mistakes alluded
to in the early part of the following letter, some
days had to be spent in doing nothing, it is easy
to imagine how his spirit chafed at what appeared
to be a needless absence from home. Yet this
had its compensation, as it gave him more of the
company of his host, a venerable saint of God.

Not only so, but Mr. Hoare used to tell of the
remarkable way in which his aged hostess comforted
him concerning the great trouble which was just
beginning to overshadow his life. Making him
sit beside her on the sofa, she persuaded him to
open all his anxiety and grief to her; and then,

in a motherly way, gave him such loving advice
and deep consolation that he was enabled to look
forward more calmly to the sorrow, and returned
home strengthened in faith to meet the trials
which were thickening around him.

"Cork, *May 26th,* 1862.

" . . . However, I am repaid by the affection of the
dear old Dean * and Mrs. Newman, with whom I am
staying. I have greatly enjoyed my visit, and she has
been most loving and sympathising. Indeed she has
done me real good, and given me valuable help by the
way. It is a pleasant and profitable thing to be with
those whose race is nearly run, and to hear their views
of life, when they look back on it from the borders of
eternity. She seems to take a different view of it to
what I do, who am in the midst of all the cares of my
pilgrimage.

"I thought of you and home all day yesterday with
much affection, though without much time for especial
prayer, for I was about all day, having preached twice,
and been two hours in the afternoon to hear Mr.
Denham Smith. I must tell you all about it when I
get home ; but it is a curious thing that I heard him
tell precisely the same stories about conversion that
Miss Saunders mentioned. There was something very
pleasing about it all, and parts of it were very powerful.
But I confess I did not see wherein lay the secret
of that remarkable success which God seems to have
bestowed on him. Perhaps he is more in prayer than
we are. But let us be thankful for what God has done,
and take courage.

---

* The Very Rev. Horace Townsend Newman.

"I fully hope (D.V.) to be at T. W. on Saturday, but I shall not expect any of you dear daughters to meet me then, as I expect to find the house thoroughly uncomfortable, and shall most probably take up my quarters with some of the people. I rejoice to think of our settling at home again before very long, and am quite of opinion that the change home may do your dearest mother as much good as the change away. But how we are to take care of her and prevent her overfatiguing herself I know not. Of one thing, however, I am sure—viz. that we have dear, loving, and most helpful daughters, whose delight will be to be helpful. Most fully do I appreciate it, and most heartily do I thank God for it. Give my dearest love to all, and most especially to your mother; to Gurney also if he is with you. I am quite delighted at his Greek.

"Most affectionate

"E. H."

It must not be supposed, however, that the parish suffered because other places profited. On the contrary, these brief trips were fitted in between his parochial duties, and by his work for others fresh energy seemed to be diffused into things at home. The newspapers might record his name at a meeting at the other end of England, but the following evening would see him at the night school or in his pulpit, or at what he seemed to love best of all, his Men's Bible Class. He had a genius for teaching; whether it was children, or ladies, or undergraduates, or working men, it made no difference—the instruction was suited skilfully to every sort of mind. Many a former curate who reads these words will remember the Men's Bible Class on Tuesday evenings. "All sorts and conditions of men" were there, a score or two at least: labourers, shop-assistants, artisans, clerks; there perhaps an ex-Indian judge, here a medical man; beside the Vicar sat his curates, who were always present; and then, after a hymn and prayer, the subject of last week was resumed, and in a simple conversational way the story of Abraham, or some other Scripture character, seemed to make the individual stand out before us like a man of our acquaintance, with difficulties and temptations which we felt were like our own.

There was no reading round, but a little friendly questioning to bring out the thoughts of the men.

On one of these occasions an elderly man of remarkable appearance made some striking observation on the subject of the evening; subsequent inquiries revealed a former student for the priesthood in the Romish Church, who, being unable to "swallow" the dogma of the Immaculate Conception when first promulgated, had been turned out of the College in Rome and afterwards joined the Church of England.

Mr. Hoare loved to address men, and was never more at home than when preaching at Cambridge to the undergraduates or addressing meetings of clergy, or, best of all, speaking in his own church at the monthly Men's Services on Sunday afternoons. His choice of subjects and of texts was very striking, *e.g.* to the Mayor and Corporation upon "The wisdom that delivered the city," to the Fire Brigades upon "Escape for thy life, lest thou be consumed," to the Volunteers upon "Soldiers of Christ," to the Friendly Societies on "A workman that needeth not to be ashamed," etc.

These discourses were delivered with a solemnity, earnestness, and simple eloquence peculiarly his own, and were accompanied by gesture and tone of voice that made them intensely striking. No one who heard these addresses could ever forget them.

At the close of the first ten years of work in Tunbridge Wells came the great sorrow of his life.

Mrs. Hoare had been his truest help in the family and the parish, bringing up her ten children with wise and loving care, ruling her household and holding open house for every guest, and yet holding mothers' meetings and visiting the sick and dying of the large parish of Holy Trinity (which then included the whole town). No one ever saw her in a hurry, none who wanted advice were turned away, and not a single duty seemed ever forgotten. In 1862 alarming symptoms appeared. Medical advice was taken; treatment and rest were tried, but in vain; the disease rapidly progressed, and after a cure was pronounced to be beyond medical skill, Mrs. Hoare resumed such of her parish work as was still within the compass of her strength, with the remark that, since rest was useless and her time was now short, she must work so long as power lasted! The loss of such a wife was indeed a deep sorrow, and the entries in his journal testify to the grief that wrung the husband's heart.

On July 27th, 1863, she passed away, her last words calmly uttered—" Lord Jesus, receive my spirit."

The journal ends with her last message to her children : " I shall look for you at heaven's gate."

A few months afterwards Mr. Hoare wrote a touching and beautiful sketch of his beloved wife entitled " Sacred Memorials " ; it was not published, but had a large circulation, finding its way even beyond this country.

The one great consolation in this overwhelming sorrow was, however, able to uphold him. The same truths which had strengthened her for an active life sustained her in suffering, and gave her unruffled peace to the end. The peace, the presence, and the power of the Lord Jesus Christ gave power to the faint and made him strong in the Lord. For twenty-four years they had worked side by side, and in the thirty-one years that remained he sometimes gently spoke of her as present though unseen, and joining in prayer for his work.

Towards the close of the year, when sending a line of welcome to his eldest daughter on her return home, he closes with these words, which have a pathetic power when read in the light of the recent bereavement :—

"T. W., *November 27th*, 1863.

"If there is so much pleasure in meeting those dear to us after these short separations, what will be the joy of the great reunion at the coming of the Lord!"

CHAPTER X

DOMESTIC LIFE AND FOREIGN TOURS

IT was a delightful thing to see Mr. Hoare in the midst of his family. Some of us remember only the later years of his life, but the enjoyment which he then took in the company of his grand-children was very charming to witness. Those, however, who recollect the time when his ten boys and girls were growing up around him, speak with much pleasure of the way in which he threw him-self into all their feelings and pursuits, and the skill which he evinced in drawing out their cha-racters. He tried hard, as he touchingly says in one of his letters, to be "father and mother in one." In the bringing up of his children religion formed such a bright part of their life that allusions to it came in quite naturally into ordinary conver-sation. On one occasion, five years before Mrs. Hoare's death, he makes the following entry in his journal :—

"*September 19th*, 1858.—Very much interested to-day by —— [one of his younger boys]. I was talking at dinner about the great geological periods of creation.

He said, ' But it took place in one week.' I answered,
' Those days were probably long periods, as it says,
" One day is with the Lord as a thousand years, and a
thousand years as one day." ' He said, ' I thought that
meant that with the Lord we should be so happy that a
thousand years would seem like one day, they would
pass so quickly ! ' "

How God blessed his efforts is known to all
who are acquainted with his family.

The following letter refers to these happy
relationships :—

" T. W., *March 3rd*, 1864.

" MY DEAR DAUGHTERS,—I cannot say how often we
think of you, and how pleased I was to hear of your safe
arrival and enjoyment at Oxford. I know few places in
all England with more objects of interest than Oxford,
and I have no doubt you will thoroughly enjoy your
week there. We are getting on comfortably, though I
have had rather too much of clerical meetings, having
one on Monday and one to-day. But I hope it has been
in the Lord's service. On Monday we went through
Romans xi., and I certainly thought that the Prophetics
had studied the chapter better than the Clericals. But I
was quite confirmed in the exposition at the Prophetical.
I suppose Annie has told you of all our home doings.
We really have got on very comfortably, but it seems
very strange to have seven away out of the ten. I
suppose, however, if God preserves me, I must look
forward to more than that in future. The course of life
seems to be that a person begins alone, and then, when
God gives him the blessing of such a union as I have had,
the house fills year after year, till at length the tide turns

and the dispersion begins, till at last sometimes the question arises who shall be the companion of the aged father. But we have not come to that yet, or near it ; and when it does come, if it ever does, I am sure it will be to draw us heavenward, and wean me more and more from earth to heaven. I am sure I have been far too much tied down below. Truly I may say, ' My soul cleaveth unto the dust ' ; but I think I already feel something of the weaning power, and I trust I may feel it more and more. However, I scarcely ought to write so to you ; but rather to thank God for the present mercies, for the past lovingkindness, and for my dear, dear daughters, who, I am sure, do all that daughters can to make my home happy. Dear love to you both, and to your uncle and aunt.

" Your most affectionate Father,

" E. H."

In 1864 Mr. Hoare, accompanied by a brother and two of his sons, went for a tour in Switzerland. It was on their return that the first meeting took place between the writer and his future Vicar (as has been intimated in the Preface) ; and Mr. Hoare used to say, with reference to the mournful circumstances connected with that day, that he often asked himself, " Why should I be permitted to bring my boys back in health and strength, while this other father brings back only one of the two who went out on their holiday ? "

The following letters were written at this time :—

"Lucerne, *August 4th*, 1864.

" My dear Girls,—We failed in catching the night train at Paris, so were obliged to come on yesterday by day to Basle, and to-day to this lovely place, which looks more beautiful than ever. I certainly think it is the most beautiful place I know in the world. To-morrow we strike into the mountains. . . . Everything thus far has prospered with us, but my heart hungers after home ; and I don't know how it is, but I always feel my loss most when I am away. I hardly knew how to bear it at Plymouth. I suppose the reason is that the thoughts are always dwelling on home and all its interests, so that all connected with it is more felt than ever. The boys are very bright and very agreeable, Edward being full of his conversation with the French, to his own great delight, and their great amusement. He travelled many hours yesterday in a carriage away from us, in order that he might ride with a large French family who had a compartment to themselves. Gurney is not so conversable, but has every appearance of being pre-eminently happy. We are now preparing to go up the Rigi for the night, and the whole party are gone to purchase alpenstocks. Would not you like to be going with us ? But, oh ! if it lasts so hot, I wonder how much there will be left of us when we reach the top. Dear love to all. Tell Lily I hope she will look after my garden as well as her own, and tell the bees we are getting on well, and met with excellent honey. Also you may tell —— of this as the right time of year to plant some Melilotus Leucantha, and also some good strawberries. Let me know how the sunflowers are, and the rose-cuttings.

" Dearest love to all.

" Most affectionate

" E. H."

Family-letter from abroad :—

"ST. LUC, *August 16th*, 1864.

"MY DEAREST SONS AND DAUGHTERS,—'Homeward Bound' is always a pleasant sound, and so it is on this occasion, however pleasant our journey may have been, for I have been quite homesick for some days, and, like a schoolboy, have been counting the days till my return. I fully hope to be home on Saturday, but I cannot say at what time, as we have lost all reckoning as to hours. Indeed we may fail altogether, as we are acting contrary to my general rule, and propose to travel by the last train all the way from Basle, so that if anything fails at any point we shall be thrown out altogether. But I trust we shall arrive all right, and dear uncle with us. . . . I hope we may be home by the 6.20, but I cannot say positively, as I know nothing.

"I cannot say how I rejoice at the good accounts I hear from you. I have thought of you all with the utmost interest, and prayed for you with a father's love. Tell the dear boys how pleased I have been to hear such good accounts of them. They little know how they have added to the pleasure of my journey, for if I had felt an anxiety respecting them, I could not have enjoyed even this beautiful country. Tell —— and —— likewise how very much I have been pleased with your report of them, and thank —— and —— for their letters.

" We had a splendid week last week, and many sacred remembrances of our happy journey together, and when we came to Zermatt it seemed so like old times that I could almost have looked out for you. The mountains seemed more beautiful than ever; but there they stand fixed, and know nothing of the changes that have taken place in the hearts and homes of those that look at them. But there is one thing more fixed and more permanent

than they are ; I mean the love of God in Christ Jesus.
In it therefore we will seek to trust more and more, and
I am sure He will never fail us, as He has never done yet,
and we shall never be disappointed.   I have accepted
the Archbishop's invitation, and I hope —— will enjoy
her visit.   As for myself, I had sooner remain at home.
But it is clearly right to go, and indeed I propose to
make an effort and go out more than I have done lately.
The boys send their very dear love, though they do not
seem much disposed to express it on paper.   That they
leave to me.   If any very nice person turns up who may
be disposed to preach once on Sunday, it would be very
acceptable ; but I hope to reach home prepared.

"Dear love to all.

> "Most affectionate
> > "E. H."

Letter to his sons :—

> "Sierre, *August 16th*, 1864.

"My dear Boys,—I have been so greatly pleased by
the good report that I have had of you that I must write
one line to tell you so.   I am quite thankful for it, and
I have no doubt you have had a happy holiday in consequence.   I made some lines on the mountains to show
that the way to be happy is to seek each other's happiness :—

> "'When all begin to seek their own,
> Then each must seek it quite alone ;
> But when all seek to please each other,
> Then each is helped by every brother.'

"We have found this to be quite the case in travelling,
for it is quite necessary when we travel to think of all
the party, and strive to please every one.   But I must
not moralise, but tell you something of our journey.   We

have not had many adventures; but we have climbed
up some terrible hills, and I can assure you it has been
hard work.   Up, up, up; puff, puff, puff; grunt, grunt,
grunt; and still the farther you go, the mountains grow
higher and higher.   You think sometimes you are near
the top, and, when you get there, you find another top
higher still, and then another, till you get quite tired of
tops.   And coming down is hard work too.   The mountains are covered with great loose stones, so that by the
time you are at the bottom you are glad enough of a
resting-place.   We go to bed very early, the boys about
eight, and I about nine.   But then we make up for it at
the other end, and by five o'clock, when you are all fast
asleep, we are all moving, and sometimes almost off.
The middle of the day is so hot, as our hands and faces
will prove to you, that we can scarcely travel in the
middle of the day, unless we be high up in the mountains, where the air is so beautifully fresh that we can do
almost anything.   We meet with a great many travellers,
many of whom are wandering over the glaciers.   They
are a queer-looking set, with immense boots with large
nails in them, with wideawakes and green veils tied over
them, with a long pole in their hand with a spike at one
end and an axe at the other.   Then you see their guide
marching behind with a similar axe, and a long rope on
his back, which is used to strap the whole party together
if they cross any dangerous place, so that, if one falls,
the others may hold him up.   And tremendous slips
they sometimes have.   A few days ago four men slipped
and slid four hundred feet, more than twice the length
of our garden, down a steep piece of ice with a huge
precipice at the bottom, so that they would have been
dashed to pieces if they had not stopped.   But happily
two of them struck their axes into the ice just in time,
and so they hung on, close by the edge of the precipice,

and were saved. I suppose some time or other I shall hear of you two being Alpine travellers. Gurney and Ted seem quite ready to begin;—but my time is past, and I must content myself with going only to those places where I can climb with poor wind and old legs. However, at Zermatt we met with Mr. and Mrs. ——, who had been wandering over the highest glaciers, she being strapped by a rope to the guides. I suppose she liked it; but I am not sure it was quite the right place for a lady.

" Well ! I hope we shall all be together, if God permit, on Saturday, and bring all our things with us, but some are already left behind, and others are waiting for us on the road, as we have taken hardly any luggage, so that a good many of our preparations were of no use at all. Since Monday morning we have had only a knapsack between us, so you may imagine we have not been very smart, and our evening dress has not been of the gayest kind. I fear also it has not always been of the cleanest, for we have not had things enough to change nearly so often as we should have liked. But we look forward to a glorious wash on Saturday. But one disadvantage of our having so little luggage is that we cannot bring home any Swiss curiosities. We have had enough to do to get our own absolute necessaries across the mountains; so we shall be obliged to come back quite empty-handed. But we shall come not empty-hearted, but full of love to all my dear ones. Good-bye. May God bless and keep you !

" Most affectionate

" E. H."

The following letters have an individual interest of their own :—

"Tunbridge Wells, *February 1st,* 1866.

"I am sure it is very profitable as well as pleasant to have an occasional change in those we hear, and on the strength of this conviction I propose to take a weekday holiday for next seven weeks, as Mr. Burgess is to preach for me next Wednesday, and other brethren during Lent. So I hope to buckle to and get through Pusey on Daniel, if good friend Jacques is not reading it. I quite enjoy the thoughts of it, though really I ought to be thankful for our Wednesday evenings, though I must admit they are an effort to me."

"Tunbridge Wells, *May 20th,* 1867.

"We have been getting on capitally, and had really a very pleasant Sunday. Campbell's sermon was quite first-rate, and made a great impression on all who heard it. But I greatly fear he will not come as curate. I should esteem it a very great favour if the Lord were to send me some one who would give a little fresh fire to me as well as the people, for I sometimes find my own energies flag, and greatly desire to have some fresh zeal infused among us. Numbers of people wandered to other churches, but I believe no one regretted their worship in the Hall or Schoolroom.* We sang the hymn 'Jesus, where'er Thy people meet,' and I believe we beheld His 'mercy-seat.' The girls are going to Mr. —— this evening with Brodie. I am going to stay at home, for I do not like the thought of sitting there for three hours. How strange it is the people think two hours too long for church, but like three hours for a lecture! I suppose they enjoy the one more than the other, and that makes all the difference. I am afraid they will find Heaven very dull."

---

* Trinity Church being temporarily closed for repairs.

"WOODFORD GREEN, *September 5th*, 1867.

"It has been a great joy to me to hear such good reports of all the party, and I hope you will tell them all so. There is no text in the Bible which I can enter into more fully than this, 'I have no greater joy than to know that my children walk in truth.' To hear of and to witness your well-doing is the greatest joy I have in life, and if it please God to grant that we may all be one together for eternity, it will take eternity to express my thankfulness."

On hearing of the sudden death of a friend :—

"YORK, *May 24th*, 1869.

"How rapidly and how unexpectedly do the greatest dangers take place! Truly we are living on the brink of eternity, and a few hours may find us in the midst of it. May the Lord keep us with our loins girt and our lamps burning, and we ourselves as those that wait for their Lord. I am thankful to say I have got on very comfortably, but I am too old to talk all day, and nothing suits me so well as home. I sometimes think I must give up travelling altogether; but then when I find how much my poor services seem to be valued I have my misgivings. We have had really noble collections, no less than £78 in one little church holding little more than two hundred persons, the richest of whom were shop-keepers and professional men; and £60 in another church where the congregation, though rather larger, was very much of the same character. We have therefore still much to learn at home, and none more than I have. It seems that we are only at the beginning, at the very threshold of heavenly knowledge, but what we can see on the threshold is enough to fill the soul with praise and gratitude."

"TUNBRIDGE WELLS, *April 26th,* 1870.

" I have really been regretting your absence from the feast of fat things which we have lately been enjoying at home, for I consider we have had privileges of a very high order.

" Our Passion Week services were most profitable, and following as they did on Mr. Langston's Lent sermons, they tended, I trust, to put a seal on impressions already formed, though I cannot say I have yet had the joy of discovering any cases of marked conversion as their consequence. I have, however, met with those who I think have been aroused to further progress, and who acknowledge the help given with real thankfulness.

" I trust also that our C.M.S. anniversary may be regarded as a token of progress. There has been an amazing amount of interest amongst our younger parishioners on the subject of the African Bishop,* so that yesterday the Mission-room was quite full, and again both the Trinity rooms in the evening. There were so many last night that there were several standing by the door of the girls' room, and a collection of £14, containing an immense amount of copper. I confess I was anxious about our collection in church, especially when I found that we had not exceeded that of last year in the morning, but we picked up nobly in the afternoon and evening. In the evening alone there was £45, so that before we left church the collection reached £120, and there were £11 additional sent on Monday morning. I hope I may regard it as the fruit of all the

---

* The Right Rev. Samuel Crowther, D.D.

admirable sermons that we have lately heard, and if so
I shall regard it with peculiar thanksgiving, as showing
that there has been not merely religious excitement but
true religious principle at work amongst the people.
And this is what we all want. It is to be living under
the combined influence of principle and emotion, of
deep feeling produced in the soul by strong conviction
of Christian truth.

"I have been very much urged to go to Cheltenham,
and if I go I should immediately set out for my long
journey. But I do so enjoy my quiet work at home that
I sometimes think I must never go out again. I ought,
however, to be thankful for the privilege of being permitted to do the Lord's work anywhere."

In the autumn of 1870 Mr. Hoare, accompanied
by one of his daughters, crossed the Atlantic, and
spent nearly three months in a pleasant tour
through the United States. It was a delightful
holiday, and was the means of greatly strengthening and refreshing him for work at home. He had
many good introductions, and went about seeing
all that he could of the people, public institutions,
and Church work, but beyond an occasional sermon
Mr. Hoare made it a time of rest. No letters
appear to have been preserved relating to this
tour.

To Lady Buxton, after her son's death :—

"TUNBRIDGE WELLS, *August 22nd*, 1871.

"I have thought of you so much lately and so affectionately that I must send you one line of loving remem

brance, for I know how pleasant a thing it is to be
remembered by those we love, especially when the
remembrance leads to prayer. I am persuaded that very
many have prayed for you under this very heavy sorrow.
There are so many who feel the bitterness of it, all of
whom connect you with it so intimately that I am persuaded there has seldom been a mourner more generally
or more affectionately remembered before God.

"I think that solemn day at Fox Warren was, on the
whole, very satisfactory. To me it was inexpressibly
affecting to be surrounded by all the beauties of the
most charming place, with his mind speaking in every
brick and almost in every tree. I was so glad that I
had paid him a visit there only a few weeks before—such
a pleasant visit, and so remarkable for the charm of his
society, although, poor dear fellow, I confess I was terri-
fied about his health. But now all that is over, and, oh!
how it does bring before us the overwhelming interest of
the Heavenly Home!

> "'My Heavenly Home is bright and fair;
>   No pain or death can enter there.'

"I never remember to have felt more deeply the difference between things which can and which cannot be
shaken. Oh, who can tell the blessing of an unshaken
hope, an unshaken safety, an unshaken inheritance, and
an unshaken home, all resting on unshaken promises
and the unshaken covenant of God! These things which
cannot be shaken must remain, and they will remain
when all fair homes of this pleasant world are passed
away for ever. May God keep us by His own grace
grasping them with an unshaken faith, that, when Christ
either comes to us or summons us to Him, we may meet
Him without surprise and receive an abundant entrance
into His Kingdom."

Extracts from family-letters :—

"PATTERDALE, *September 14th*, 1871.

"I have received two very earnest invitations to Edinburgh, and one to Australia. I do not suppose that I shall accept either of them, certainly not the latter until my return ; but if I accept the former it will delay my return a week. But I do not think it likely.

"Our journey thus far has been most prosperous. We have had beautiful weather, and a very happy party : Keswick and Derwentwater on Tuesday, Helvellyn and Ambleside yesterday, and Bowness and Patterdale to-day. As usual we have had several affectionate greetings, amongst others one from Sir —— ——, whom we met at Keswick. We were both very friendly, but it was impossible not to feel that we were both under constraint from the sense of great divergence. We both scrupulously avoided any points of difference, but both showed clearly that there were too many rocks on which we might split at any moment. And yet I feel reproved by the zeal he had shown in his endeavours to do good to his guide. I am sure there are many lessons which we may learn from those who widely differ from us, and the more we value the blessed truths which God has made known to us, the more humbled we ought to feel at the want of fervour with which we endeavour to maintain them.

"To-morrow we hope to reach Carlisle, and I hope I may be prospered there. But I find it very difficult to work up much zeal about the Jews. What I do feel is entirely the result of Scriptural conviction, and not of any personal interest. The Jew in Scripture is certainly a much more interesting character than the Jew in Petticoat Lane. But we profess to act on Scriptural principles, and therefore ought to persevere, even though it be in the dark."

"I am greatly pleased by your letter of this morning. It was indeed a most profitable sermon of Mr. Edmonstone's, and I have felt the powerful influence on my own mind of it and the life of Agnes Jones. I trust, therefore, that my Cromer visit has been thus far really for good, and I feel, myself, a fresh stimulus for the sacred work to which the Lord has called us."

"I have been thinking of you all day in your return to the dear old home, and have almost felt disposed to envy you, for I am satisfied with holiday-making and begin to long for home. However, I have consented to return to Cromer from Nottingham, to pay a visit of a few days to your Uncle Richard, so that I expect to enjoy the hospitality of three of my brothers, which is very satisfactory to me. Nothing could have exceeded the kindness of all parties, and I am not without a hope that there has been some blessing on my ministry. But I cannot say it has been a time of rest, and I feel the want of repose more than I do at home. I suppose this is why I write so slowly, so badly, and with such difficulty that I am sure I never should do for Secretary to the C.M.S.*: the first long letter would knock me up for the day."

"I have been venturing on a speech this morning in

---

* A subject on which he had been approached by the Committee.

which I think the Lord prospered me. I desired to speak for Him, and I was certainly most kindly received."*

"You need not be at all frightened about the Dean, for it is on Wednesday the 25th that he comes to us. The sermon, etc., is on the 26th, and on that day we ought to have an S.P.G. luncheon. I think it would be well to ask the Committee soon. The list may be found in the S.P.G. report, under the head 'Local' on the top shelf.

"I feel doubly interested in the thought of my return, and trust it may be with a greater realisation of our completeness in Christ Jesus and of the blessedness of working not merely for Him but in Him. I felt this most remarkably at Nottingham, and I believe it resulted in power, at all events on one occasion referred to in the paper which I have asked —— to send to you.

"The Congress was very interesting, but too exciting. The week was one of great exhaustion, though I am thankful I was there, and I believe God gave power to those who were endeavouring to be witnesses for the truth. I cannot doubt but on the whole they did well and carried the people with them. With only one exception, they spoke with wisdom and power, like men who were being prayed for, as indeed we all were by many in the Hall. But the close attention, the hot room, the many friends, and the anxiety as to the issue took a great deal out of me, so that I am to-day really enjoying a quiet morning over my letters.

"Amongst others I saw a great deal of the Bishop of Sydney, and found him very strong about the Australian idea.† He says it is the very thing that he has long

---

* Nottingham Church Congress.

† An invitation from some of the Australian Bishops to undertake a series of Missions in their dioceses.

desired for his own diocese. But I do not yet see the call of God sufficiently clearly to have my judgment really inclined to it. If the Lord makes His way plain, I hope to be ready to go, but God forbid that I should go one step without His orders."

From the Archbishop of Canterbury :—

"ADDINGTON PARK, CROYDON, *September 24th,* 1868.

" To REV. ED. HOARE.

" DEAR MR. HOARE,—It will give me very great pleasure if you will accept the office of Honorary Canon of Canterbury, to which your standing in the diocese and the services which you have rendered to the Church by your zeal and ability in the discharge of your ministerial functions amply entitle you.

"Believe me, dear Mr. Hoare,
"Very sincerely yours,
"C. T CANTUAR."

The offer of an Honorary Canonry in Canterbury Cathedral, made in 1868 by Archbishop Longley, was the only dignity which he ever received ; why this should have been the case is a question that has often been asked, and to which no satisfactory answer has ever been made. Canon Hoare would have made an admirable Bishop : he was a born ruler and administrator ; his intellectual powers and wide sympathies (for which those who knew him superficially gave him no credit), together with his power of inspiring enthusiasm in all his subordinates, would have been good qualities for that high position, and not the least advantages

which he possessed were a fine presence and commanding personality.

But he neither sought nor wished for promotion,
and remained to the last what he loved to be, a
pastor in the midst of a devoted flock, with more
opportunities of preaching the Gospel of Christ
at home and throughout England than fell to
the lot of most men, and, as one remarked to him
when the subject happened to be referred to in
a newspaper, " Man has not promoted you, but
God has, by permitting you to be the means of
bringing blessing to more souls than any one whom
I know." Looking at the subject in that aspect,
it is impossible to deny that his exceptional
talents were specially suited to the sphere which
he adorned, and thus we may believe that God
overruled the apparent neglect of men for the
greater advancement of His truth.

CHAPTER XI

PAROCHIAL MISSIONS

FIVE-AND-TWENTY years ago parochial missions were in a different position from that in which they stand at present.

There were very few mission preachers, and they had a good many difficulties to contend with. Some looked askance at the new movement and thought it savoured of Rome ; others deemed it " exciting," and unworthy of the calm atmosphere of the Church of England.

It had not then been reduced to a science : missioners adopted their own individual methods, as seemed best to them. Canon Hoare at an early stage of the history of the movement recognised its vast possibilities, and believed that it was just what was wanted to save the Church from stagnation, and arouse men from that dangerous respectability which enables them to repeat the General Confession, but which declines to particularise. All through his ministry his aim had been to reach individuals, and he saw the opportunities of so doing in the work of a mission.

The first invitation which he accepted was that given by the Vicar of Holy Trinity, Nottingham, on the occasion of a general mission throughout that town in 1872. Being his first, it was a time of the most intense and thrilling interest, and the letters describing it are therefore given at more length than those that refer to later missions. Not that this work lost any of its freshness to him ; during the twelve years that followed he undertook similar missions frequently, sometimes twice in a year. The opportunity was always fraught with the deepest and most prayerful interest to the preacher ; his congregation, moreover, will remember how he used to return to them after such occasions, not wearied, but fresher than ever, and all aflame with spirituality, power, and love.

His scheme of subjects for a mission was very wisely drawn up ; some of these have been printed, and evince great knowledge of human nature. The writer well remembers how that, when he was going to undertake a mission for the first time, Canon Hoare sent for him and said, " Tell me your order of sermons and Bible-readings." It was mentioned in detail ; he replied, " I see very little about the ' New Life.' " He was referred to the subject of " consecration." " Well," said he, " if you will take my advice, you will leave that out. I say little about ' consecration,' because that is man's work. Make the life which is God's gift one entire subject ; its necessity, its source, and its reality ; and conse-

cration will follow." His advice was taken, with
the happiest results.

To his daughters :—

"TRINITY VICARAGE, NOTTINGHAM, *February 6th,* 1872.

"I think I may thus far give a thankful report of my
journey. As I passed through London I had a most
interesting and encouraging conversation with Mr. ——,
and a pleasant journey down to this place with ——.
We arrived just in time to have a hurried cup of tea, and
go off to the public prayer-meeting in the Exchange Hall.
This was a wonderful sight : the large Hall was crammed
full, and many were unable to gain admittance. It was a
very striking contrast to the busy market outside. There
was a great deal of singing from a very nice little book of
the S.P.C.K., and a remarkable address from old Aitken.
The best part of it was an exposition of Asa's prayer :
the rest was awakening, and, I hope, profitable, very
earnest and very affectionate, but it did not move me,
though some people said it almost threw them into
hysterics. I offered a prayer myself, and three others
besides Aitken. I liked them all thoroughly, and came
away, I hope, the better, though the meeting had lasted
nearly two hours. So having come here and received a
most warm welcome from my pleasant host (Rev. Allan
Smith) and hostess, I lay down and awoke fresh and
happy for the Sunday's work. Mrs. Smith is daughter
of my old friend Mr. Linton of Oxford, and even you
could not make me more comfortable than she does !

"Well ! Sunday dawned upon us, and at 10.30 service
began. The church is not so large as our own, and was
not so well filled, but they were pleased with the attendance. I preached on the deep sleep in Isaiah xxix., and
I believe the Lord was with us. They were attentive all

through, and towards the close many of them were much affected, so much so that I gave notice I would have a Bible class in the church at 3.45 p.m. for a re-consideration of the subject. The Lord's Supper was very solemn, and many were in tears, especially two old gentlemen whom I hope to be able to see during the week. So we went home thankful.

"The Bible class in the afternoon was well attended. There must have been more than a hundred present, including several gentlemen, so that I was well repaid for the effort, though very tired when it was over and scarcely up to the Evening Service. However, when the time came I was fresh again, and I believe the Lord helped me. There was a larger congregation than in the morning, but I did not see the same evidence of impression. I preached on the old subject, Exod. xii. 23, and, though there was deep attention, I did not perceive the same emotion. Then followed the prayer-meeting: this was most interesting. The large room was quite full, and during certain periods of silence I heard the sound of weeping in many parts of it. Mr. Smith gave a short address and offered prayer; I did the same, and longed to know how to manage such a meeting. After a time I dismissed them, and invited any to remain who liked. But they all seemed unwilling to go, and it was some time before they began to move. But at last the room was cleared, and then what should I see but two clergymen with their faces covered, in trouble about their souls. One proved to be a most deeply interesting case. He told me his difficulties without any reserve, and at length went away declaring himself satisfied. I really believe he learned the way of peace.

"Meanwhile Mr. Smith was speaking to four adults one by one, and I then found a row of five young people waiting for me. In three of them, especially one, I thought there was great reality, but I had not time to speak with them separately, and I cannot say I was satisfied with the interview. I hope to see one of them again to-night, when I trust there may be more decisive results.

" All this quite freshened me up, so that I was ready and in good heart this morning to start off for the service in Adams' Factory at eight. The place was quite full, so that there must have been about three hundred present. As they all dispersed immediately to their work, I had no opportunity of any personal intercourse, but they listened with great attention, and I can only hope the Lord gave His blessing.

" I am now enjoying a quiet morning, writing, reading, thinking, and praying ; remembering with great affection my dear friends at home who are praying for me, and most especially the three dear daughters left at home to help their father by their prayers and each other by their mutual help. May the Lord be with you ! "

"Trinity Vicarage, Nottingham, *February 9th*, 1872.

" I can hardly tell you what an interesting week I have had. It has been without doubt the most encouraging in my whole ministry. I never knew so many persons awakened under my sermons in so short a time, and I am thankful to say that many of them, and many more who have been previously anxious, have been brought to see the way of life in Christ Jesus their Saviour. I cannot say how deeply I thank God for it, or how it has stirred me up to look out more hopefully for a great blessing at home, and also amongst the young men at Cambridge. I hope you all continue to pray for me.

" Last night I had first a strong middle-aged man come to speak to me under deep conviction of sin ; and

then a most respectable woman who had no peace in her
soul. These two took so long that I was obliged to send
for another clergyman to come and help me with the
remainder, as there were sixteen waiting in the outer
room to see me.

"The greater part of the morning has been occupied
by my Bible class, but I had one hour for inquirers,
during which there came one of the leading gentlemen
of Nottingham, and a most interesting inquirer who
had been in deep anxiety for years, and who, I believe,
through God's mercy left the vestry at peace in Christ
Jesus. Oh, what can I render unto the Lord for all
His goodness to me! Dear love to the dear sisters and
to all who pray for us."

"CAMBRIDGE, *February* 12*th*, 1872.

"I hope to be home, if it please God, to-morrow by
express, and look forward with the deepest interest to my
return. One thing is clear, and that is—we must seek to
go forward, and look out for far greater results than ever.

"Saturday was a sacred day. I went in the morning
on my way to church to see some of those who had
been awakened, and found them peacefully trusting in
their blessed Saviour.

"I then went to the church to see any that might
come to me, and my whole hour was filled up by most
interesting cases, one of a most touching character. At
11.30 I gave a short parting address in the church to
about a hundred people, and at twelve left for the train,
after the most kind and grateful farewells from numbers
of people who wished to thank me for my ministry. It
has been a new era in my life, and I trust has done me
great good.

"I arrived here after five o'clock, swallowed some dinner,
and hurried off to the gownsmen's meeting, which began

at six. I did not know how to turn my mind to a new subject, but still I hope the Lord helped me, and it gave me the opportunity of inviting the young men to meet me on Sunday night.

"Well! Sunday came, and I believe the Lord was with us. There was a large morning congregation, and many of the people were deeply moved. Oh, how I longed to ask them to come and open their griefs! but the Vicar would not give me leave to do so, so I was obliged to leave them to God, and perhaps that was better.

"In the evening I stood up in dear old Simeon's pulpit. The church was crammed with gownsmen, and I believe the Holy Spirit was with us. I then had a cup of tea in Carlos' rooms, and went off to the meeting of gownsmen. The room was quite full. I gave them an address on Justification and Sanctification, illustrated by some facts in my Nottingham experience. I believe that I might have had many coming to me for help if I had only invited them ; but I was stupid, and did not do it.

"But one dear fellow seemed as if he could not go away : he came and took me by the hand, and would not let go. The others all left the room, and then he poured out the troubles of his soul. I thank God his difficulties were removed, and we walked home together blessing and praising God. Oh, what shall I render unto the Lord for all His goodness to me ! "

The following extract describes a return visit three months later to the scene of his first Mission :—

"NOTTINGHAM, *May* 30*th*, 1872.

"But I have no words to describe the interest of my short visit here. Nothing could be more satisfactory.

I found almost all those in whom I trusted a work was begun standing fast and thankful in the Lord. Many of them were so transformed from the look of gloom and depression which they had in February to a look of peaceful, confiding thankfulness, that I could scarcely believe they were the same persons ; and their affection, their gratitude, and their pleasure in meeting me again were truly touching to my heart."

Leeds Church Congress :—

"LEEDS, *October 8th,* 1872.

" In almost an hour I am going down to the battle, as weak as David, but I hope to find the help of David's God. There is an enormous gathering for the Congress, and people of all classes will be there. Oh, how earnestly I hope and pray that the Blessed Spirit will rest on all there who are called to speak for their blessed Saviour ! "

Mission at Hull :—

"HULL, *November 25th,* 1872.

" Many thanks both to you and —— for your letters, for I delight to hear from you, and think of you with most heartfelt and loving prayers.

" I had a very pleasant, quiet, unfatiguing journey, quite by myself all the way from London, so that I had no temptation or obligation to talk. At Tranby I had a most affectionate and brotherly welcome, and came on here on Saturday, full of hope and thanksgiving for the privilege of speaking to so many people about their souls.

" Immediately on my arrival I went to a meeting of Communicants, very much like our own, and then to a very uninteresting conference of the clergy; so we did not really begin work till yesterday. In the morning there was a fine congregation, and in the evening one still larger, with a prayer-meeting after it, in a large hall which was so full many could not get in. As a mode of intercourse with the people it of course completely failed, but as an indication of their interest it was very encouraging, and I am happy to say that, one way or another, I have already met with several persons anxious about their state, and I am thankful to be able to add that some of them have gone home with the expression of great satisfaction to their souls as the result of what they have been taught.

"I have therefore great reason to be thankful for a beginning, and from what I have seen of the first droppings of the shower I cannot help hoping that there is a real blessing in store.

"Immense pains have been taken all over the town, and much prayer offered, so that we have a right to look for great things.

"My throat is not at all the worse for yesterday, and, if anything, better; but I tumbled about all night with a very hot head after the excitement of the day.

"My host and hostess are most kind and agreeable: they make me exceedingly comfortable, and are people quite able to carry out their hospitable intentions, so that I am very well off; but I am not sure that Thorold is not wise in going into a lodging, so as to avoid the necessity of conversation, for I really believe that talking fatigues more than preaching, and I sometimes long to be alone, or at all events to be able to get away into my own study just when I please. But I ought not to say so, for I am as comfortable as man can make me. Pray for me, that I may have wisdom and power given to me."

Specimen of one of Canon Hoare's " Mission Subjects " :—

St. Dunstan's Mission.—*November 12th to 22nd*, 1880.

Nov. 12*th.*—To Communicants.   Psalm cv. 40 : " He satisfied them with the bread of heaven."

Nov. 13*th.*—Prayer-Meeting.   Psalm xcvii. 5 : " The hills melted like wax at the presence of the Lord."

Nov. 14*th.*—*M.*   Jonah ii. 9 : " Salvation is of the Lord."   A Divine Saviour ; Salvation ; Revelation ; Application.

  E.   Gen. xlii. 21 : " We are verily guilty." Conscience—may be seared, 1 Tim. iv. 2 ; defiled, Titus i. 15 ; aroused, John viii. 9 ; purged, Heb. x. 22.

Nov. 15*th.*—*M.*   Propitiation : (1) Divine, Rom. iii. 25 ; (2) Complete, Heb. ix. 12 ; (3) Final, Heb. ix. 28 ; (4) Satisfies conscience, Heb. ix. 14 ; (5) Sufficient, Heb. x. 18.

  E.   Heb. xii. 24 : " The blood of sprinkling." Speaks of complete atonement, full remission of sin, Heb. x. 22, ix. 22.

Nov. 16*th.*—*M.*   Forgiveness :   (1) Present, Psalm xxxii. 1 ; (2) Complete, Micah vii. 19 ; (3) Dependent on atonement, Rom. iii. 25 ; (4) First gift of the New Covenant, Jer. xxxi. 34— " for."

  A.   To Mothers.   Heb. ii. 13 : " I will put my trust in the Lord. . . . Behold, I and the children whom Thou hast given me."

  E.   Job ix. 29 : " If I be wicked, why then labour I in vain ? "   (1) The difficulty ; (2) The remedy—" the Daysman " or Mediator, ver. 33.

Nov. 17*th.*—*M.*   Justification, Rom. v. 1-10 : (1) Five

blessings from, vv. 1-5; (2) Through recon-
ciliation, ver. 10; (3) To whom given, vv. 6,
8, 10; (4) When given, vv. 6, 8—"yet."

　　E. John v. 28, 29: "The hour is coming."
(1) The voice; (2) The resurrection; (3) The
separation.

Nov. 18*th.*—*M.* The New Birth, John iii. 1-16: (1)
The necessity, ver. 7; (2) A spiritual change,
ver. 6; (3) By the sovereign power of the
Holy Ghost, vv. 5, 8; (4) Found before the
Cross of Christ, vv. 14-16.

　　A. To Church-Workers. Zech. iv. 1-10.
(1) "By My spirit"; (2) The mountain removed; (3) Christ will finish His work;
(4) Small things; (5) Christ the King and
Priest supplies all, ver. 3.

　　E. John v. 25: "The dead shall hear."
(1) Dead conscience; affections; hope, etc.;
(2) The dead hear; (3) The dead live.

Nov. 19*th.*—*M.* Sanctification: (1) In the heart, Psalm
xl. 8; (2) The standard, 1 John iii. 3; (3) The
difficulty, 1 John i. 8; (4) Progressive,
2 Peter iii. 18; (5) By the use of Scripture,
John xvii. 17; (6) By the sight of the Lord
Jesus, 2 Cor. iii. 18; (7) Must follow, not
precede forgiveness, Jer. xxxi. 33, 34.

　　E. Matt. xxvii. 46: "My God, My God,
why hast Thou forsaken Me?" (1) The im-
putation of sin to Christ; (2) The certainty
of complete satisfaction; (3) The burden of
unforgiven sin.

Nov. 20*th.*—Prayer-Meeting. Psalm xxxiv.: The song of
the delivered.

Nov. 21*st.*—*M.* Psalm cxix. 94: "I am Thine." (1) By
the gift of the Father, John xvii. 2; (2) By

redemption through the Son, 1 Cor. vi. 20 ;
(3) By the life-giving power of the Holy Ghost,
John vi. 63 ; (4) By personal surrender to
God, Rom. xii. 1.

A. To Men only.   2 Cor. vi. 18 : " I will
be a Father unto you."

E. Exod. xxi. 5 : " I love my master ; I
will not go out free."   (1) The new master ;
(2) The old master.

Nov. 22nd.—Jude 24 : " Him that is able to keep you
from falling."

Summary : (1) Finished propitiation ; (2) Free
gift ; (3) Life-giving power of the Holy Ghost.

CHAPTER XII

PARISH WORK

SOME men are in great request as preachers and speakers outside their parishes, but for some reason or other they are not very useful at home.

It was not so with the subject of this memoir. The prophet in this case was honoured in his own country. On Sunday mornings, three-quarters of an hour before service began, many aged and poor parishioners might be seen making their way into the church to secure good seats. In Holy Trinity the free seats are more in number than those that are appropriated, and some of the former are in the best part of the church; all these were filled long before the hour for the commencement of service. As eleven o'clock drew near the congregation were in their places, and the aisles were filled with strangers in every available spot waiting in the hope of some possible seat. It was a common thing in the summer for as many as a hundred to go away unable to get accommodation. The writer well remembers the profound impression which the Sundays used to make upon his mind.

The old Vicar and his curates were in the vestry in good time robed and ready ;* having knelt in prayer, there was a silent interval, and exactly to the moment when the clock in the tower struck, the vestry door was opened and they passed out into the church.

Sometimes this was a slow work, as the people stood close together ; some were sitting on the pulpit stairs, and the clergy had to thread their way to the chancel rails.

When service began the cushions at the rails were all occupied by worshippers kneeling upon them. Canon Hoare generally took part in the service, which was conducted in the simple old-fashioned way, read, not "toned down" in the manner now so prevalent.

When the preacher ascended the high pulpit it was an impressive thing to see that great congregation, over sixteen hundred in number, ranged beneath in the body of the building and around him in the deep galleries, waiting for his words. His prayer before the sermon was a very striking one, and it was always in the following words : "Almighty God, our Heavenly Father, who hast purchased to Thyself an universal Church by the precious blood of Thy dear Son, and hast

---

* Over the door in the vestry there hung the well-known lines :—

> " I'll preach as though I ne'er should preach again,
> And as a dying man to dying men."

promised that the Holy Spirit should abide with us
for ever : may we now enjoy His sacred presence !
May He direct the word which shall now be spoken,
and apply it with Divine power to all our hearts,
through Jesus Christ our Lord. Amen."

Those sermons were wonderful, delivered so well
that few could believe them to be written discourses, which they were ; with changes of tone
which made the sentences impress themselves
upon the memory ; the manner so solemn, as
befitted the ambassador, and yet so pleading,
as became the father. The eloquent language
attracted the intellectual mind, and the remarkable
simplicity of expression appealed to the simplest
understanding. The *matter* of these sermons was,
however, their great charm.

The atonement wrought by Christ was their
great theme. Many preachers, when enlarging
upon other subjects, bring in this doctrine at the
close of their discourse, but with Canon Hoare the
great foundation of our faith, viz. the substitution
of Christ for the sinner, and His finished work of
propitiation applied by the Holy Spirit, was always
visible, not as a thing to be brought in at the
end, but *already there*, as the centre and pivot of
all that he said ; hence no doubt the power of his
words, and withal as a thing much to be observed
was the extraordinary freshness with which he was
able to present, Sunday after Sunday, the old story
of the Cross, old but ever new.

Very powerful were those discourses, for they were full of teaching. The preacher was a deep student of his Bible,—" After diligently working down into it for fifty years," he used to say, " I am still only scratching the surface ! "—and he possessed moreover an unusual power of imparting knowledge ; he was pre-eminently a teacher, and among the many privileges which his curates enjoyed none was so great as the Scriptural teaching which they received in their Vicar's sermons. After the preacher had concluded there was a short prayer, followed by the blessing, and then, with nothing to take away the impression of the solemn words to which they had listened, the congregation dispersed. There were three or four services in the Parish Church every Sunday, besides the shortened Morning Service in the hospital and Mission Service in the large Parish Room ; there were also five Sunday Schools, and many classes on the same day for old and young men, women, and senior girls.

Though in his vigorous days he always preached twice, he was in the habit of opening the principal boys' school every Sunday morning, and in the afternoon visiting one or other of the various schools and classes, finishing all by slipping into the afternoon service in time to hear the sermon preached by one of his curates. By these means he kept in touch with everything going on in the parish.

The weekday work was enormous and varied.
The Parish Room, so called—really a large building
containing a hall and different rooms—was occupied nearly every hour of every day in some part
or other ; and in the parish at large every conceiv-
able kind of agency for the temporal and spiritual
good of rich and poor was to be found, all animated
by real energy and spiritual power. Many a time
have the workers heard from their Vicar's lips,
" Let us not be content with machinery ; what we
want is *Life.*"

The Sunday Evening Services in the Parish
Room were deeply interesting. For half an hour
beforehand the volunteer choir sang hymns to
attract the people in, and workers went into bar-
rooms and common lodging-houses to bring in any
who would come.

It was a very moving sight, about three hundred
people, some of them degraded in vice, packed
close together, joining in the familiar hymns, and
listening with attention to the speaker. Canon
Hoare often said that, intensely as he delighted
in the opportunity, it was at times more than he
could bear to realise the depth of sin in which
many lived who were gathered together at these
services—the responsibility of the preacher seemed
on such an occasion to be so enormous.

Except as occasional workers, he never would
allow the regular church-goers to attend the Mission
Room services. " This service is not for you," he

used to say ; " it is a stepping-stone to the church."
And such it was. The process of transformation
used to be watched with interest in those cases where
some poor degraded creature, either there or at the
Temperance meetings, was led to " take the first
turn to the right, and then go straight on," as
Bishop Wilberforce once tersely put it. Soon the
ragged clothing improved, the whole appearance
altered ; after a while it might be said of such
that, clothed and in their right mind, they sat
at the feet of Jesus ; and then by degrees moving
on to the church, they might be seen at the Lord's
Table, or sitting in the adult Confirmation Class in
preparation for that sacred privilege.

There were low slums in that parish, but, as
Canon Hoare used often to say, " The Church of
England can and does reach the lowest of the low,
and can bring the Gospel to bear upon the vilest,
without the aid of a fiddle or a flag !" One practical difficulty met him at first in the Parish (or
Mission) Room services. Many a poor tramp,
weary and footsore, used to say when asked to
come in : " I have eaten nothing since the morning.
Can you give me food ? I want that more than the
service." When these answers were reported to
him Mr. Hoare used to say, " And if I were in
their place I should make the same reply." It then
became a matter of consideration what could be
done to remove this difficulty, and yet not give
anything like a bribe to induce people to come to

these services for a paltry motive. After a great
deal of thought and consultation with the workers,
it was determined to give a slice of bread and
cheese to any poor hungry ones who were not
residents, but passing through the place, and in the
cold weather a mug of coffee was added. This plan
worked admirably ; only a few asked for the food,
but those received it, and what had been a very
real hindrance at the first was satisfactorily
removed.

Most if not all of our Religious Societies were
well supported in the parish, but the three in which
Mr. Hoare seemed to take the warmest interest
were the Church Missionary Society, the Church
Pastoral Aid Society, and the Irish Church Missions.
For the first and last of these three there were,
besides the Great Hall meetings, crowded gatherings
for the poorer parishioners in the Parish Room.
Canon Hoare was an incorporated member of the
S.P.G., and had an annual sermon for that society,
but of course the Church Missionary Society had
the love of his whole heart. What he was to that
society every one knows, and he infused some
of his missionary enthusiasm into the town, and
especially his own parish.

The Church Missionary Society anniversary
was indeed a "field-day." Long prepared for, it
was anticipated with keen interest ; the best
deputations came down, and nearly every church
in the town joined in the celebration. Canon

Hoare generally preached in the old Chapel of
Ease in the morning, but always occupied his own
pulpit in the evening of that day, and what a
thronged congregation there was on these occasions!
The whole soul of the preacher seemed to go forth
in his subject, and his hearers were thrilled by the
trumpet call of that missionary sermon. In later
years the thought of his dearly loved son and
daughter working for God in China brought a
special and personal interest into his words—not
that he spoke of them, but somehow one could
feel that they were in his thoughts. The collections
on these occasions were very large ; in former
years £100 was thought the proper thing as the
result of the Anniversary Services in Trinity
Church, but gradually the amount crept up until
about ten years before his death, when on one
anniversary, in his absence through illness, it was
suggested by the evening preacher that it would
be a cheer to their beloved Vicar if £200 were
reached ; and right liberally was the appeal
answered. After the sermon two gentlemen came
into the vestry to inquire the amount collected,
" for," said they, " whatever the deficit may be,
we will make it £200 " ; but their kindly help was
not needed, as more than that sum was already
counted out upon the vestry table!

From that day £200 was looked upon as the
proper sum from Trinity Church for the Church
Missionary Society anniversary.

The parish schools for boys, girls, and infants were all first-rate, and Canon Hoare prided himself upon having the best boys' school in the diocese; but he was not content with the welfare of his own schools—it was his wish to strengthen all Church schools in the town. We hear now a good deal about the confederation of Church schools. More than twenty-five years ago the Vicar of Holy Trinity started such a confederation. Every Church school in Tunbridge Wells elected its members, and sent them to the periodic meetings, where matters of interest were discussed, weak points strengthened, and preparation made for dangers that threatened. This was only one of the many things in which his statesmanlike ability showed itself; Edward Hoare was one of those "men that had understanding of the times, to know what (the spiritual) Israel ought to do." The power of such men is readily felt and acknowledged. "All their brethren are at their commandment."

It would be impossible to write about the work in Holy Trinity parish without alluding to the Ladies' Bible Class. This was a remarkable feature of his ministry, and, like most of his works, was going on before it had been suggested or thought of in other places.

This was not a Bible-reading, but a class for teaching by preparation beforehand, and at the time by question and answer. The answering was, of course, not compulsory, but nearly every one present in the large assembly of ladies took part.

The teaching was marvellous; sometimes it was a topic or a life in Scripture, sometimes a portion of the Prayer-Book or the Articles. The mastery of the subject and the power of conveying the same clear knowledge to other minds were very striking. Some have even said that they considered this class to have been his greatest work in Tunbridge Wells. The enthusiastic letters which have been received during the past thirty years from generations of young people who, having been taught by him, went forth into life educated and fortified in religious truth, testify to the fact that these classes formed in many an instance the real turning-point of life.

Twice in the period that he was Vicar of Holy Trinity a Parochial Mission was held, the respective missioners being the Rev. Rowley Hill, afterwards Bishop of Sodor and Man, and the Rev. H. Webb Peploe. Each time it was a grand success, greatly owing, under God, to the prayer and preparation which preceded it. The second mission was remarkable for the number of men whom it reached; at the services for men only there used to be two thousand listeners crammed into the church. Being well followed up, these missions left a glorious mark in the parish. Canon Hoare used often to quote the words of some foreign pastor, "The Church of England is the best in the world at

throwing the net, but the worst at drawing it in,"
and he always added, " Let *us* not fall into that error,
but draw in the net " ; and so he did. How familiar
to the ears of his old curates were the words that
he often said on Sunday morning from the pulpit
at the close of some instructive sermon, " If there
are any who would like this matter explained
further, I shall be glad to see them this afternoon
in the Parish Room at a quarter past four " ; and
he has often remarked, " I have never given this
notice without getting some earnest souls who
wanted help."

" Pray for people and look out for God's answer,"
was the direction that he used to give to his
workers, and in this lay surely one of the secrets of
his great success as a pastor. The characteristic
of Holy Trinity parish was " Life " ; the Holy Spirit
was manifestly at work in the place, blessing the
various agencies among rich and poor, young and
old, arousing, renewing, converting, and edifying.

One of his loving fellow-workers thus recalls an
experience of this in the earlier years of Canon
Hoare's ministry at Tunbridge Wells :—

" I recollect well a great spiritual movement that took
place over the whole parish, then undivided except
by St. John's. People, men and women, came to us,
chiefly of course to him, asking for help in their spiritual
state—people who had been living entirely secular lives.
There seemed to have been no special cause for it—no
mission—no exciting preaching ; it was caused by his

careful parish work and ministry. This went on for, I think, about two months ; we kept it very quiet, spoke of it only to a few prayerful people, but they were praying for it ; at length, however, it got out, and a few unwise persons—some of whom were Church people and some were not—got down Revivalists and hired the Town Hall to throw excitement into the work. Immediately it ceased ! I build no theory or argument upon the fact, I merely say what I noticed."

The same writer continues thus :—

" About that time we began the Evening Communion, and I recollect well our astonishment at the result. Such a number of new faces whom either we did not know or never saw at Holy Communion ! Servants, lodging-house keepers, wives of working men, whom practically we had been excommunicating by having the Holy Communion only at the hours when we had hitherto celebrated it."

All who had the sacred privilege of working with Canon Hoare in his splendidly ordered parish will agree in this, that two clauses of our Church's Creeds were ever before his eyes : one was the note of all his preaching ; the other, the motive and reward of all his work.

" I believe in the Forgiveness of Sins."

" I believe in the Holy Ghost, the Lord, and Giver of Life."

This chapter, which describes some of the parochial work of the parish, would not be complete without a reference to a great organisation

which, though not of the parish, yet annually
assembled in it, viz. "The Aggregate Clerical
Meeting." Shortly after his appointment to
Tunbridge Wells, at a time when no conferences
of clergy, now so common, had been thought of,
the idea of the great spiritual benefit to be gained
by such an annual gathering made Mr. Hoare
determine to try the experiment. Having consulted with some friends, he sent invitations to
the members of seven "Clerical Societies" in the
neighbouring parts of Kent, Sussex, and Surrey,
to assemble in Tunbridge Wells in the month of
June for a series of meetings, not for the public,
but for themselves, lasting over two days, with
a sermon in Trinity Church on the evening of
the first day and a celebration of the Holy
Communion in the morning of the day following.
All invited guests were given hospitality in the
houses of kind friends. The Conference thus
assembled met annually for about forty years,
and from the first to the last meeting Canon
Hoare was its President, although on two
occasions illness obliged him to depute another
as the chairman. From its small beginning it
soon spread, sending its invitations through the
South-East of England, although drawing the
greater part of its members (who numbered
altogether nearly five hundred) from the three
counties named above. Laymen too, "introduced
by a clergyman," were invited to attend, and gladly

availed themselves of the opportunity. Most of the great Evangelical men have preached at its annual gatherings, and papers and addresses of the greatest possible interest have been given at these meetings. All however who have attended on these occasions will agree in this, that the one thing to which every one looked forward was the closing address of the President. Precious words were always given him to speak, full of spiritual experience and loving exhortation.

The value of conferences like these is now acknowledged everywhere, but it is only due to the one whose memory we affectionately cherish that the credit of originating them should be here given to him whose foreseeing mind recognised the blessings such meetings would confer.

CHAPTER XIII

THE BORDERLAND

THE most important crisis of Canon Hoare's life was now drawing near—a time which, though it seemed to be full of trouble, was really a period of blessing to himself, to his congregation, and to a far wider circle than his own devoted people.

In a former chapter there was a reference to the invitation which, issuing first from his old friend Bishop Perry of Melbourne, was taken up by other Australian prelates, viz. that Canon Hoare should visit Australia in about two years' time and make a mission tour throughout their dioceses in the principal towns. The project assumed a tangible shape, and details began to be considered ; the whole thing, including the journeys each way, was calculated to take ten months. He *was* absent from his parish for almost exactly the very period, and at the very same time during which the Australian tour would have taken place, but his absence was due to the consequences of that Roman fever which nearly cost him his life.

When Canon Hoare first spoke of this to the writer it was with the deepest solemnity; he said: "I am never quite satisfied in my mind as to whether the Lord had not a specially humbling message for me in that fever; the Australian plan was given up because I thought I ought not to be so long away from my parish, and it has sometimes seemed to me as if He, by laying me by for the very time that I should otherwise have been away, may have meant me to learn that my presence here is not so important after all, and that He can carry on His work by other hands." This is thoroughly characteristic of the way in which our beloved friend seemed always on the alert to detect his own weak points, as well as to gain from trial its intended blessing. Australia was given up, and several months afterwards he decided to take a short holiday in Rome during part of Lent.

The following letters describe his enjoyment of the place, but at the same time we can detect signs of the penumbra of the dark shadow that was swiftly approaching.

To his eldest son :—

"Rome, *March* 3*rd*, 1873.

"So after all my misgivings, doubts, and hesitations, here I am really in Rome, and already profoundly interested in the place. We arrived on Friday evening and put up at a new hotel opposite the Russie, where alone we could find a resting-place; and to-day we have moved into some lodgings at the top of one of the highest houses on the top of the highest hill in Rome. We have been triumphing in the thought of our fresh air, but the conceit of some of us has been a little diminished this morning by, being told that there is nothing so unwholesome in Rome, that nothing is so healthy there as a low and crowded situation, and that no Roman would accept our privileges for love or money; but this we keep to ourselves.

"On Saturday K—— and I went to St. Peter's, and my expectations were more than realised by the magnificent area and perfect proportions. There is something most solemnising in the magnitude and vast open space perfectly uninterrupted by any arrangement for worshippers, and a second visit this afternoon has only confirmed my first impressions. I thought to-day that it appeared to have grown since I saw it on Saturday.

"Then we went to the Forum, which I have been feasting upon again to-day. I imagine that the excavations have been extended since you were here, but I doubt whether in the Forum much has been discovered. And really nothing is wanting. But how strange that the villain Phocas, whose edict has led to so much discussion, should be the one whose one column should stand out by itself in the best preservation of them all! But all one's ideas of human greatness are dwarfed by the Coliseum. What must the place have been when crowded with people! It must have contained all the inhabitants of the city, and a good many over, and must have illustrated St. Paul's expression ' so great a cloud of witnesses.' I suppose that Christian martyrs did not much care for lookers-on, but had their minds wholly absorbed by their God and the wild beasts which were to devour them, but it must have been an awful ordeal to face such a host of enemies, and how inconceivable it is that such thousands could be brought together for the pleasure of seeing their fellow-men torn to pieces!

Truly man is a fallen creature, born far above the beasts, but fallen far below them !

" I was greatly entertained by an American gentleman, who said to me that as they had gone so far in America as to give the suffrage to every man, they had better go a little further and give it to all the horses, for intelligent persons might drive them to the poll, which they could not do with ignorant men."

To his eldest daughter :—

" ROME, *March* 16*th*, 1873.

" We have all been greatly interested by your report of the ordination.* It seems to me that everything was ordered for us exactly as we could have wished, and if I had sat down to plan it for myself I do not think I could have planned anything more completely to my mind. So blessed be God for the abundance and carefulness of His mercy ! How I have thought of our young clergyman to-day ! I wonder whether he has been preaching. He has not written much to me, but I cannot be surprised at that when I consider the absorption of his mind. What a delightful birthday for him !

" I am sorry to say I cannot give a very good report of myself. Rome has thoroughly disagreed with me, and the disagreement has brought on so much pain in my back that between the two I have had very little power of enjoyment. Still there has been so much to enjoy that, notwithstanding everything, I have enjoyed a great deal very much indeed. But the thing I should enjoy more than anything in the world would be to get home, and I am very much disposed to turn my steps homeward instead of going on to Naples. But nothing

---

* Of his son the Rev. J. Gurney Hoare.

is fixed at present, or even discussed. It is only a floating idea in my mind, and may come to nothing.

"It has been strange to spend a second Sunday in retirement. I was engaged to preach both days, but could not venture on either, and now I should not be surprised if I left Rome without opening my lips in public. How different God's plans are from ours! My plan was that I should be so very useful, and carry on here the same blessed work the Lord granted at home. But God's plan was to keep me still and to let me learn quietly by myself. And I really hope He has been teaching me, and that these two Sundays especially have not been without their blessing. I am quite sure that those who teach most have the greatest need of learning the deep things of God and the secret windings of their own hearts.

"I have not told you about Rome, for you know a great deal about it better than I do. The great, grand old ruins stand out as magnificent as ever, speaking witnesses to the failure of the world's greatness. 'Broken greatness' seems written on them all. And modern Popery goes on its way, I should really think, more idolatrous than ever—the most vulgar, tawdry travesty of the simple Christianity of the Catacombs. But I am not going to write a book, so hoping that God has been teaching you at church as I believe He has been teaching me at home, and wishing you every one every possible blessing,

"I remain, etc.,

"E. Hoare."

Mr. Hoare returned to Tunbridge Wells for Passion Week, and was stricken down by the deadly fever which had taken hold of him in Rome. For

several weeks he was desperately ill. Sir William
Jenner came down two or three times to see him,
and the daily bulletins were looked for by the
whole town with the deepest anxiety. A daily
prayer-meeting was instituted, and was thronged
by those who joined in the most earnest supplica-
tions to Almighty God for his restoration. He
recovered, being to all appearance simply prayed
back to life by his people. The physician before
named considered it a most remarkable case, for his
patient had lingered too long on the Borderland to
make recovery seem possible. In the summer, so
soon as he could travel, he was taken away for
change, and he did not return until the autumn,
nor even then to work.

The following letter from Archbishop Tait was
one of very many that poured in upon him at this
time, and the Aggregate Clerical Meeting, which
he had instituted several years before and of which
he was President, presented him with an illuminated
address signed by some hundreds of clergy, in
which they thanked God for his recovery and
welcomed him back to health.

From Archbishop Tait :—

"Stonehouse, St. Peter's, Thanet.
"June 6th, 1873.

" 'The Rev. Canon Hoare.

" My dear Mr. Hoare,—Your long and trying illness
has made us feel much for you and your family. I trust

that now our Heavenly Father is restoring you to health. May He long continue to you and to us the blessing of your preservation in health and usefulness amongst us ; and may He in health and sickness give you every support from the Holy Spirit.

"Yours sincerely,

"A. C. Cantuar."

To one of his daughters :—

"Hampstead, *August* 13*th*, 1873.

"You and I have had so little correspondence lately that you must almost forget the sight of my handwriting, and though, I am sorry to say, the want of practice has led to a great disinclination to exert myself or to take any trouble, I really must begin again.

"We are still here, and not at sea, as we proposed to be, for last night it was so stormy that the family in general and your uncle in particular decreed we should not go by ship. I do not think K—— is sorry. So now we propose to go by train, which I always declared I would not do. But the pair of sons and daughters is more than any resolutions can withstand, so (D.V.) we go to York to-night and Newcastle to-morrow.

"On Sunday I hope I may hear Gurney preach : when shall I be doing it again myself? It seems sometimes as if I had forgotten how.

"Remember me very particularly to the Parrys. I have often thought of the Bishop's * visits to me when I was ill, and sometimes regret that I did not invite more good ministers to visit me. But I doubt very much whether I was capable of receiving much good. Indeed I am humbled to find even now how little power of receiving I appear to have. I have been talking to

---

* The Bishop of Dover.

people with a view to my own improvement, but I am very stupid. Some things I cannot understand at all, as, e.g., this new doctrine of 'Perfection.' I cannot criticise it, for I have not yet discovered what it is or what its advocates really mean. I have been talking to E——, A—— G——, and Me—— about it, but I do not know that I understand much more in consequence; and I have been reading a very interesting American biography, but that has not helped me much more. So I begin to think I must be content with the old paths, those blessed paths in which so many saints of God have walked and followed Christ. Let me and my dear ones be found walking there in the new and living way, and we may well indeed be thankful. May nothing ever turn us to the right hand or to the left, but be taking a step forward! For what other purpose has this sickness been sent? Oh, thanks be to His Name!"

"CROMER. *October 2nd*, 1873.

"I do not suppose I shall reach home till Friday or Saturday. I am not surprised at your feelings about yourself, for we have all had a shake which must leave its loosenings. Besides which we are not going home as usual to full work and happy activity, and it is impossible not to feel the difference. But there is no reason why we should not be returning to a winter of peculiar enjoyment. There is a joy in work, but there is great peace in quiet, and if the Lord grant His presence we may be more happy together than if we were under the full pressure of the ministry. I believe that we shall all be of one mind in the Lord, as we have ever been in former times, and I am looking forward to very great enjoyment.

"It is delightful to me to hear how much God has

blessed Mr. Money's ministry,* and most pleasant to find how God has made my absence such a blessing to the people.

"I enclose you Robinson's letter, as I think you will be interested by it. Certainly he has been a capital curate and friend, and I have to be most truly thankful for his help. The Lord sent him when He foresaw I should need him, and so He will always provide."

It has been mentioned that, during Canon Hoare's illness, the whole town was stirred with affectionate anxiety on his behalf. Prayer was offered up for his recovery in the churches and all the Nonconformist places of worship, and the common testimony to his character, in the conversation that was heard in the shop and the street, was that it was not his preaching nor his intellectual powers which appealed to their feelings so much as the sterling integrity and faithful consistency of his Christian life.

Towards the end of November Mr. Hoare preached for the first time after his recovery, and his friends rejoiced to see that few traces remained of his long and alarming illness. His sermon was entitled "The Best Teacher," and in the course of it the preacher said : "I believe that lately God has been teaching us all. He teaches at different times and in different ways. His teaching is not always

---

* The Rev. Canon Money, who took charge of the parish during the summer.

the same in form. Sometimes He gives His teaching by the voice of His teachers, and sometimes by
their silence; sometimes by giving them power,
and sometimes by taking it away. Now I believe
that He has taught us all by His blessing on the
ministry in this church during the twenty years we
have worshipped together, for it was twenty years
yesterday since I became incumbent of this parish.
I thank God I believe He has taught many of you
during that time by my own preaching, and I
thank Him with my whole heart for the blessed
results which He has given in His mercy. But I
am not sure that this last year has not been the
most teaching year of the twenty. I am not sure
that He has not taught us all more by laying me
on one side than He did by permitting me to
preach. He has certainly taught us how He
answers prayer, in a manner that no preaching
could ever have done, and we meet this day with
such an encouragement to pray as many of us
never had before. But that is not the only lesson
that God has been teaching us during the year.
I know not how it has been with you, but for my
own part I recognise many others which He has
deeply impressed on my convictions. I do not
mean to say that He has taught me new truths,
but that He has made old truths, the grand old
truths of the Gospel that I have loved for years,
more precious than ever, and has filled my soul
with an earnest desire, if it please Him to restore

me to my ministry, to preach those truths as I have never done yet."

After that sermon he never flagged, but steadily rose again in health, and in the years that followed many a one was known to say that, although his preaching had always been clear, powerful, and convincing, yet after his illness it had gained a special characteristic—now he always seemed to speak as one who had come from the Saviour's presence and had heard His voice.

CHAPTER XIV

BOOKS AND SPEECHES

CANON HOARE never published any large theological work, but whenever any event " was in the air," or some religious point was brought into special prominence, a small book on the subject was sure to appear, written with his masterful clearness and power, that just served the needed purpose and put into men's hands the teaching which they sought.

A few of the best-known of these little books are the following : *upon the Prayer-Book*—" Baptism," " Doctrine of the Lord's Supper," " Absolution and Confession," " Our Protestant Church," " Morning and Evening Prayer," " Articles of the Church of England " ; *upon the Bible*—" Witnesses to Truth," " Inspiration " ; *upon Prophecy*—" Rome, Turkey, and Jerusalem," " Palestine, Egypt, and Assyria," " Egypt and the Prophecies " ; *upon the Religious Life*—" Redemption," " Sanctification," " Conformity to the World " ; and many others, some of which have had a great circulation.

His papers read at Diocesan Conferences and before large gatherings of clergy at Islington and

all over England were models of clear thought
and well-expressed ideas; if these could be collected
together they would form a valuable handbook
upon the most important spiritual and practical
subjects.

But although Canon Hoare was widely known
by his small books and papers, and by the stream
of visitors that attended Trinity Church during
their sojourn at Tunbridge Wells, it was as a
regular Congress speaker that he was familiar to
members of the Church of England at large.
His writings were read by the same sort of people
who came to hear him preach, people for the most
part with religious views like his own; but at
Church Congresses all shades of opinion are
represented, and although at earlier gatherings of
this sort violent partisans tried to put down
speakers of the Evangelical party by " exhibiting,"
as a witty Dean expressed it, " symptoms of the
foot and mouth disease ! " yet better feelings
gained the day, and soon the calm and fearless
speeches of many whose names will readily occur
to the reader caused them to receive a welcome
even from opponents. Ill-advised attempts were
made at first by members of their own party
to hinder Evangelical men from attending the
Congress, but wiser counsels prevailed, and Canon
Hoare was one of those who felt that, unless he
and other leaders were willing and able to stand
up in defence of their principles on the Congress

platform, the days of Evangelical truth were
numbered. The sagacity of this view soon became
apparent, and it has led to a kindlier feeling
between men holding different theological opinions,
as well as to a diffusion in unexpected quarters
of teaching such as that which men like Canon
Hoare were well qualified to give.

The Vicar of Holy Trinity was asked on various
occasions to speak at the Devotional Meeting that
always closes the Congress week, and in reference
to this the present Dean of Norwich once said
to the writer, " I always call Canon Hoare the
Grand Amen."

Extracts from family-letters :—

"FAREHAM, *October 12th*, 1874.

"At Brighton I was most kindly and comfortably
entertained, but I cannot say I enjoyed the Congress.
There was an immense attendance, and such a crowd
that it was almost more than I could bear. The result
was that I heard but a portion of what was said, and
with that portion I must confess I was ill satisfied.
The Evangelical clergy had to sit hour after hour listening to all kinds of things without the opportunity of
saying a word. I was the only one called up on the
subject of Church services, though a great number had
sent in their cards, and I should think nearly ten
Ritualists and High Churchmen were called up one after
another. I did not in the least satisfy myself, though,
as I had trusted it in the Lord's hands, I am satisfied
that that which I said He gave me, and there I leave
it. But the result was very painful, for as the audience

did not know of all the cards, it appeared as if I was the only speaker on our side and my poor words the best that could be produced. I am not surprised at those who prefer to go quietly on their way and do the Lord's work at home. But are we not to fight manfully? Yet how are we to do it if our hands are tied as they were there?"

"TUNBRIDGE WELLS, *August 6th*, 1875.

"I hope you may have a happy Sunday. I propose to preach on the Song of the Redeemed in Rev. v. 9, as the winding-up of my course of sermons on Redemption. My subject is 'What do they think of it in Heaven?' and I fear there is a great contrast between their thoughts and ours. If it fills the praises of those who know most about it, surely it ought to fill the hearts of us who are saved through its power!"

"TUNBRIDGE WELLS, *May 26th*, 1876.

"I fear I shall not be home to welcome you on Thursday, but hope to arrive that evening if God prospers me on my long journey to Southport and back. I am sure my paper ought to be very good, if I go such a long way to deliver it! I am thankful to say it is completed, and as good as I know how to make it; so I hope the Lord will accept it and make it useful.* I certainly have been producing a great deal lately, but by no means with uniform success. The Lord has not let me feel that I have the power in my own hand, and has sometimes thoroughly humbled me, more especially in my speech for the Jews, which was a failure. But I was encouraged in my sermon about them which I preached last Sunday and which is being printed."

* The title of the paper was "The Effect of the Externals of Religion on Public Worship."

"OTTERY ST. MARY, *October 7th,* 1876.

"I am writing this letter, though I am not sure that I shall not be with you as soon as it is. But I know you will be glad to hear from me if I can reach London in time for the post.

"I rejoice to think the Congress * is over, and am thankful also that I went to it. I believe that the paper was accepted of the Lord. It provoked no controversy, and was most kindly spoken of next day by one of the Ritualistic speakers: I had great reason therefore to be thankful. Some of our people did admirably, manifestly helped of the Lord, and I do not think the truth suffered. But we sadly wanted more Evangelicals; the Ritualists put on a number of young men, many of them foolish fellows and poor speakers, but they got more people on their legs than we did.

"Now for a race between my letter and myself; I wonder which will win!"

(MISSION), "MANCHESTER, *January 30th,* 1877.

"You will be thankful to hear that the Lord is prospering us. We have had some desperate weather, and the congregations have of course been much less than they would have been. But you know I am not dependent on numbers, and have sometimes found the richest of blessings amidst a little flock on a stormy night. I hope we had such an one last night. It is almost impossible that the weather could have been rougher, but there was a capital congregation, considering, and profound attention. I believe also that there are many seriously impressed and others already greatly helped in their faith."

* Exeter.

"York, *May* 29*th*, 1877.

"I am delighted to hear a good report of you all, and rejoice to think how happy you must be now that the work is finished and the scaffold down. Notwithstanding all hindrances, it is an easier matter to beautify the outside than to reform that which is within. We cannot set the heart right with Portland cement!

"I cannot say much about myself. I hope the Lord may have given His blessing, but I have not had the sense of power as in former days: possibly I have not sought it so much from the Lord; possibly people expect more from me, and are disappointed at what they hear.

"It is curious to find how 'Rome, Turkey, and Jerusalem' is read and thought about. I hear of it in all directions, and people express a great interest in it.

"The owner of the enclosed letter was also interested about 'Inspiration,' as he remembered the address when originally given, and I promised to send him a copy."

"Caterham, *April* 14*th*, 1878.

"I hope you are enjoying a peaceful Sunday; but I cannot bear to be away from you, for I do not feel very happy about you. I have felt afraid that I was not sufficiently grateful for all your kind care of me, and that I sometimes seemed cross when I ought to have been full of gratitude! But I did not feel poorly enough to justify all the care that was taken of me. I hope I may be all right by the time I come home, and that if I am not I may at all events be in a more thankful and submissive spirit. I think it is a very possible thing that a man living with a party of young people does not always realise what they are feeling, and so does not show that tender sympathy which is the beautiful peculiarity of a mother's love. But I have often prayed

that I may be a mother as well as a father to you all,
and, I trust, may be enabled to meet your hearts'
desires more fully than I have ever done yet.

"But, oh! what a wonderful mercy it is that in the
recollection of all our defects and failings we may fall
back on the finished Atonement! 'The Lord hath laid
on Him the iniquity of us all.' There is a resting-place
for sons, for daughters, and, blessed be God, for fathers."

> "King's Lynn, *October 9th,* 1878.

"I hope that you have been interested about the
Congress, and have read carefully Canon Tristram's
most interesting speech in the *Times* of Saturday. It is
one of the most remarkable addresses I ever met with,
and I rejoice to find how well it is reported in the
secular papers. Do read it together, if you have not
done so already.

"I do not know what to say of my own speech, and
am puzzled by the way in which it was received. My
own friends were most cordial, but what astonished
me most was that —— —— and ——* came after
the meeting and thanked me for it.† What it was for
which they felt grateful I cannot imagine. I delight to
hope that God may have helped them to see His
Gospel more plainly than before; but He knows, and
He only."

In the year 1879 there came an earnest request
for a Mission Tour in some of the dioceses in

---

* Two of the most advanced men of the opposite party.

† The words used by one (accompanied by a cordial grasp
of the hand) were, "You little know how much I owe to you;
I thank God for truths which you have taught me"—words
that reflected equal lustre upon the speaker and him to whom
they were addressed.

India, similar to the one alluded to on a previous page as emanating from Australia. He was anxious to accept the invitation, but his medical adviser in London, Sir William Jenner, absolutely forbade the undertaking, and it had to be given up.

The description of the death of an old and valued servant is very characteristic. The writer well remembers the calm that pervaded the household next morning, and the mingled sorrow at the loss of a faithful friend and yet of thanksgiving at the thought of one of their household being called to the Palace of the King.

"TUNBRIDGE WELLS, *March 8th*, 1880.

"I hope you all enjoyed a happy and peaceful Sunday yesterday, as we did at home, notwithstanding the solemn, but peaceful, event with which ours concluded. F—— had passed a bad night and felt poorly in the morning, but she came to prayers as usual. She did not go to church, and H—— went to Dr. Marsack for some medicine. During the day she lay on her bed a good deal; but when we went to evening church she was in the kitchen with S——, sitting in her chair, reading her Bible. S—— went into the pantry for two or three minutes, and when she returned there was our faithful friend with not a muscle moved or a feature changed, but the spirit gone. Her Bible was open at the text on which I had been preaching in the morning (2 Cor. v. 1, 6); and so, gently and without the slightest struggle, the knowledge by faith was exchanged for that by sight and she entered into the visible presence of her Lord. . . .

"When I came home from Southborough I found her laid out in the little room, looking just the same as usual, with a perfectly peaceful, tranquil appearance, with no more disturbance of expression than a little child shows in its sleep.

"I need not tell you what a sense of solemnity there was last night throughout the house. We have all deeply felt it, but I must say that thankfulness prevails, for all who knew her had felt anxious for her future. How graciously does God deal with His children! and how needless are our anxieties!"

In the Ladies' Bible Class, when going through Acts xvi., he had urged upon his people the duty of ever looking out for opportunities of speaking for God. "Lydia" was the case in point, and the apostle's readiness to make a personal appeal was shown to be God's plan for this woman, who, residing in the very place which St. Paul was not allowed to visit, was yet brought all the way to Philippi to meet God's messenger there. This will explain some passages in the following letter to his daughters :—

"SCARBOROUGH, *July 12th*, 1880.

"I have been thinking of you unceasingly ever since I left home, and am more and more amazed at my ever having done so. How I could bring myself to it I cannot imagine; but I hope it is for the Lord's service.

"I have been looking out for 'Lydia' all the way, but not very successfully. When I got into the train at Tunbridge Wells there was a nice-looking lady who fixed her eyes on me so steadfastly, as if wishing to speak to me ; so I soon opened the way, but I found the poor thing was out of her mind, being taken to London.

" In the next train there was a lady with her servant, very tearful, so as she sat opposite me I took the opportunity of a civil word about the window, but as soon as she could she got away to the other side of the carriage, so there was no opening there. But I am not sure that ' Lydia ' may not be in this house, for there is a lady staying here, and both she and my hostess are eager for conversation on the great truths of the Gospel.

" I had a pleasant, quiet Sunday. The place is perfectly charming ; the house and garden delightful, with the most lovely view of the sea and the opposite hills, so that I do not know how to tear myself away from my bedroom window.

" The church is very nice, but sadly small. . . . There were good congregations, but not a crowd. I preached in the evening, and I certainly could not have desired a better congregation. I hope the Lord was with us, bestowing His blessing.

" I heard in the morning a very good, practical sermon on the causes of restraint in prayer :—

> " Allowed sin,
> " Unbelief,
> " Worldliness,
> " Business,
> " Temper.

" It was all true and profitable, but I should have been more profited if he had helped us to overcome them."

" NEWCASTLE-ON-TYNE, *October 4th*, 1881.

" As for the Congress, I cannot say I like the thought of it, though I hope the Lord will make use of it and of me in it. I have been thinking of my text last

Sunday, 'Shall your brethren go to war, and shall ye sit here?' so I am rejoiced to act with my brethren, and I trust the Lord may unite us in His service, and give us not only meekness of wisdom but the wisdom of meekness."

"CROMER, *October* 10*th*, 1881.

"I am rejoiced to hear of your happy visit to that dear home at Canterbury. I cannot say with what thankfulness I think on all the grace which our God and Saviour has shown there, and how delighted I am that you all should have the unspeakable joy of being employed as the Lord's agents for conveying the glad tidings of life to precious souls.

"I return you Mr. Stock's letter, as you wish it, though I am more inclined to put it in the fire, for it frightens me. But I believe the Lord was with me on the occasion to which he refers, and there was one very remarkable circumstance about it which he did not know.

"Dr. Bardsley and I had both sent in our cards, and I saw that he was eager to speak. About twenty minutes before the close of the meeting the Bishop turned to me and said that he could just manage to find a place for me. So I told him he had better call Bardsley instead, which he did. So B. spoke, and some other man after him, when the Bishop turned round again and said, 'I think after all I can find time for you.' All this made me the last speaker of the day. Off I went, and I believe before the Lord; He seemed to give me the ears and the good-will of the people at the very first sentence. I was enabled to say exactly what I wished, till at length, speaking of toleration, I said, 'But if men introduce a ritual intended to symbolise Rome——' when two or three persons cried out 'No, no.' But their objection only roused the whole multitude to what seemed like an almost unanimous cheer, which went on so long that at length the bell rang without my being able to finish my sentence, and there the discussion ended. So I lifted up my heart to the Lord and thanked Him for His mercy.

"I sent in my card next day on 'Reformation Principles,' but the Bishop of Carlisle, who was chairman, did not call me up.

"On Friday I read my paper.* Of course there was no excitement about that, but quite as much cause for thanksgiving, for several persons, amongst them Archdeacon ——, came to me in the evening and thanked me for it as having been a real help to them in their own souls. So I am come away with a thankful heart and a longing desire to spend what time remains as a firm and faithful witness for truth."

Few speeches at a congress can have aroused more excitement than Canon Hoare's famous impromptu address at Derby in 1882, and none probably have been so far-reaching in their effect. The enthusiasm aroused in the vast audience was electrical; cheers and shouts of applause interrupted the speaker at every sentence.

The same night it was being sold about the streets of Derby as a separate publication, next day it was in all the papers word for word, and during the twelve months that followed letters came in large numbers from nearly every part of the world, thanking him for his manly and vigorous words, in

* On "Helps and Hindrances to the Spiritual Life."

14

which he did not merely "hold the fort," but carried the war into the camp of those who wished to bring our Church back into the dominion of Rome.

Commenting upon it, the *Guardian* of that date said : "No one, whether agreeing with Canon Hoare or not, could fail to be struck with admiration at the courage and skill with which he grappled his antagonist."

The speaker who followed allowed himself to utter words which in calmer moments he would never have said ; it is hardly possible that one who rose, as he expressed it, "to pour oil upon the troubled waters," could have otherwise stated that Canon Hoare's friends would hold up as a very "mark of the beast such a frequent use of the Holy Communion" as Mr. Wood and his friends advocated ; and this said to one who always had weekly Communion in his church, and who, when a young man at Richmond, had been the first in his diocese to institute an early celebration !

"CROMER, *October* 10*th*, 1882.
(After Church Congress at Derby.)

"I enclose you four letters received by this morning's post, and now, as that speech to which they refer has manifestly made a great impression, I wish to put on record the Lord's dealings with me in the matter, for they have tended very greatly to the confirmation of my faith, and, I hope, given me a lift for the remainder of my life.

"When I was first asked to take part at the Congress the Secretary asked me to choose a subject from a list sent to me. I marked three, any one of which I should be prepared to undertake, one being the Liturgy, to which my attention had been directed at the Bible class and preparation for my Lent sermons. Thus God was preparing me then.

"When the list came out I was disappointed that I had a speech and not a paper, and felt the responsibility of my position, as I was the only speaker on the list, and there were four papers to precede me, by Hope, Bickersteth, Wood, and Venables.

"You all know what difficulty I felt in preparation. I did all I could to be prepared, and continually committed it to God, but I felt doubtful all the way through whether all my preparation would be of any value.

"So we went on till the day came. I awoke very early under the sense that I had important work before me, and as I lay still in the dark I was able to cast the whole matter into the hands of the Lord. After breakfast I went to preside at the prayer-meeting, and spoke to them of the Lord's love for the Church, in Ephesians v. The room was very full, and when we knelt down to pray I was solemnised more than I can tell you by all who prayed praying for me especially : I was the one subject of their prayers.

"I never can forget the prayer of one of them that the Lord would make me His mouthpiece and put His thoughts into my mind. This was very delightful to me, but it made me think something was coming ; so I left the morning meeting and went home for a quiet hour before luncheon. I then polished up my weapons, finished off my opening and conclusion, and spread it all out before the Lord, in happy remembrance of the good man's prayer.

"At length the meeting began. Hope was very bad, but did not give much that I could lay hold on. But when Wood began he at once pronounced our Communion Service to be a meagre deposit of the 'Use of Sarum,' and said he did not want to suggest the improvement of our Liturgy, but the adoption as an alternative service of the First Book of Edward VI. I sat listening to him, taking careful notes, and hoped that by the time Venables had done I should be ready. But what was my astonishment when I heard my name called by the Bishop as soon as Wood sat down. I said to him, 'It is not my turn,' but he replied, 'You had better go on.' I do not know his motive; perhaps it was that he wished Wood answered. So there I was in the face of the vast assembly without a minute's notice. But was not the Lord with me? and would He not answer the good man's prayer? So I put down my Prayer-Book, notes and everything—and away! The people gave me a most kind welcome, and, as I have been told since, many dear friends throughout the hall lifted up their hearts in prayer for me. I saw in a moment what I had to say; it was as clear to me as if I had studied it for months: nor had I the slightest difficulty for words, except once when I failed in quoting accurately the thirty-first Article. I was hissed and met with noisy opposition. But that did not matter in the least; the mass of the people was with me, and so was the Lord.

"Mr. Wood had put a weapon in my hand which was irresistible. I was encouraged as I went along with most hearty and enthusiastic cheers, till at length when I had done the people went on cheering as if they never could leave off. Oh, how I thought of the good man's prayers, and how I realised the privilege of being an instrument in the hand of the Lord! This thought has made me feel quite satisfied since. I should have liked not to have slipped in the Article, and there are many things that have occurred since to me, some that I might have added and some that I might have said better, but I have been satisfied in the thought that the Lord gave me what to say and that I said what He wished me to have said. So I do not fret over the omissions or defects, but accept it with thankfulness from Him.

"I cannot describe the expressions of thankfulness from multitudes of my friends after the meeting, or the deeply solemn feeling at the prayer-meeting next morning, when again I was the principal subject of it, but this time in thankful acknowledgment of the help which the Lord had given.

"Well! I have written you a long letter about my own proceedings, but I would rather say about the Lord's dealings with me, and that justifies its length. I hope the whole history will lead us all to trust Him more simply than ever to put words into our lips and thoughts into our minds, and so to employ us for His own most sacred service."

The following is the text of the speech, taken from the Church Congress Report :—

"Your lordship has called upon me before my time; but I am prepared, my lord, to go on if you think it right that I should. At the same time, I may add that I am called upon by surprise, for I expected to have to discuss the suggestions for Liturgical Improvements which it was likely would have been made by the Rev. Mr. Venables. At the same time, however, I am prepared to accept the position, as appointed for me in the providence of God. I consider that this debate is a most important one for the Church of England. I think that the speech of Mr. Wood, to which we have

just listened, is one of the most important speeches that
I have ever heard delivered at a Church Congress. We
used to be told that what was originally called the
Tractarian movement, but which has since been called
the Ritualistic movement, was an effort of pious and
devoted men to rise above our poor Churchmanship, and
to bring out in better development the true principles
of the Church of England. We always, with that
happiness which accompanies a clear conscience,
maintained that we were the true representatives of the
Church of England. We acted upon its principles, and
taught its truth. But still, we have had to bear a
certain amount of reproach, and we have not been able
to overcome the old prejudices. This day, however,
we have been told by Mr. Wood, the President of the
English Church Union, that our beautiful English
Church Service is ' meagre ': that there is nothing more
meagre than our existing Liturgy ; that our Holy Communion Service—in which we have taken so much
delight—is a mutilated, an inferior, and a defective
Service. [Cries of 'No, no.'] I say 'Yes,' and this
great assembly has heard what Mr. Wood has said.
We have been told to-day that we are to go back to
the Liturgy and to the Communion Office of 1549,
instead of accepting that of the year 1552, and finally
revised in 1662. And, now, will you just look for one
moment at the first Liturgy of Edward the Sixth ?

" We were told to-day that it was a falling-off from
the use of Sarum. We are therefore, it seems, to look
upon the use of Sarum—that old Popish Liturgy—I
say that old Popish Liturgy, which existed in the diocese
of Salisbury, as the model at which we are to aim. To
this use of Sarum the Reformers applied the pruning-
knife, and I cannot say that they left much of the
Office of Sarum. There were certain very fine passages

in it, and they retained them. But they brought out a
new Communion Office in 1549. There were, however,
certain defects still left.

"But as time went on, and the Reformers saw more
and more of the blessed truth of God, they then said
that the thing must be thoroughly done, and it was of
no use to carry out mere half-measures. So, thank
God, they did not stop at the First Book of Edward.
I am very much disposed to think that, if Mr. Wood
gets it, he won't stop there either. And now that we
have enjoyed the Prayer-Book as the Reformers gave
it us for these three centuries past, we are told that we
are to hark back again. Of this I am fully persuaded,
that the Churchmen of England are not prepared for
such retrogression. You must consider what has been
said by Mr. Beresford-Hope on this subject; he and I
have sparred about this matter before now. Mr.
Beresford-Hope knows just as well as I do that there
is no such thing as an altar in the Church of England.
And I will tell you also what Mr. Wood and his friends
know very well. They know as well as I do that if
they can but coax us back to those three years—to
1549, to the First Book of Edward—that there they
will find an altar. And that is one reason why they
wish for it. The Reformers knew very well that an altar
was essentially connected with a sacrifice. And they
knew this also, that while they were prepared to offer
the sacrifice of praise and thanksgiving, the sacrifice of
propitiation was completed for ever. And they believed,
further, that the doctrine of the mass was a lying
abomination, or rather I would say, a 'blasphemous
fable and dangerous deceit.' Now, then, my lord, we
fully know our ground, and where it is we have to stand.
We have, therefore, learned something at this Church
Congress. We know where we are. We go home

to-day knowing with what a power and with what an intention we have to contend. We know what Mr. Wood has told us. He has told us as plainly as possible that the object is to bring back the Church of England from the Reformed Church of 1552; to stop just a little by the way in the refreshment room of 1549, and then we are to plunge head-foremost right into the use of Sarum. Now, then, my lord, what shall we say to this? Shall we have it? or shall we not? What, I ask, shall we say to this? Shall we stick by the blessed truths that we have received, and for which our Reformers died? Shall we cling to the dear old Office Book, in which we have hundreds and thousands of times poured out our whole hearts before God? Shall we unite heart and soul as witnesses for Christ while we come to His Holy Table, and hold there communion with Him? or shall we begin by half-and-half retrograde measures until we go right back into the arms of Rome? My lord, I say no more; but I wish to thank Mr. Wood for having spoken out so plainly on this subject, and for thus having let us know this day what are the real intentions of the English Church Union."

CHAPTER XV

BLINDNESS AND SECOND ILLNESS

THE annual Confirmation times were looked upon by Canon Hoare as the most important occasions, and the ten or twelve weeks of preparation as a season whose value was simply inestimable.

Large numbers were prepared by him personally every year, and it was beautiful to see the tender individual interest which he showed in every case. Before the day of Confirmation, at the private interview with each, he noted down in a special book his opinion of the case. He was once asked when he made this diagnosis. He replied: "As they walk from the door to the chair beside me, I get a view of their character and disposition; the conversation which I have with them afterwards gives me a further insight, and I hardly ever find the estimate wrong." Many who read these lines will remember the earnest prayer, and then the fatherly grasp of the hand and loving blessing with which those interviews ended.

All through the weeks and months of preparation the candidates were remembered at the weekly prayer-meeting in the Parish Room, and on the Sunday previous to Confirmation they were commended to the prayers of the congregation and a sermon was specially devoted to the subject. On the day itself there was an early prayer-meeting, to which all candidates came, and afterwards every arrangement was made to keep the newly confirmed free from outside influences that might too soon remove good impressions ; the evening was spent, after tea in the Parish Room, in the singing of hymns and listening to various addresses. Every year his interest in the subject was fresh as ever, and at the age of eighty-one his sermon on Confirmation, which was afterwards printed and a copy sent by him to the present Archbishop of Canterbury (and acknowledged by him in one of the following letters), was so remarkable in its power and teaching as to receive a special notice in one of the Archbishop's recent Charges—an honour most gratifying to the preacher and probably nearly unique.

To one of his daughters :—

"BALACHULISH, N.B., *September* 13*th*, 1883.

"I hope you will enjoy a delightful Sunday at Thun. I do not look forward with much pleasure to ours, for I do not like the Scotch Church services. I was greatly distressed last Sunday at Oban. Oh, how earnest I should be that visitors to Tunbridge Wells should have the pure Gospel of the grace of God ! It is grievous to think what many people are condemned to hear ! May God make us faithful to His truth ! "

"TUNBRIDGE WELLS, *June 4th*, 1885.

" I am getting on very comfortably with Confirmation candidates. The Trinity school-girls are improved. They are excellent in their knowledge, well up in the Catechism, in which they used to be so sadly defective. Of course it is extremely difficult for an old man like me to get into the secrets of their young hearts, but many of them, I believe, are more than in earnest, for I feel sure they are really resting on their Saviour. Poor dears ! I hope they will be kept, but they are likely to be terribly exposed to all kinds of religious unsettlement. The Salvation Army is going to have a grand ' Battle ' next week, and the rank and file is to consist of ' saved drunkards, liars, swearers, poachers, parsons, sailors, and nailers ' ! ! So we are classed with queer company ! Is it of God ? or is it strange fire ? that is the question. But who can wonder if our young people are perplexed and confused ? "

Written at the death-bed of his brother Joseph :—

"HAMPSTEAD, *January 16th*, 1886.

" I could not come home to-day, for I could not leave him in his low estate, though I am not like some of them, in immediate apprehension of any change. I fear there may be still before us deeper depths than we have known yet, unless the Lord mercifully lifts him over them, as He did Miss Courthope. He is generally wandering, but frequently revives in a most curious manner when I speak to him. I firmly believe that minds clouded like his very often have a perception of heavenly things, and most especially of the sweet name of Jesus.

"I went this morning to C.M.S. on the subject of the February Meetings. It was very edifying, but I had to come away very quickly, as I wanted to be back. People were all most kind, so much so that I hardly knew how to bear it.

"Since then I have been to see Bishop Perry, who was very unwell yesterday, I believe from riding home after a tiring day at Islington in a cold hansom-cab when he had a carriage and pair in his stable wanting exercise! Such is mankind. I tell him that I am obliged to knock about in cabs and 'busses because I cannot afford anything better, but he ought not to think of it.

"When we shall be home no one knows. I do not think I can come home for Sunday if things go on as they are now doing, unless I am obliged to do so, and I see nothing to indicate any immediate change. But we are in the Lord's hands, hour by hour, with eternity full in view and the Lord Jesus almost visible. May we each one abide in His love!"

"HAMPSTEAD, *January* 21*st*, 1886.

"Joseph at rest in the Lord."

"TUNBRIDGE WELLS, *March* 5*th*, 1887.

"I hope you are still prospering and that you have had as beautiful weather as we have had. I consider that the beautiful bright sunshine of our dear old England is to be preferred to that of the South of France, more especially if the latter is accompanied by earthquakes as a variety, and certainly we have all been enjoying it here. Last Sunday was one of the most lovely days I can remember, and I hope it was one in which we enjoyed some sunshine in our souls. All the week too has been bright and happy, though we have had some fogs in the morning—just enough to teach us

how God can clear away all that obscures the sunshine of His love. On Wednesday we had a most
profitable sermon from Mr. Russell."

"Marden Hill, Hertford, *August* 30*th*, 1887.

"Nothing can be kinder or more affectionate than
everybody here. H—— and M—— are most pleasant,
and I would not have missed coming to them here on
any account, as I consider that at Cromer every one is
in a non-natural condition and here they are in their own
home. I wonder whether there is the same difference
between myself at home and abroad. I suppose there
is, though I do not see it.

"I hope you are enjoying Brittany. You surely did
not leave Guernsey on your left as you were crossing.
If you did I suppose it was to avoid rocks ; and maybe
we should all prosper more if we were more careful to
avoid temptations as well as to overcome them ; and
I hope the Lord may so direct the path of every one of
us that we may be kept from danger and guided safe
into the haven of peace. I have been exceedingly
impressed with these words in Jeremiah x. : 'The way
of man is not in himself : it is not in man that walketh
to direct his steps.' So my way, and your way, is not
in ourselves, and I trust the Lord may direct all our
steps for His own glory."

"St. Bernard's, Caterham, *October* 14*th*, 1887.

"I return Miss T——'s enclosure. Pray tell her that
her confidence need not be in the least shaken by the
proposed visit to the Old Catholics, for they are thorough
Protestants in many respects. They withdrew from the
Church of Rome on the decree of Papal Infallibility
(I think in the year 1870), under that very remarkable
man Dr. Döllinger, and have been excommunicated by

it. They call themselves 'Old Catholics' to distinguish themselves from the New, or Roman, Catholics, and they claim to hold the Catholic faith as it was before Rome introduced its errors. We ought, therefore, to rejoice at our Bishops taking them in hand."

To his daughters :—

"York, *May 27th,* 1888.

"I know not why it is, but my heart is so full for you all that I cannot forbear from writing to tell you. You have been constantly in my thoughts since I left home, and oh, how I have desired that the Lord may give to each one of you every possible happiness! I thank God that I believe He has given us a very happy home, and one that can stand comparison with others; but I long to make it happier still and to do all that a father can do to help each one of you and to promote that loving, joyous spirit which is the sacred privilege of a Christian home. Certainly it has entwined itself very closely round my own heart ; and now that I am away I seem to feel it more than ever. May the Lord be with you all, not only while I am with you, but when I am gathered to my own Home with the Lord Jesus!

"I am thankful that I have been prospered, and am quite well and had an easy journey. Everybody has been most kind, and I hope the Lord has accompanied the ministry. The morning sermon was a long way off and not exciting : I felt for the good man, for he seemed discouraged.

"The Evening Service in the Minster was magnificent. There was a grand congregation, and what with the noble building and fine music there was enough to make a profound impression, even if there had been no sermon.

"But I hope they had the Gospel in addition ; I

certainly desired to give it to them, and they appeared to me very attentive. I do not feel in much heart for speech-making to-day, for I am utterly out of practice. But 'what have I that I have not received?' so I must open my mouth to receive my message, and I hope the Lord will give it me."

"TUNBRIDGE WELLS, *August 22nd*, 1888.

" I rejoice to hear that you are prospering and enjoying Chamounix. I cannot doubt that you have a most pleasant, happy, and loving party, and I shall heartily enjoy a few bright days with you and another look at those lovely mountains. There they stand unchanged, while all their admirers pass by and are gone. What a picture of what is going on in life! There is only One who is not a mere passer-by; but, thanks to God, He is unchangeable, and we need never pass away from Him.

"We had a very comfortable Sunday. I preached in the morning about Jehoshaphat, to my own great interest. But in the afternoon I had a very poor attendance of men, and preached the feeblest of sermons. I hope it may have confounded the mighty, for it certainly was one of the weak things of the world, and contributed nothing to the self-elevation of the preacher.

"I am now off to church to preach on holiness. May God make us partakers of His holiness!"

In the autumn of 1888 his blindness began. The doctors stated that it was due to no illness, but just a sudden failure of power. He could at first see figures and large objects more or less, and detect a placard on a wall, but faces were indiscernible and reading and writing an impossibility.

Yet it made no difference in his manner or character, and his life was immediately adjusted to the new state of things. The writer well remembers coming into the Vicarage study one morning, and finding the vigorous old man of seventy-six commencing the task of *learning the Bible by heart!* " It was so important to have all quotations exact." This work was continued for some months, but when it was suggested that there would be less labour and more profit in learning the raised type for the blind, the former plan was discontinued, volumes of the latter sort were procured, the characters mastered, and for the seven years remaining the beloved study was resumed under circumstances that would have discouraged most men of his age. Blindness did not stop his work— nothing of the kind ; the regular Bible and annual Confirmation classes were continued as before, the weekday and Sunday sermons as regularly prepared and preached. His daughters read to him passages from books bearing upon the subject that he had in hand, and he arranged and classified it in his own mind. Gentlemen and ladies in his congregation gladly undertook to come at stated hours and read to him books of various sorts, and so he kept abreast with all that was going on in the world of literature, and, as was his wont, met it for praise or censure in his sermons.

On Sundays it was touching to see the venerable old man ascending the pulpit, giving out his text, and then preaching with all his old fire and vigour. The accuracy with which he quoted his texts made it hard to believe that the preacher was blind. The same accuracy was remarkable in another way. There were few things in which Canon Hoare took more interest than in helping the younger clergy. All through his career his Greek Testament readings have been sources of great blessing and help. In the last few years of his life, since his blindness, he revived these readings, going rapidly through a book or group of passages dealing with a subject. There are several now in Tunbridge Wells who remember gratefully and lovingly those early half-hours once a week ; they can see him in his study-chair, surrounded by six or eight of the junior clergy with pencils and note-books—the mortal eyes sightless, but the eyes of his understanding being opened, and from his lips pouring forth a stream of words almost too rapid to take down, as he sketched forth the scheme, say, of the Epistle to the Hebrews, and then going into the details chapter after chapter, pointing out the notes of exegesis and different readings, and the light thrown by the Revised Version on each.

It was at this time, as the first birthday after his blindness drew near, that several members of his loving congregation subscribed together and pur-chased a splendid gold repeater watch, striking the hours, quarters, and half-quarters, as a birthday present for their old Vicar. The following letter, written with the aid of the typewriter which he had also learned to use after the loss of his eyesight, shows how much he appreciated this further proof of their affection :—

"TRINITY VICARAGE, *June* 5*th*, 1889.

"MY DEAR MRS. PERKINS,—I hear that you have been the one chosen by your friends to convey to me the beautiful gift which I received this morning, so to you I must send my answer, and ask you to be so very kind as to assure all the dear people who have taken a share in it of the very great pleasure that their gift has given me. It was so kind of you all to think of me, and to mark by a birthday offering your loving interest in my welfare. But, as for your sending me such a beautiful present, I never for one moment thought of such a thing. You have, however, selected a most useful and valuable form for your kindness.

"For many years I have been dependent on a repeater for securing, day by day, the sacred morning hours before breakfast; and many an hour has been secured to the study of God's most holy Word through the use of an old repeater left to me (as a legacy) by the dear uncle who gave me my title to my first curacy.

"But the old watch, like the old master, has worn out, and I have been put to the greatest inconvenience; so that, if ever I have left home, I have been obliged to carry two watches—one for the day and the other for night.

"But now, by your gift, the difficulty is removed; and, if ever it please God to restore to me the privilege of spending my winter mornings in the study of His Word, I shall find it to be of inestimable value.

"Most heartily, therefore, do I thank all our friends

through you, and trust that they may enjoy as happy and sacred morning hours as our Heavenly Father has so often given to me.

"Believe me, my dear Mrs. Perkins,

"Very faithfully yours,

"E. HOARE."

In 1889 Canon Hoare was laid low by a severe illness which all expected to be the last. His family assembled around him, and his people thought that they never would see him again.

At this time, when all his friends thought that his call had really come, many letters were received at the Vicarage expressing the warmest sympathy and containing assurances of fervent prayers. The Archbishop of Canterbury wrote as follows to the Rev. J. Gurney Hoare, who was at Tunbridge Wells :—

"LAMBETH, *June 12th,* 1889.

"MY DEAR MR. HOARE,—Pray give my love and the assurance of my loving prayers to your dear father.

"I had your letter this morning at Hereford.

"As some old writer says, it is ' like the descending of ripe and wholesome fruits from a vigorous and steadfast tree' when God calls to Him so single-minded and true a servant—all contests over, and charity having triumphed more and more to the end. Tell him, as you think fit, how much I have always felt that he helped and comforted me in my trying place. I have always had his sympathy and genial counsel, and his *prayers*. And his strength has been *consecrated* to the last. In what honour he passes to the last peace! May it be wholly ἀνώδυνος, as the old Greek prayers say. Once more you are all sure of our prayers, and of the prayers of how many through Christ who loves him ever.

       " Most sincerely yours,

            " E. W. Cantuar."

Again his congregation assembled in daily prayer-meeting, as before; and when it was supposed impossible that he could live out the day the C.M.S. Committee met and poured out their petitions to God, asking that their veteran friend and adviser might yet be spared if it were His will.

The prayer was answered, and once more he rose from the bed of sickness, wonderfully unchanged. Compared with past years, we saw that the outward man was perishing, but we saw also that the inward man was being renewed day by day. Before long he was again in the pulpit, and it was more than three years after this that he preached the sermon upon "Confirmation" to which reference has been already made, as well as one upon the "Agnus Dei," delivered after the Archbishop of Canterbury's famous judgment.

To Bishop Perry :—

          " Tunbridge Wells, *January 10th,* 1890.

" My very dear Friend,—I cannot tell you how much I have felt about dear Carus. When we think of his age we cannot be surprised, and when we think of his love, his fidelity, his maintenance of the truth, and his great attractiveness we know not how to part with so valuable and pleasant a companion. But as far as

you and I are concerned the parting is not likely to
be for very long. As we see one after another of our
old friends gathered to their rest, it would be madness
in us to forget how near we ourselves may be to the
banks of the river, or to lose sight for a single moment
of the blessed Hope set before us in Christ Jesus.
I trust we may all be kept looking for that blessed
Hope and the glorious reunion of the Resurrection
morning and of the Coming of the Lord. I must acknowledge that for my own part I find myself better able
to realise the prospect of that final reunion than the
thought of our gathering before the Throne in the
intermediate waiting time ; but I am persuaded that both
are taught in Scripture, and that when we are no longer
entangled in the body we shall see wonderful things
in the spiritual world, and when we do how shall we
ever praise God enough for His marvellous love in
making a perfect atonement for people so unworthy
as we are ! I don't know how it is with others, but
I find myself there is scarcely any sentence in the
Prayer-Book which so expresses my own mind as those
words, ' We are not worthy so much as to gather up
the crumbs under Thy table '; but, thanks be to God !
we depend upon the worthiness of that blessed Saviour
by whom every claim of the whole law is more than
satisfied. Remember me most affectionately to Mrs.
Perry, and believe me

" Your loving and faithful Friend,

" E. HOARE."

Letter to Bishop Parry after seeing a report in
the papers that he was dangerously ill :—

"DEAR EDWARD,—We are all truly sorry to hear
that you are not so well. . . . But how can we thank

God enough for the unspeakable privilege of knowing that all such matters are safe in the hand of the Lord! I often think of those words of St. Paul, 'We know that all things work together for good,' etc. He did not say 'we think,' or 'we hope,' but 'we *know*,' thereby expressing the full persuasion of his soul in the infinite love and perfect power of our blessed Saviour in combining all things so that they may work together for our good. I delight in the thought that it is our privilege to rest in that full, calm, deliberate persuasion, and that, looking away from everything in ourselves, we may look to Him in peaceful trust, as an eternal object that will not vary with our own variations of thought and feeling. May He keep you in His own right hand, and raise you up if it be His will; and above all, whenever the time of our departure comes, and it must come to us both before very long, may He fulfil present persuasion by giving us an abundant entrance into His everlasting Kingdom.

> "Believe me most faithfully yours,
>
> "E. Hoare."

To Mr. Storr, upon hearing of the wonderful collections for the C.M.S. in Matfield and Brenchley:—

"*February 24th.*

"Dear Mr. Storr,—I wonder whether there is any information respecting the things of this world given to those who are at rest with their Saviour? If there is 'joy in Heaven over one sinner that repenteth,' may we not believe that there is also joy when the Lord's work is prospered among His people that are on earth? If it be so, I am sure your dear father's heart will be gladdened by the good report sent me in your letter. It is delightful to see the permanent results of faithful work such as his was at Brenchley. He is gone, but the light which he lighted is still burning, and I hope will long continue to burn to the glory of God."

To one of his daughters :—

"NEWCASTLE, *July* 31*st*, 1890.

" May the Lord grant you a very happy birthday, and follow it up by the very best of new years! I wonder where we shall all be this time next year; one thing only do I know, *i.e.* that we shall be safe in the Lord's hands, so that all will be well. If safe in Him we shall be safe anywhere, whether in Heaven or on earth, whether in the Home above or in some dear old dwelling here. Let the Spirit of God be on the tabernacle and all will be well.

" We are prospering, and hope to return on Tuesday. I have quite given up all thought of Stirling, and am looking forward to home with great pleasure."

[Written with the aid of a typewriter.]

"TUNBRIDGE WELLS, *August*, 1890.

" What do you think of this ? I have been contriving a plan for writing without seeing : I hope it will answer, but as yet I get on very slowly."

[Also typewritten.]

" TENCHLEY, *October* 12*th*, 1891.

" I am thinking of you very much in your return to our dear old home, and trust the Lord Himself is with you. I do not like the thought of your being alone, but there is a great difference between being *alone* and being *lonely*, and lonely we need never be if only we have the companionship of our Father in Heaven, and that I trust you are enjoying.

" We are hoping to return on Thursday, if God permit : I trust it will please Him to grant it.

"Let us all pray that there may not merely be three sisters, but the three sister-graces, Faith, Hope, and Love, abiding together in our happy home."

"THOUGHTS ON OLD AGE.—1891.

"Its temptations :—

"1. *Indisposition to exertion.*—In many cases there is real physical inability. The old muscles are worn out, so that 'the grasshopper becomes a burden,' and every movement requires effort. The natural result of this is, we move as little as possible and are glad to have as much as possible done for us. But there is very often a still worse result—namely, that we are apt to leave things undone altogether ; we do not like to give in, but when the time comes for action we shrink from the exertion.

"2. *Selfishness.*—Aged people meet with a great amount of attention : their comfort is a matter of continual thought to many loving hearts. Household arrangements are all made to suit them ; young people are exceedingly kind to them ; they read to them, write for them, help them in every possible manner, and do all in their power to minister to their happiness and comfort. The result is that the old man is apt to consider himself as much as others."

In his latter years there was an added joy in visiting the homes of his married sons and daughters.

The circle of interest widened in sympathy with the joys and sorrows of his grandchildren, and it is no small proof of the tenderness and strength of his character that a man of his age, with so much to occupy his mind in public and private

things, could find time for letters to the boys and
girls of the second generation. The two following
letters are instances of this.

To one of his grandsons :—

"TUNBRIDGE WELLS, *February 7th,* 1890.

"DEAR CHRIS.,—I have been thinking of you every
day, and praying to our Heavenly Father to make you a
good and happy boy.

"I know it is a very sad thing for you to lose Louis,
but I have also been thinking what a delightful duty it
puts upon you, for now you have your father and mother
all to yourself, and are the only boy at home to attend
to them and try to make them happy. I think this
is a great pleasure and privilege, and I expect to have a
nice letter some day from your mother to say that dear
Chris. is so good and attentive that he makes the home
quite cheerful. But we are such fallen creatures that
you cannot do this unless the Lord Himself helps you.
So I trust He will do so, and make you a joy to your
father and mother.

"Your affectionate Grandfather,

"E. HOARE."

To one of his granddaughters :—

"TUNBRIDGE WELLS, *February 24th,* 1891.

"DEAR LETTICE,—I am very glad to hear that you
are so happy and prosperous, and I often think what a
happy arrangement it has been for your early education.
I am sure we ought all to be very grateful to your uncle
and aunt for their kindness in making it. How much
kindness we meet with in life ! I am sure there is kindness for the old, for I am receiving it every day, and I am

equally sure there is kindness for the young, for I am constantly meeting with persons who are spending their whole lives in making them happy. But what are we to think of the lovingkindness of the Lord? David says it is better than life, and so I hope you will find it. You have a name that means joy, and I hope the joy may be, not in your name only, but in your heart. For the last two days I have had a great joy in my home, and I shall leave it to you to guess what it is. It is the visit of a lady for whom I feel a great affection. She has sons and daughters who are great friends of mine, so that I wish she had brought some of them with her. You must guess who it can be, and also find David's words about lovingkindness (Psalm lxiii. 3).

> "The loving old Grandfather,
>
> "E. H."

Extracts from letters to his married daughters:—

"TUNBRIDGE WELLS, *November* 11*th*, 1890.

"I have thought a great deal of you in your re-settlement at home, and I trust that you have returned for a happy, holy, and useful winter.

"I look back with the greatest pleasure to my pleasant visit when all the boys were at home, and I trust that the same happy, peaceful spirit may be the abiding characteristic of your family.

". . . I often think of the promise, 'They shall bring forth fruit in old age,' and most earnestly do I desire that my old age may be a fruitful season, but I am inclined to regard anything I can do as little more than the gleaning of grapes when the vintage is done. I trust, however, that whatever is left may be diligently used for the glory of my Blessed Saviour.

" Give my dear love to Robert, and also to Chris. and Lettice.

" Your most affectionate Father,

" E. HOARE."

" TUNBRIDGE WELLS, *August 29th,* 1891.

" I have very much enjoyed your letters, though I have been slow in acknowledging them, for I find type-writing to be both slow work and very tiring to the brain. But I am glad of it, as it makes me sometimes fancy that I am independent. But independence is not the gift for me just now, for I am dependent for everything, and have to be unspeakably thankful for such loving care-takers on whom I may depend.

" Above all, how ought my heart to overflow with gratitude to that loving Father on whom it is my joy to depend for everything ! Daughters can do a great deal, and would do more if they could, but He can do every-thing and does supply all my need according to His riches in glory by Christ Jesus.

" I trust all the dear sons are prospering, and the tutor doing well. I wonder whether we shall meet any-where this autumn. I do not feel much pluck in me for Norfolk ; my home is so comfortable that I am not eager to leave it. But there is an idea in people's minds that we ought to go out in the autumn, so I suppose I shall go somewhere, though I do not at present know where. I am very thankful for my two visits to the North. They helped me to realise better the great interests for which to be continually in prayer. I was very happy with you and your sons. May our gracious God bless you all !

" Your loving Father,

" E. H."

". . . Most heartily do I respond to all your loving wishes for a rich Christmas blessing on our whole party. We have enjoyed a very happy Christmas together. We have had with us E—— and his family, and very pleasant have they all been. We have thought continually of the homes of the absent, and many a time both by day and by night has my heart been lifted for you all. I have thought very much of you and all your boys, and cannot doubt that you have had a very merry party. God grant that they may all know the joy of the Lord! I am very sorry to hear of your disappointment. . . . I never forget the advice given me by my grandmother—never to act without seeking the guidance of the Lord, and after acting never to re-open the subject. She would have said that your great mistake is in distressing yourselves now about your decision made two years ago. So as you sought His guidance trust Him to have given it, and push away regrets.

" The Lord be with you all !

" Your loving Father,

" E. H."

" My typewriter is none the better for its journey, so that I have been unable to write and thank you both for my very happy visit. I most thoroughly enjoyed it, and throughout the whole of my visitation tour there has been nothing on which I look back with more genuine pleasure than I do on those happy days at Chenies. I thought the village lovely. I was greatly pleased with the meeting of Communicants and with the Church Services. I delighted in the children, and am looking forward with the greatest pleasure to their visit; and I greatly enjoyed all my pleasant intercourse with you both, which I valued the more as I have seen less of R—— lately than of you, so that I was glad to enjoy his thoughts on many points of interest.

" May the Lord bless you abundantly both in your home and in your parish ! With dear love to the children,

" Your most loving Father,

" E. H."

" Tenchley, Limpsfield, *December 28th,* 1892.

" We had a very happy day at home, lovely weather, the very perfection of a Christmas Day, and I trust a good deal of sunshine within. I preached to the people on the sacred Name of Jesus, and I gave them what was new to myself, and, if I mistake not, new also to most of them, so we had fresh thoughts on an old subject. What a remarkable feature this is in Scripture ! It is full of old truths, but is always bringing them out in newness and freshness to those who will take the trouble to study it.

" Dear love to Robert and the boys.

" Your most loving Father,

" E. H."

From the Archbishop of Canterbury :—

"Deal Castle, *April 13th,* 1893.

"To the Rev. Canon Hoare.

" My dear Canon Hoare,—It was very kind and thoughtful of you to send me your two sermons, in which I was sure to take a great interest. I have read them both with much satisfaction. I think the ' Agnus Dei ' ought to be very useful. It puts that great hymn in its right position, and it shows the fallacy of certain deductions drawn from the fact that there were no legal grounds on which it could be decided that it was impossible for it to be used. I daresay you have noticed that Richard Baxter (not exactly a Ritualist) did not hesitate to make use of that same passage from St. John in his draft Communion Service.

"The sermon on Confirmation I think most serviceable; its instruction most clear, and the remarks on what the Gift *is* very impressive. I am glad you teach that that beautiful passage in the Epistle to the Ephesians refers to the event recorded in the Acts. And what a motive it supplies, and what a basis for the Christian life!

"Thank you very much; I think no one can read that sermon without feeling that Scripture and its true teaching leaves more and more to us, in spite of all fears of 'Criticism.'

"Sincerely yours,

"E. Cantuar."

The following letter was to a lady in the United States who had written gratefully about some of his prophetical books, and asked for guidance on various points, as well as for some larger work on the same subject written by him :—

"Tunbridge Wells, *May 29th,* 1893.

"To Miss Gray.

"My dear Madam,—I have received your letter with very great interest and thankfulness. How little do we know either the *where* or the *how* or the *when* it may please God to make use of any effort in His service, and how little I thought that my two small books had found their way to the hearts of any of God's people in America! I am the clergyman of a large parish, and they were printed chiefly for the use of my own parishioners, and God has made use of them in His own way and far beyond my expectations. I am thankful to say that the coming of our blessed Lord is more and more the joy of my heart, as I am persuaded it is the central part of our Christian hope. I trust it has pervaded the whole of my ministry; but I have not published anything to be called a book upon the subject, though fragments have been occasionally printed in our local press. I am sending you the sermons recently printed, though only one refers directly to the Advent of our Lord. I am very glad to hear of your meeting for the Study of the Prophetic Word. At one time we had such meetings here, at which we discussed with great brotherly freedom the bright hope pointed out to us in Prophecy, and I believe I learnt more from those Christian conferences than I have ever done from all the books in my library. I trust the Lord may grant you all a similar blessing, so that when our blessed Saviour returns in His glory you may be able to greet Him with the words: 'Lo, this is our God; we have waited for Him, and He will save us.' 'This is the Lord; we have waited for Him: we will be glad and rejoice in His Salvation.'

"Believe me very faithfully yours,

"E. HOARE."

To one who was losing her sight :—

"MARDEN, *June 8th*, 1893.

"DEAREST ——,— May the Lord give you a happy birthday to-morrow! You have your heavy trial hanging over you, but I trust that in God's leading you may have a bright and happy year, and may have a clearer

sight of your Heavenly Father's boundless love than you
have yet enjoyed.   I trust that we may both have the
eyes of our understanding enlightened, that we may
know better what is the hope of our calling, and what
the riches of the glory of His inheritance in the saints.
It is my unceasing prayer that I may see these things
clearer and clearer.   And I am sure that, if He manifest
Himself more clearly to my soul, I shall be more than
repaid for the failure of my earthly vision.   Your case is
different to mine, for you have every hope of complete
restoration of sight.   But we are one in the desire for
heavenly light, and I trust the Lord *may* give it to you
abundantly through the new year, and that I too may
enjoy a share."

Extract from a letter to one of his married
daughters :—

"TUNBRIDGE WELLS, *August* 3rd, 1893.

"We thank Him also very heartily for the happy week
spent with you.   It was absolutely impossible that
greater care and kindness should have been shown to
the old man, and I wish you to know how successful
you were in giving me a comfortable, pleasant, and
happy week, so that I was well repaid for the effort of
the two long journeys, and shall ever retain a happy
memory of that pleasant visit.

"I was very glad to see as much as I did of the three
dear sons, and felt exceedingly interested for them all, as
I could see in each one that he had a special claim
on our loving and earnest prayers.

"It was also a great gratification to me to make the
acquaintance of your future daughter.   Oh, how I hope
that the voice of rejoicing and salvation will be in their
'tabernacle'!   With dear love to them all, to the two

boys arriving from school, and above all to yourselves at
the head of such a family,

"Your most loving Father,

"E. HOARE."

The autumn of 1893 was remarkable for the
number of visits which Mr. Hoare paid among
relatives in Norfolk and elsewhere. He spoke of
it as one of the pleasantest holidays that he had
ever spent.

Earlham, his mother's old home, a name so
familiar to many through Mr. Hare's recent
volumes on the Gurney family, was revisited, and
he delighted in pointing out places in the house
that reminded him of childish romps and adventures. A week was spent at Cromer, where, as
usual, a great gathering of the clans took place.
Here he met his beloved sister-in-law Lady Parry,
and, at the house of his favourite cousin, Lady
Buxton, he gave a Bible-reading in her spacious
drawing-room to a gathering of some fifty or sixty
friends and relatives.

An eye-witness has described this impressive
scene. The old man, blind, but mighty in the
Scriptures, took for his subject the prayers for
"teaching" contained in the 119th Psalm, and
those who listened felt that he had been taught of
God, and that another prayer in the same Psalm
had been answered in his case : God had opened
his eyes and permitted him to see wondrous things
in His law.

16

The Sunday following he preached in the grand old church at Cromer. Many remember that occasion ; and when the writer paid a visit to that place a year later, he met an old man who spoke of this sermon with enthusiasm, and said that he thought it one of the best that he had ever heard from the aged preacher's lips.

No less than seven homes of his children and relatives were visited by him at this time, and it was from one of them, towards the close of this pleasant holiday, that the following letter to one of his daughters was written :—

"AYLSHAM, *September 21st*, 1893.

" I am very glad to hear of your prosperous settlement at Lynton. It is the place where your dear mother and I spent our first Sunday after our marriage, and I preached in the church, to the great satisfaction of the Vicar, who, I think, was Mr. Pears, afterwards Master of Repton : you appear to have gone to the other church. . . . Magee's sermons have been very interesting, though I doubt whether they would meet the wants of those who are hungering and thirsting for life ; they aim too much at intellectual brilliancy, and it is not by excellency of speech that souls are won.

" We came yesterday to this beautiful home. Certainly the lines are fallen unto them in very pleasant places, and I trust they have a goodly heritage in many souls won to their Saviour. But they have their difficulties, and who has not ? As long as human nature is what it is, we shall find them everywhere, though different in different places."

The following letter illustrates the affectionate

feelings between the pastor and his people so manifest in this parish :—

"THE VICARAGE, *Decemb r* 13*th*, 1893

"*My dearly beloved Friends, the Members of our Communicants' Union, and other Communicants in our
Church,*—

"I have been looking forward with the greatest possible pleasure to the prospect of our Advent gathering
arranged for to-morrow, but it has pleased our Heavenly
Father to take from me all hope of being present.

"I have greatly enjoyed those gatherings on former
occasions, when it has pleased God to manifest Himself
and His own grace in a peculiar manner to our souls.
They have also been a source of especial pleasure, as
they have given an opportunity for that loving, friendly
intercourse which is so delightful amongst Christian
friends, and so difficult of attainment in large parishes
and large congregations.

"I cannot be with you to-morrow in bodily presence,
but may I not thankfully adopt the first part of those
words of St. Paul in Col. ii. 5-7, 'For though I be
absent in the flesh, yet am I with you in the spirit,
joying and beholding your order, and the steadfastness
of your faith in Christ'? and may we not all accept this
exhortation in the latter part, 'As ye have therefore
received Christ Jesus the Lord, so walk ye in Him:
rooted and built up in Him, and stablished in the faith,
as ye have been taught, abounding therein with thanksgiving'?

"You observe he does not address us as persons for
the first time seeking to know Christ, but as those who
have received Him, and are permitted to walk, or spend
their lives, in union with Him. If this be the case

with us, how should our thanksgivings abound in every possible effort for His glory !

"With much affection, and many prayers,

"From your faithful Friend and Vicar,

"E. HOARE."

It was at this time, when his bodily health was so feeble, his step slow and head bowed, that a visitor who had never heard him preach came to Trinity Church.

Knowing his reputation, the stranger had great expectations, but at first sight his heart fell within him ; as he afterwards acknowledged, "I could not *believe* that old man in the pew was going to preach, but he got up into the pulpit with some difficulty, and *then*, it was the power of God !"

A clergyman friend who had known him intimately for forty years said of the aged preacher that "his ministry had grown in power up to the very end." The chief cause of this was doubtless the life of prayer in which he moved and had his being. All who knew him were aware of this, and certainly he who has been permitted to peruse the sacred pages of his journal can no longer feel surprised at the marvellous success which attended that prayer-steeped ministry.

While upon this subject it is worthy of record that he often told those whom he wanted to help in their preaching that he *prayed over his sermons more even than he prepared them*, and the latter part took several hours of his time. When blindness came upon him, and others had to read for him and take down his thoughts for the preparation of his sermons, it was his custom to stand up by his study table and say : " Here is my mind, Lord ; take it and use it. Thou knowest who will be there ; give me the right thoughts and words, that I may speak as Thy messenger, for Christ's sake !" And this prayer too was answered.

The following letters, written in the last few months of his life, show the clearness of his mind and width of his sympathy up to the end.

To the Rev. C. H. Dearsly, who asks, "How far is it Scriptural that female evangelists should address large mixed assemblies—or men only?"

"January 19th, 1894.

" Mrs. Fry used to draw a wide distinction between 'prophesying,' as in Acts ii. 17, and 'teaching,' as in 1 Tim. ii. 12, as she believed the former to be an appeal called forth in a special manner by the Holy Spirit, and so she justified her own ministry. I have often thought that there is some truth in her distinction, and I have never felt able to put a hindrance in the way of what may possibly be the movement of the Holy Spirit ; so I have thought it safer to be passive in the matter, and not to forbid even though I have felt unable to support."

To the late Dean of Canterbury on the death of his wife :—

" My dear Dean,—I trust the Lord is with you in your great trial, and will be with you unto the end.

I believe that no one has the least idea of what the trial
is, until they are called to pass through it.   Its depth
is learned only by experience.   There were two lessons
taught me when it pleased my Heavenly Father to send
it to me.   I never had any idea of the magnitude of
the trial, and what it was to lose one who had been for
so many years a wise counsellor and a most loving
wife and mother.   But I never knew the extent to
which a Heavenly Father could supply all my need
'according to His riches in glory by Christ Jesus.'
I look back upon the thirty years that have elapsed
since my great bereavement, and am utterly unable to
count up the tokens of His love and tender thought-
fulness during the whole of that period.   And so,
my dear friend, I am persuaded that you may trust
Him entirely.   You may trust Him for your eternity;
you may trust Him also for the short remainder of your
pilgrimage upon earth.   You may trust Him to do well
for yourself and your daughters.   You may trust Him
as your faithful Friend and your most wise Counsellor;
and so trusting you will never be disappointed, but He
will be both with you and yours continually, guiding you
with His counsel, and afterward receiving you to glory.
Remember me very particularly to your daughters.

"Most faithfully yours,

"E. HOARE."

To the Rev. H. E. Williamson, Hon. Sec. of the
West Kent C.M.S. Union:—

"TUNBRIDGE WELLS, April 11th, 1894.

"DEAR WILLIAMSON,—I am exceedingly sorry to be
quite unable to attend the Union of Unions to-morrow
at Canterbury.   I have greatly enjoyed the meetings of
our own Union in former times, and firmly believe that

we have been favoured with the presence of that loving Redeemer whose Name we desire to make known throughout the world. I should also have greatly enjoyed the meeting with our dear brethren of East Kent under the presidency of our beloved Dean, in his noble Cathedral; but I cannot venture upon the undertaking, and must look forward to the gathering of that more perfect Union which I hope is shortly to take place, at the Coming of our Lord and Saviour. Remember me to all the dear brethren, and believe me to be very faithfully yours, " E. HOARE."

NOTES OF CONFIRMATION LECTURES.

These notes are intended to assist Candidates in preparing for the Classes. Each of the Chapters mentioned contains a text on the subject of the Lecture.

LECTURE I.—*The Sinfulness of Man.*

Man is sinful.   1. In nature: Psalm li.; Rom. viii.
  „   2. In heart: Matt. xv.; Jer. xvii.
  „   3. In thought: Gen. vi.
  „   4. In word: James iii.
  „   5. In act: Rom. iii.
  „   6. Under God's wrath: Eph. ii.

Therefore requires two things, viz. Forgiveness of Sin and Change of Heart.

LECTURE II.—*Forgiveness of Sin.*

1. The blessing of it: Psalm xxxii.
2. Examples of it: Mark ii.; Luke vii.; Luke xviii.
3. Given us because our sins were laid on the Lord Jesus Christ as our substitute: Isa. liii.; 2 Cor. v.; Gal. iii.; Eph. i.; 1 Peter ii.

LECTURE III.—*Change of Heart.*

1. Necessary : John iii.
2. Compared to Birth : John iii.
        ,,   Resurrection : Eph. ii.
        ,,   Creation : Eph. ii. ; 2 Cor. v.
3. Wrought by God the Holy Spirit : John i. ; John iii. ; Ezek. xxxvi.
4. Prayer for it : Psalm li.

LECTURE IV.—*First Promise made in Baptism.*

RENUNCIATION.

We promise to renounce three things.
1. The devil : Gen. iii. ; John viii. ; 1 Peter v. ; 1 John iii.
2. The world : Rom. xii. ; 1 John ii. ; Psalm xvii.
3. The flesh : Rom. viii. ; Gal. v.

LECTURE V.—*Second Promise made in Baptism.*

FAITH.

We promise to believe in the Lord Jesus.
1. The three articles of Christian faith : Catechism.
2. Examples of faith : Gen. xv. ; Rom. iv. ; Matt. viii. ; Matt. xv. ; Luke i. ; Luke vii.
3. Salvation given through faith : John iii. ; Acts viii. ; Acts xvi. ; Eph. ii.

LECTURE VI.—*Third Promise made in Baptism.*

OBEDIENCE.

We promise to obey the Commandments.
We should obey them In both their parts : Matt. xxii., and Church Catechism.
    ,,   From the heart : Deut. xi. ; Rom. vi. ; Eph. vi.
    ,,   With delight : Psalm xl. ; Psalm cxix.

We should obey them In all things : Josh. xxii. ; Gen. vi.

      „   From love : John xiv. ; Rom. xiii. ;
                    2 Cor. v.

LECTURE VII.—*Prayer.*

Promises to prayer : Luke xi. ; John xiv. ; John xvi.
Prayer should be From the heart : Matt. xv.

      „   Earnest : James v.
      „   Persevering : Luke xviii. ; Eph. vi.
      „   In humility : Luke xviii.
      „   In faith : Matt. xxi. ; James i.
      „   In the name of Jesus : John xiv.

LECTURE VIII.—*The Sacrament of the Lord's Supper.*

Was appointed by the Lord Himself : Matt. xxvi. ;
        1 Cor. xi.
Is an act of obedience : Mark xiv. ; Luke xxii.
Is a sign, or emblem : 1 Cor. xi.
Is an act of loving remembrance : 1 Cor. xi.
Is a means of feeding on the Lord Jesus : 1 Cor. x.
Is an opportunity of intercourse with the Lord ; Luke xxiv.
Is a means of fellowship with each other : 1 Cor. x.
Is a help to joy : Acts ii.

LECTURE IX.—*On receiving the Lord's Supper unworthily.*

Danger of receiving it unworthily : 1 Cor. xi. "Damna-
        tion" here means "chastening" : ver. 32.
To receive it unworthily is to receive it—
Without repentance, without faith, without seriousness,
        without love : 1 Cor. xi.
You may be young Christians, but not come unworthily :
        Matt. xxvi. ; Acts ii.
You may be unworthy to come, but not come unworthily :
        Luke vii. ; Luke xv.

LECTURE X.—*Confirmation Service.*

The laying on of hands : Acts viii. ; Acts xix. ; Heb. vi.
The blessing to be expected : Acts viii. ; Acts xix.
Decision for God : Isa. xliv.
The prayers in Confirmation Service.

  For the Holy Spirit.
  For strength.
  For defence.
  For perseverance.
  For growth in grace.

CHAPTER XVI

REMINISCENCES

THERE are numerous anecdotes and incidents connected with Canon Hoare's lengthened ministry at Tunbridge Wells, which illustrate his many-sided character in a remarkable way. A few of these selected from the great stock of reminiscence in the minds of his people may be of interest to the reader.

   *   *   *   *

On one occasion banns of marriage were put up in Trinity Church between a workman recently come to the town and a young woman whose widowed mother lived in the parish of Holy Trinity.

When the banns had been twice called an anonymous letter was received by the Vicar, which stated that the man was already married. Careful inquiry having proved that this was true, and that his wife and family were living in another town, the Vicar made up his mind to punish the delinquent in a novel way. The couple whose banns had been called were sent for, and Canon Hoare told the girl the whole story in her false lover's presence. It was received with indignant incredulity, but the proofs were unanswerable. Turning upon her companion, she sobbed out, " James, James, I never believed you could have done this." The man tried to brazen it out, and laughingly said, " Well, I suppose we need not have the banns published again ? " " *Indeed they shall be read again*," was the Vicar's reply.

By this time the man was getting uncomfortable under the piercing eye that was fixed upon him, and he said, " Well, come along, Polly ; it's time for us to be going." " Indeed it *is* time for you to be going," said the Vicar, "and you had better be sharp about it too, but Polly shall not go with you." With these words he pointed to the door, towards which the offender made with remarkable rapidity. When he was gone Mr. Hoare turned to the girl, and, taking her out on the other side of the house from that by which the man had left, bid her go home with all speed.

Next Sunday morning in the vestry Canon Hoare called the clerk aside and gave him some directions ; then, having said to the curates " I'll read the banns to-day," he took that part of the service in which they occur. Having finished the second lesson, it was observed that in an unusually loud voice and with great distinctness he read out : " I publish the banns of marriage between James ——, *bachelor*, and Mary Ann ——, spinster, both of this parish. These are for the third time of asking. If any of you know cause or just impediment why these two persons should not be joined together in holy matrimony, ye are to declare it." At this moment the whole congregation were electrified by a loud voice at the end of the church calling out, " I forbid the banns of James —— and Mary Ann ——!" "Well, come into the vestry after service and state your reasons," was the reply.

The news fled like wild-fire over the parish, and the man got so unmercifully (yet deservedly) jeered and hooted by his fellow-workmen that he had to fly from the town. It may be added, as a curious and significant fact, that it was not the immorality of the proceeding which aroused this feeling, but " Jim —— has let the parson do him out of three and sixpence, for he paid for the banns, but couldn't get tied ! "

*   *   *   *   *

Another anecdote which has got into print somewhat incorrectly is the following. The parish clerk was one day in attendance at a funeral in Holy Trinity Cemetery when he noticed a gentleman walking about apparently looking for something. He accosted him, and asked if he could help him in any way. The other replied, in a very cheery and brisk way : " Yes, you can ; in fact I am looking for a nice sunny place for my grave. I am going to die soon, the doctors tell me, and I want to get a pleasant place to be buried in." The clerk

was somewhat astounded at the tone and manner
of the visitor, but suggested various sites. One
was soon selected, and in the same cheerful way
the gentleman went on, striking the ground as he
spoke : "Capital, just the place ; here it shall be ;
I shall be put in here, and that will be the end
of me." The clerk responded quietly, "Are you
quite sure of that, sir? for I am not." "Yes, quite
sure," was the answer, and then a discussion ensued
between the two ; when it had lasted a few minutes
the official said, "Well, sir, I may not be able to
convince you that you are wrong, but I know
my Vicar could." "Oh, I want none of your
parsons," said the visitor ; "but who *is* your
Vicar?" "The Reverend Edward Hoare, sir."
"Hoare, Edward Hoare—did he come from Hampstead?" "Yes, sir, I believe he did." "How
astonishing !" muttered the gentleman, and then
speaking aloud, "Why, he and I were friends when
we were boys !" Having asked the way to the
vicarage that he might call upon him, the visitor
went his way.

The meeting between the two old boyish
acquaintances was very interesting, but when the
gentleman stated the circumstance of his meeting
with the clerk, Mr. Hoare replied, "You have
made arrangements about your body ; have you
been as diligent about your soul?" It soon came
out that, brought up, like his old friend, as a
Quaker, but without his religious advantages, he

had drifted into open scepticism. Now, however, the loving, earnest words that he heard made a great impression, and he begged Mr. Hoare to come and visit him.

Several weeks passed by, and one day the clerk received a message from his Vicar, "There will be an adult baptism in the service to-morrow." His feelings can be imagined when he saw quietly standing by the font the gentleman whom he had seen in the cemetery! the defiant, cheery manner gone, but instead of that a peaceful, happy look upon his face. The illness soon progressed, but his friend of olden days visited him continually up to the end, and had the joy of knowing that he died resting happily upon his Saviour. In his will he bequeathed to Mr. Hoare the valuable proof copy of Landseer's picture "Saved," as a significant memento of what he had been permitted to do for his old friend.

* * * * *

The writer once heard it remarked of a certain clergyman that his many curates were like so many sentinels posted over the country to warn people of the danger of approaching him! The exact reverse was the case with Canon Hoare : if any one wished to get an enthusiastic description of the Vicar, they had only to go to one of his past or present curates. He was "a hero to his valets" : so considerate and thoughtful of their wants and circumstances, and yet so vigilant about their work,

knowing exactly how it was done, and never failing
to notice an omission, yet doing it all so kindly.
The quarter's cheque was always enclosed in an
envelope, with a slip of paper on which were written
words like these, " With many thanks for all your
invaluable help."

This may be a trifling thing, but it means a great
deal. Canon Hoare was like a father to his curates,
and was beloved by them ; he never lost an opportunity of putting them forward, and if need be of
standing up in their defence. There are some who
remember well an incident at a general meeting of
subscribers to the hospital many years ago. Some
one present had spoken very wrongly and imper-
tinently of one of the curates, making suggestions
of evil in his remarks.

At the close of the speeches that followed, the
chairman got up. He was watched closely as he
slowly took off his overcoat, and with great
deliberation folded it up and placed it on the
back of his chair. The room was very still as, drawing himself to his full height and looking keenly
round the room, he fixed his gaze upon the former
speaker, and gave him in words the most terrible
castigation that the unfortunate individual ever
received in his life. It was well administered, and
equally well deserved.

The fact that in all parochial work he was
leader, not director—saying " Come " instead of
" Go "—was one of the causes of his influence with

his curates. It is related that at some wedding in the parish church, when the bridegroom, a stranger to the place, was paying the fees in the vestry, he made the remark, " I think the man who does the work ought to get the pay." This greatly tickled the two curates present, who could not help laughing at the idea of their Vicar seated in his arm-chair while they laboured in the parish, and simultaneously both exclaimed, " The Vicar does more than both of us put together ! "

＊　＊　＊　＊　＊

The simplicity of the services at Holy Trinity have been already noticed. The preacher wore the black gown, not that he had any objection to the surplice in the pulpit, as he used that dress without hesitation in other churches, but because he felt that he was too old to make changes. " I knew many of the old Evangelical Fathers," he used to say; " I preached Charles Simeon's funeral sermon in his own church at Cambridge ; so that I feel as if I were connected with them, and I will keep up the old gown which I have been used to all my life."

But although this seemed but a trifle to him, he never ceased to express his disapproval of what are commonly called " musical services." On one occasion, at some conference or meeting of clergy, he followed the reader of a paper who had advocated the introduction of an intoned service, and commenced his reply with these words : " For the discussion of this subject I possess the important

qualification of being an *unmusical* man !" He then
continued in the same strain, and impressed this
point upon the clergy, that they had to deal with
as many unmusical people as musical in their
congregations.   All could speak, but only a limited
number could sing ; therefore, by arranging a service
for the musical, they really closed the lips of those
who were not so.   At another time, also in public,
he said : " The proper use of music is in praise and
thanksgiving.   People are so eager in these days
to introduce as much music as possible that they
have applied it to prayer, the reading of Scripture,
and even to the Creed.   All this I believe to be a
mistake.   We delight in thorough congregational
singing, but the essence of prayer is to be perfectly
natural, to realise that we are speaking to God,
and forget all beside.   Who can imagine the poor
publican waiting to hear the note of the organ, or
the trumpet, before he smote upon his breast and
said, 'God be merciful to me a sinner !'"

＊　　　＊　　　＊　　　＊　　　＊

As a chairman Canon Hoare was unequalled.
His kindness to opponents and his fairness in
stating their case disarmed prejudice and won
their approbation.   A barrister who had been
contending vigorously against some project which
Canon Hoare was anxious to advance said at the
close of a meeting in which he was taking part : " I
have no more to say.   Mr. Hoare has handled his
brief ably, and I retire from my former opposition."

Some now in Tunbridge Wells will remember a meeting of publicans who had been invited by the Vicar to come to the Parish Room and discuss in a friendly way the Bill for the Sunday closing of public-houses. They proved an unpleasant audience, and often indulged in bitter and insolent observations, all of which he took in the most gentle Christian spirit. At last one fellow shouted out: "You clergy are the biggest Sabbath-breakers going; you are working hard all Sunday, and why shouldn't we?" "No, no," answered the chairman with a beautiful smile, "what we do on Sunday is not work; it's *happy rest* from first to last." A Nonconformist who was present remarked afterwards to the writer that he would never forget that look nor those words as long as he lived.

* * * * *

In questions relating to the interests of the town or of the country at large he was always to the front, gauging public opinion and leading it in the right direction. In actual politics he took no part until the Home Rule question was brought to the front by Mr. Gladstone; then he lectured in the Great Hall against it, and more than once spoke in public on the same topic. Again, when in 1885 the Liberation Society announced a lecture by Mr. Guinness Rogers, and the Great Hall was filled with a noisy, excited audience, at the close of the lecture Canon Hoare ascended the platform; and though at first his words could scarcely be heard in the tumult of cheers and hootings, yet his manliness and skill in debate soon gained way for him, and though the lecturer and chairman both made insulting remarks, he so entirely turned the tables upon them that, when the Liberationist motion was put to the meeting, it was rejected by a majority, and the whole thing collapsed ignominiously.

*   *   *   *   *

Many years previous to the event just narrated, when the Volunteer movement was making itself felt throughout the country, a large meeting was held in Tunbridge Wells to consider the question of establishing a Volunteer Corps. The chairman, a local magistrate, threw cold water on the proposal by reminding them that all their strength was needed for foreign service.

Mr. Hoare then got up and said that he entirely disagreed with the chairman ; proceeding in a very vigorous speech to show the horrors of a foreign invasion, and the duty of every true Englishman to defend his country, he concluded by declaring that he hoped the first invader who landed on the shores of Kent might be shot by a Tunbridge Wells Volunteer ! The speaker was well supported by the Rev. B. F. Smith, then Vicar of Rusthall (now Archdeacon of Maidstone).

A well-known medical man in the town then got up and said : " I came to the meeting in a doubtful state of mind, and though my courage failed under the depressing remarks of the chairman, it has now completely revived under the bold leadership of Captain Hoare and Lieutenant Smith!" The motion was carried by acclamation.

*   *   *   *   *

The following anecdote has reference to the extraordinary influence which he wielded over the town of Tunbridge Wells at large. His strong religious character may be said to have moulded the place. Two gentlemen were conversing at Sevenoaks Station, just before the train left the platform. One was heard to say to the other, "How is it that you have no theatre at Tunbridge Wells? A large town like that should have a theatre." "Oh," responded his companion, "it would never pay. Tunbridge Wells is too religious a place for a theatre."

*   *   *   *   *

Yet this man, when he came first as Vicar of Holy Trinity, met with much discouragement. The District Visitors came in a body and tendered their resignations, and the first remarks which he overheard about his sermons as he passed a group of parishioners at night on his way home from church were, "Oh, what a dreary sermon!" "Yes, and *I* thought it would never end!" It is hard for us now to believe this possible, and still harder perhaps to remember that even in late years, after all his services, two of the Evangelical newspapers used to write suspiciously of him,— one sneering at "the three Canons" Ryle, Garbett,

and Hoare as " Neo-Evangelicals "; the other
in a flaring leader actually calling him and the
writer of these lines (who was proud to be in
such company) "traitors to the Church of England"! Both these journals are now in different
hands, but it is a humiliating thought that one
who had done so much for Evangelical truth
should have been thus treated by those who professed to aid its progress. It has often been
noticed that a lofty mountain seems nothing very
remarkable when you stand at its base, but as the
traveller departs and it recedes from sight, it towers
above the lesser peaks and almost seems to stand
alone. So the character of a truly great man,
although valued, cannot be measured during his
life; it is as the years pass by that we see how
much higher he was than all his fellows.

CHAPTER XVII

PROMOTION

DURING the last year of his life it was evident to all that "old Mr. Valiant-for-truth," as some one had aptly named him, was growing more feeble in body, and it was apparent that the end of his faithful warfare could not be far distant.

Some thought that he ought to resign and leave the parish in younger hands, but it was more generally felt that the grief of leaving his work would be too much for him, and many believed that he would be allowed to die in harness: and so it was.

At the Easter Vestry he spoke feelingly of his approaching end and his desire for a suitable successor, and when he thanked his hearers for what he described as their toleration of the failings of an old man who was doing all that his strength would allow, all present were visibly affected.

The next week he went for a few days to Eastbourne, and thence dictated the following letters. How descriptive were their closing words of the continual attitude of our beloved friend's mind!

To one of his daughters :—

"EASTBOURNE, *April* 18*th*, 1894.

"We have had a comfortable night in our very comfortable quarters; I think you did indeed do well for us. I cannot imagine anything that would have suited us better.

"The day seems most beautiful, the sun shining brightly; those we love most hearty in their welcome, and everything cheerful all around us, so that I hope we may go home at the end of our week refreshed and invigorated for any work that the Lord may have in store for us. But at present our work consists in idleness, and I propose to devote myself to it with much diligence!

"All whom I have seen recommend a bath-chair, and I should not be surprised if I were to follow their advice before I go home, but I little know what is in store for me. Only let me enjoy the lovingkindness of my Heavenly Father, and we may safely leave the rest in His loving hand."

To a friend who was in ill-health :—

"EASTBOURNE, *April* 21*st*, 1894.

"I can heartily sympathise with you in the pain of giving up one after another the different objects in which you have been interested, and I can feel for you the more as I have been lately passing through the same process.

"I am obliged to hand over to others a great deal of the work in which I used to take delight. But I believe it is good for us, and that the ties to earth are being loosened in order that we may be the more ready for the Lord's summons when He shall call us to depart and to be with Christ.

"So let us think more of what we are likely to find

in Heaven than of the pain of parting with those things which have been a joy to us upon earth. . . .

"E. HOARE."

On Trinity Sunday, May 20th, he preached for the last time. The occasion was the anniversary of the British and Foreign Bible Society, of which, as we have seen, he was ever a staunch friend. At the close of the sermon he seemed to be rather exhausted, and his faithful parish clerk (who had served under him all through his ministry in Tunbridge Wells) hastened up the steps and helped him down. He never again entered that church where for forty-one years he had faithfully declared all the counsel of God. Of that ministry it may be truly said that its "record is on high." Few men have had so many opportunities of preaching the Gospel, and few have used them as he did.

After this there was a marked decline in strength. He knew that the tabernacle was being taken down, and made preparations accordingly. Two of his brother-clergy were asked by him to pay a pastoral visit weekly, and they will always thank God for this privilege ; it was beautiful to see the calm, steady trust—"I know *whom* I have believed." On these occasions they received more than they gave, and as some passage of help or comfort was dwelt upon the old saint of God would himself go on, and bring out some new light upon the passage, for to the very last he was "mighty in the Scriptures."

On St. Peter's Day, a week before his death, when the Sunday School Teachers' Association met as usual for their annual gathering in his garden, he saw them for a few minutes, and then from his room sent out this touching message : " Earthly pastors pass away, but remember Him of whom it is said, '*He, because He abideth ever, hath His priesthood unchangeable.*'" Surely this public testimony was a fitting sequel to his life's ministry !

A few weeks of weariness, and then the end came. The usual " Good-night " was said the night before, and early in the morning of July 7th, as he slept peacefully, the brave and faithful spirit passed away.

When a man's whole career has been given to God, we are not careful to ask for his last words, yet his were characteristic of the humble but unwavering trust that filled his heart. Replying to some inquiry he said, " I am perfectly at rest on every point."

God had bestowed many privileges and honours upon His servant during his life ; the greatest of all —even to be with Him—He granted during that quiet slumber, for " so He giveth unto His beloved in their sleep."

CHAPTER XVIII

TRIBUTES

IT is impossible to describe the feeling exhibited in Tunbridge Wells when it was
known that Canon Hoare had passed away, and
on the day of the funeral the town witnessed
such a display of universal sorrow and respect
as it had never seen before. To enumerate even
the deputations from different parts of England
and to describe the component parts of the huge
procession of mourners would occupy pages of this
book.

It is enough to say that everything which could
be done by the Mayor and Corporation and inhabitants of the town to declare their loss and
emphasise their respect was done. More than one
Bishop and over a hundred clergy walked in the
ranks of the mourners.

All testified as with one voice : " A prince and
a great man is fallen this day in Israel."

His mortal remains were laid beside those of his
beloved wife, and he who in those thirty-one years
of bereavement used sometimes to say, " In spirit

we have never been parted," was now in spirit
reunited to her, and that for ever.

*   *   *   *   *

A little book published at this time * contains
in full all that was said and done with reference
to him who had passed away.   There are to be
found in it the funeral sermons preached all over
the town, in church and chapel alike, as well as
sketches of his character and career in their special
bearing upon the town, whose particular reputation
had been so much formed by him.   It is a touching
tribute of affection and respect, and is well worthy
of perusal.

Hundreds of letters poured in upon the bereaved
family, from all parts of England, and indeed from
the ends of the earth.   Extracts from these interesting tributes of affection would form of themselves
a volume ; it is therefore impossible to give them
to the reader, but all testified with one voice to the
esteem and admiration in which he was held by
those who differed from him, and to the warm love
and devotion which he inspired in all who knew
him, and whom he had guided into the ways of
peace.   One expression may be mentioned which
was overheard in the conversation of two gentlemen
on the day of the funeral (one of them a man of
light and leading in the world).   Said the first,

---

* "In Memoriam: Rev. Canon Hoare." *Courier* Office,
Tunbridge Wells.   Price 6*d*.

"We ne'er shall look upon his like again," to which the other made reply, "Did we ever see his like before?"

The beautiful letters which follow, written on the day of Canon Hoare's death, speak for themselves :—

"LAMBETH PALACE, S.E., *July 7th*, 1894.

"MY DEAR MISS HOARE,—One word only of intense sympathy; but intense in something which swallows up sorrow.

"No one will ever have looked more joyfully on the face of Christ in Paradise.

"Sincerely yours,
"E. W. CANTUAR."

"LAMBETH PALACE, S.E.. *July 7th*.

"MY DEAR MISS HOARE,—The news has this moment reached us, and I cannot resist sending you one word of deepest sympathy. I know the Archbishop will write for himself, but the thought of the beauty into which that holy and beautiful spirit has entered lives in one so, and in spite of all your personal sorrow and loss I cannot help feeling that you are living in that thought now.

"You know how we loved him—how could we help it!—and that we do know something of all he was and is and how the joy of the Lord has been the breath of his life ; and so we may give thanks with you, may we not? though the heart must ache and the grief be keen. I must not trouble you more—God bless and keep you.

"Affectionately yours,
"MARY BENSON."

Notices of Canon Hoare's death and sketches of his life, longer or shorter, appeared in countless newspapers in England, America, and Australia. The *Record* published several articles upon his career and influence in the Church of England. One of the most happily written appeared in the columns of the *Guardian* under the familiar initials " B. F. S."

Few in the diocese of Canterbury had better knowledge of the man whom he described than the dignitary who penned those lines.

(*From " The Guardian.*")

In Memoriam.

Edward Hoare.

" By the death of Canon Hoare the Evangelical party in the Church of England loses, perhaps, its doughtiest champion in our generation. But long before his death experience and advancing years had so suffused his views with catholicity that he was even more conspicuous as a pillar of his Church than as the leader of a party.

" Born in a family in which piety was a tradition, and predisposed by his Quaker blood to think little of public opinion where it came into conflict with convictions, he inherited a vigour of mind and body of which he early gave proof when, as stroke of the Second Trinity boat, he raised it to the head of the river, and became a high Wrangler. But though a Fellowship at Trinity was fairly within his reach, he entered at once into the active duties of the ministry to which he had devoted himself, and thenceforth his energies were wholly bent on pastoral work, though not to the ex- clusion of the Mission cause abroad and the furtherance in England of those views which he believed most faithfully to reflect the mind of its Church. To the successful study of mathematics he doubtless owed the habit of boldly pressing his principles to their logical conclusions, undisturbed by those many side-issues which often perplex minds less vigorously trained in the exact sciences ; though in his case a sturdy common sense and native shrewdness did not suffer him to be betrayed thereby into practical mistakes, while his large and loving heart would never permit the strongest of his opinions to impair his affection for men whose con- clusions differed from his own, if they were otherwise worthy of it.

" It was on a foundation thus broad and solid that his commanding personality was built up, becoming a tower of strength to those who resigned themselves to his religious guidance, and attaching marvellously by its strength and sweetness converts to the religious principles which he held and advocated. How im- portant a place he held at his best in the esteem of his neighbours those will remember who witnessed the universal demonstrations of sympathy when his life was in danger from Roman fever, and the whole town was quivering with anxiety lest they should lose one whom they could so ill spare. And though the wane of his physical powers and the inevitable changes of a watering- place population may have narrowed the circle of his influence towards the last, the striking demonstrations of respect which marked his funeral bore witness not only to the deep attachment of his own congregation, but also to the widespread conviction of his brother- clergy and of all the country-side that a shining light had been quenched, whose witness for God had penetrated far beyond the range of his personal ministrations.

"Of the endeared relations between him and his congregation, who had looked up to him for spiritual direction for over forty years, only those within the magic circle of that pastoral connection could form an idea. The well-spring of personal affection which flowed forth from his loving heart towards the humblest of his flock was repaid by a personal devotion which might have proved injurious to a weaker character, less firmly rooted on the rock of truth. But there was an element of generous appreciation in a remark let fall at his funeral, that there was probably no more 'personally conducted' congregation in England than that of Trinity Church, Tunbridge Wells.

"But on wider platforms Canon Hoare's ascendency of character had been in his time not less conspicuous. In his own ruri-decanal meetings, in which he continued to take part up to within a few weeks of his death; in the diocesan conferences, at which only a year ago he bore his solemn and memorable testimony to the value of Church Schools; and at Church Congresses, where he was ever ready to step gallantly into the breach in defence of the principles of the Church which he thought to be assailed,—in these various fields of encounter the manliness of his advocacy, set off by his manifest sincerity, and by his charity towards those who differed from him, commended itself to the admiration even of those who remained unconvinced by his arguments.

"But his own pulpit was undoubtedly the vantage-ground from which he most effectively did battle for his Master's cause. Armed with a forcible, lucid, and winning mode of address, with an incomparable command of Holy Scriptures, transparently in earnest, and known of all men to live the life he preached, by the elevation of his religious character no less than by voice and gesture, 'he drew his audience upward to the sky.' Even after his eyesight failed him, and he could with difficulty mount the pulpit steps, he continued to the last, like the Apostle of love, to deliver his Master's message. And who shall say in how many hearts it found an echo among that changeful congregation, and in what remote parts of the world a generation which knew him not have been taught by their parents to call his name blessed? His beloved Mother Church has lost no more loyal, wise, persuasive, heavenly-minded son and servant—no more trusty guide of souls from earth to heaven—than our modern 'Greatheart,' Edward Hoare."

"*The Record*," *Friday, July* 13*th.*

CANON HOARE.

"The death of Canon Hoare removes from the front rank of Evangelical Churchmen a conspicuous and commanding figure. He took his degree in 1834—Fifth Wrangler. He was ordained deacon in 1837,* the year, it will be remembered, of the Queen's accession. His jubilee coincided with that of the Sovereign whom he so truly honoured; and it is neither fanciful nor fulsome to say that he held a kind of sovereign rank amongst the Evangelical clergy. One of their kings is dead. It happens sometimes to all parties to lose a man who was much more to them than to the Church at large. We do not deny that this was the case with Canon Hoare. In spite of his conspicuousness, he was not naturally the sort of man who loves to be conspicuous. He grew to greatness amongst his fellows by the influence

---

* He was ordained priest in 1837.—ED.

of character alone. His abilities were considerable; his training was excellent; his family traditions were of the best that the eighteenth century in its ripe benevolence handed on to the young religious energy of the nineteenth. That bright benevolence and beneficence shone in his face, unmingled with the eagerness of the combatant or the push and pressure of the ambitious candidate for leadership. His attitude to the Church of England at large was one of admiring loyalty, but he had no self-seeking thoughts. He dwelt, and loved to dwell, among his own people. He took his share, an honourable share, in the struggles of his own times; but the part which he took was, when it led him to scenes of controversy, always a strange and unwelcome work. But none the less, perhaps all the more for that, he did it well. The nephew of Joseph John Gurney and of Elizabeth Fry was not without a strong element of what is sturdy and staunch. That side of his character found useful expression when, at the Church Congress at Derby in 1882, he was suddenly called upon to meet the suggestion of Lord Halifax that the Bishops should allow the alternative use at the Holy Communion office in the Prayer-Book of 1549. Then, in his own name and in the name of the Evangelical party, he spoke his apologia. . . . That scene illustrates the man; and though a good deal has happened since, and the Lambeth Judgment must not be forgotten, yet that interpretation of the signs of the times remains the only reasonable reading of them, and the alternative—the Reformers or Rome—is still the only possible alternative if England is to remain a Christian country. And yet, as we have said, this was an incident.

" His work, his real work, was of another kind. Perhaps no other position in England would have suited

him quite as well as the post he held at Tunbridge
Wells. He made Tunbridge Wells the Canterbury of
West Kent, and he was the unofficial primate. For
forty years this watering-place, the once fashionable and
frivolous resort of people half whose complaints were
due to the too easy conditions of their life, has come
more and more to be the home of people whose leading
purpose is to find out how to do most for the Kingdom
of God, and have found there that a plain English
clergyman was for the most part at the back of all its
missionary energies. ' I am but one of yourselves, a
presbyter,' said Newman in his first tract. So, in his
last tract, might Canon Hoare have said. For forty
fruitful years the overshadowing influence of a good
man's life has been a kind of visible sign of a yet higher
overshadowing. Prayers and alms have marked the life
of the place, and, whatever the future may have in store,
there has been peace and truth in Tunbridge Wells in
Canon Hoare's days. Outside his own parish, his next
most influential place was, no doubt, the Committee-
room of the Church Missionary Society. There was a
time, indeed, when week by week two able men came
up to Salisbury Square, each in his own way exercising
a powerful influence upon the Cabinet deliberations.
One was the pen more than the voice, the other the
voice more than the pen, of missionary counsel. But
those were the days of Henry Venn, and in his days
counsellors for the most part found themselves anticipated. But when those days had passed away, and the
increasing missionary activity of the Church brought
new conditions, new problems, new agencies, new
methods into view, then came a time in which counsellors who had within them a living spring of energy,
readiness of mind, elasticity, hopefulness, breadth of
view, a firm belief in the future as well as a firm grip

upon the past, were invaluable, and such a man was
Canon Hoare. Things new and old were in him, as
they always are in the men who by the force of character
become guides of their fellows. The man of routine,
the mere pedant, the mere deprecator of mistakes, asks
always for a precedent. He does well to ask for it; it is
a finger-post to him. The man of wisdom makes pre-
cedents, founding them on principles of which he is
sure. In such a man the inner sight is clear, the eye is
single. When he speaks there is the ring of authority
in what he says, the highest expression of the common
sense of men.

"Who shall estimate the value of such a career?
Who shall gauge the loss to the commonwealth of the
Church of one such counsellor? It is pleasant to think
that, priceless as Canon Hoare was to his party, and
thoroughly as he was in sympathy with its aims and
sentiments, there is no deduction to be made for bitterness, for narrowness, for sour alienation from human
interests. It was his privilege to touch the life of his
times at many points: in the abundance of his interests
he multiplied himself.

"Happy in his family, in the narrower and the wider
sense of the word, happy in his friendships, happy in
his opportunities, happy in his wide sympathies with
humanity, his heart went out expansively to all who
challenged his attention. The world became one wide
field, to which he gave himself, his children, his sub-
stance, his time, his prayers. He was heart and soul
an Evangelical. But we are greatly mistaken if the
Church of England generally does not recognise in
Canon Hoare one of her truest children, not the less
for that which was part of his inheritance, the knowledge
that Christ our Lord has other sheep, not of the fold
in which he was so distinguished an under-shepherd."

THE CHURCH MISSIONARY SOCIETY.

The following minute, which was passed by the Committee of the above body at their first meeting after Canon Hoare's death, records, as far as words can do so, the deep loss that the Society has sustained by this event :—

"In addition to the deaths of long-honoured and attached friends of the Society within the last few weeks, the Bishop of Bath and Wells, Canon Lord Forster, Lord Charles Russell, and Howard Gill, the Committee record with affectionate and thankful remembrance a life consecrated to the service of our Divine Master in the removal of their beloved brother Canon Edward Hoare.

"Trained in the days of the Evangelical revival at Cambridge under Simeon, Scholefield, and Carus, Edward Hoare commenced his ministry in 1836 as curate to the Rev. Francis Cunningham, at Pakefield, where he found the genial and warm sympathy of those who were at the time engaged in the religious movement, and where he gave early evidence of the bright living missionary spirit which was so prominent a feature of his ministry in his after-life at Richmond, Ramsgate, and, finally, at Tunbridge Wells; where, for forty-one years, he was by the grace of God ever at the front of all missionary work both at home and abroad. The remarkable position of influence which he attained was not from his gifts, which were considerable, but from his grace. The features of his character may be briefly summed up as they were known in his private life, in his parochial work, in the pulpit, on the platform, and in the Committee-room of the Church Missionary Society :

godly simplicity and unflinching courage, clearness of
judgment and expression, loving sympathy and consideration for others, unfailing diligence and soundness in the
Faith, and supreme reverence for and delight in the
Word of God. These gracious qualities made his
counsels and co-operation wise, weighty, and practical.
He was in the highest sense a faithful witness to the
principles of the Reformation and the doctrine and discipline of the Church of England, and a zealous, popular,
and attractive advocate at all times of the work of his
beloved Church Missionary Society.

"The Committee commend the members of his family,
especially those who are in the Mission-field, to the very
special prayers of the Church, in the hope that a double
portion of his spirit may be imparted to his successors."

   *   *   *   *   *   *

The beloved son in the Mission-field was the
only one absent when the aged father was laid to
rest. His visit with his wife and children, three
and a half years before, had been an unspeakable
joy in the old home. During Canon Hoare's latter
years all who knew him remember the interest and
delight that he took in the work at Ningpo, and
how continually his thoughts turned to those dear
ones who had dedicated themselves to labour for
God in China. Yet—who can tell?—perhaps when
the River has been crossed time and distance have
ceased to be, and the blessed dead, being with Christ,
are nearer those who are in Christ than when they
moved among us here on earth.

   *   *   *   *   *   *

" After this it was noised abroad that Mr. Valiant-
for-truth was taken with a summons by the same
post as the other, and had this for a token that the
summons was true, 'that his pitcher was broken at
the fountain' (Eccles. xii. 6). When he understood
it he called for his friends and told them of it.
Then said he : ' I am going to my Father's ; and
though with great difficulty I have got hither, yet
now do I not repent me of all the trouble I have
been at to arrive where I am. My sword I give to
him that shall succeed me in my pilgrimage, and
my courage and skill to him that can get it. My
marks and scars I carry with me to be a witness
for me that I have fought His battles who now will
be my rewarder.'

" When the day that he must go hence was come
many accompanied him to the river-side, into which
as he went down he said, ' Death, where is thy
sting?' and as he went down deeper, he said,
' Grave, where is thy victory?'

" So he passed over, and all the trumpets sounded
for him at the other side."

    *   *   *   *   *

" I passed from them, but I found Him whom my
soul loveth" (Canticles iii. 4).

APPENDIX.

As an illustration of the hold which the name of Canon Hoare has upon the Church at large, it may be mentioned that when the suggestion was made to call the proposed New Wing of the South-Eastern College at Ramsgate after him, and to erect it as a memorial of his principles and the teaching of his life, the proposal was warmly received; contributions flowed in from India and the Antipodes, as well as from England, and in about ten months' time the needed sum of £5,000 was in the Treasurer's hands.

Printed by Hazell, Watson, & Viney, Ld., London and Aylesbury.